Wataru Watari
Illustration **Ponkan⑧**

2

Contents

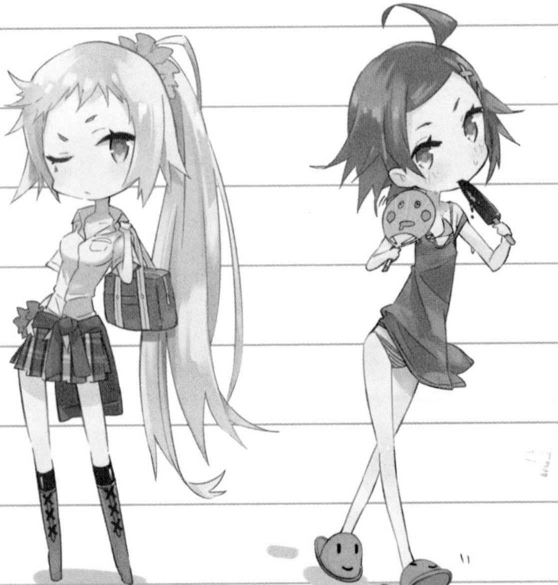

MY YOUTH R♥MANTIC C☺MEDY iS WRØNG, AS I EXPECTED

Wataru Watari
Illustration Ponkan⑧

VOLUME 2

YEN ON

NEW YORK

MY YOUTH ROMANTIC COMEDY IS WRONG, AS I EXPECTED Vol. 2

WATARU WATARI

Illustration by Ponkan⑧

Translation by Jennifer Ward

Cover art by Ponkan⑧

YAHARI ORE NO SEISHUN LOVE COME WA MACHIGATTEIRU.

Vol. 2 by Wataru WATARI

©2011 Wataru WATARI

Illustration by PONKAN⑧

All Rights Reserved.

Original Japanese edition published by SHOGAKUKAN.

English translation rights arranged with SHOGAKUKAN through Tuttle-Mori Agency, Inc, Tokyo.

English translation © 2017 by Yen Press, LLC

Yen On

1290 Avenue of the Americas

New York, NY 10104

Visit us at yenpress.com

facebook.com/yenpress

twitter.com/yenpress

yenpress.tumblr.com

instagram.com/yenpress

First Yen On Edition: May 2017

Yen On is an imprint of Yen Press, LLC.

The Yen On name and logo are trademarks of Yen Press, LLC.

Library of Congress Cataloging-in-Publication Data

Names: Watari, Wataru, author. | Ponkan 8, illustrator.

Title: My youth romantic comedy is wrong, as I expected / Wataru Watari ; illustration by Ponkan 8.

Other titles: Yahari ore no seishun love come wa machigatteiru. English

Description: New York : Yen On, 2016–

Identifiers: LCCN 2016005816 | ISBN 9780316312295 (v. 1 : paperback) | ISBN 9780316396011 (v. 2 : paperback)

Subjects: | CYAC: Optimism—Fiction. | School—Fiction.

Classification: LCC PZ7.1.W396 My 2016 | DDC [Fic]—dc23

LC record available at http://lccn.loc.gov/2016005816

ISBN: 978-0-316-39601-1

10 9 8 7 6 5 4 3 2 1

LSC-C

Printed in the United States of America

MY YOUTH R♥MANTIC COMEDY iS WRØNG, AS I EXPECTED

two

Cast of Characters

Hachiman Hikigaya.......... The main character. High school second-year. Twisted personality.

Yukino Yukinoshita.......... Captain of the Service Club. Perfect and beautiful, but her personality is a disappointment.

Yui Yuigahama.................. Hachiman's classmate. Tends to worry about what other people think.

Yoshiteru Zaimokuza......... Nerd. Thinks of Hachiman as his buddy.

Saika Totsuka.................. Tennis club. Extremely cute, however...

Saki Kawasaki.................. Hachiman's classmate. Turning delinquent?

Shizuka Hiratsuka............. Japanese teacher. Guidance counselor.

Komachi Hikigaya............. Hachiman's little sister. In middle school.

Taishi Kawasaki................. Saki Kawasaki's little brother. Goes to the same cram school as Komachi.

Prologue

Golden Week was over, and the temperature had gradually been rising of late. Students were getting rowdier during lunch, making it feel even hotter than it actually was. By nature, cool, hard-boiled guys like me don't do well in the heat, and so I headed somewhere less crowded in search of even the slightest bit of relief. The basal temperature of the human body is approximately thirty-six degrees Celsius. Put in terms of weather, that's not just a summer day; it's a sweltering heat wave. Even I couldn't handle such intense heat and humidity. Cats are the same way. When it's hot, they seek out places where no one's around. I, too, head for empty locales to seek refuge from the blistering heat. It's not because I don't fit in with the class or because I feel awkward. Not at all.

This behavior is instinctual, and actually, it's the kids who don't follow this biological imperative who are, as organisms, flawed. Basically, they're weak, so they form groups and adopt a herd mentality. Acting as a collective is the sign of a weak-willed life-form. They're no different from herbivores that move in herds so that, when attacked by a predator, they can offer up someone as a sacrifice. Innocently munching their grass, they turn their backs as friends become food.

Well, you get the idea. Strong beasts don't flock together. You've heard of a "lone wolf"? Cats are cute, and wolves are cool. In other words, loners are cute and cool.

Considering these sublimely trivial matters, I meandered along. I was on the landing that connected to the roof. Unused desks cluttered the area, leaving just enough room for one person to barely squeak through. Usually, the door to the roof was chained with a cheap padlock, and it should have been shut tight. But that day the padlock was undone, dangling from its loop. It was probably just some gaggle of airheads who'd ventured up to the roof to get loud and caterwaul at each other. What they say about those types and high places really is true.

Figuring I might as well just trap them up there, I piled up about three desks and two chairs. True to form, I was an amazing man of action. So masculine. Eek, hold me! But then I noticed that things were awfully quiet on the other side of the door. Odd. So far as I know, these normies fear quiescence like beasts fear flame. They believe silence = boring without realizing *they* are the boring ones, and so they just chatter, clamor, and frolic away. But then when they're talking to me, their lacking loquaciousness tells me, *You're kinda boring.* The hell is with that, seriously?

No, no, don't get the wrong idea; I actually like peace and quiet. And that degree of calm meant there wasn't a clique up there. Maybe no one was there at all. Being a loner means a sudden euphoria when you realize no one's around. But a loner isn't just meek in public and a monster at home. Rather, loners are just always considerate and avoid bothering others.

I relaxed the emotional barricade I'd built around myself and put my hand on the door. I was a little bit excited. It was the kind of anticipation you feel the first time you happen to stroll into a soba shop by the station, or the thrill of a deliberate expedition out of Chiba city to buy porn in Yotsukaidou. It's the characteristic delight you feel precisely because you are alone.

Beyond the door stretched the wide blue sky and the horizon. Now this was my own private roof. Rich people like having private jets and private beaches. Loners, who exist in perpetual private time, are the winners in life. Basically, I'm saying there's status in being a loner.

The May sky was thoroughly sunny, as if the world were telling me that one day I would escape this sheltered world. If you were to put it in terms of a classic movie, it was like *The Shawshank Redemption*. Not that I've seen it, but based on the title, I think it was like that. Gazing at the distant haze of the sky is rather like taking a good, hard look at your future. That's why the roof was an appropriate venue to entrust my dreams to the Workplace Tour Application Form in my hands.

The workplace visit was looming right after my next test. I committed ink to paper with the career I wanted and the workplace I wanted to tour. I always have a plan firmly in mind for my future, so there was no hesitation as my pen scratched along, and I had completed the form in under two minutes.

And that's when it happened. The wind blew. It was a fateful wind and seemed as if it were carrying away the languid air that lingered after school was over. It launched that sheet of paper on which my dreams were written into the future like a paper airplane. I make it sound poetic, but of course, I mean it blew away the form I'd just been filling out. *Hey, you stupid wind, don't give me this crap, seriously!* The paper skimmed along the ground, and just when I thought I'd caught it, it flew up high again as if toying with me.

Oh, whatever. I'd get another form and write it over. My motto is "When the going gets tough, give up," so something like this doesn't rattle me. Also, "If at first you don't succeed, give up" works, too. Shrugging my shoulders, I began walking away, when…

"Is this yours?"

I heard a voice. I glanced around, looking for the source of that slightly husky, somehow apathetic tone, but it seemed I was alone. I mean, I'm always alone, but not that way… I mean I didn't see anyone on the roof besides me.

"Over here, stupid." The voice originated overhead, scoffing at me derisively. I guess this is exactly what they mean by being talked down to.

By ascending a ladder, one could climb even higher—from the roof up to the water tower. She was leaning against the tower, fiddling with a cheap hundred-yen lighter, as she looked down on me, and when our eyes met, she quietly slipped the lighter into the pocket of her uniform.

Her long, bluish-black hair hung all the way to her waist. She went without the uniform's ribbon, leaving her blouse open at the chest with her shirttails tied loosely in the front. Her long, supple legs looked capable of a swift kick. What left an impression, though, were her listless eyes, which seemed to be idly gazing into the distance. There was a mole like a teardrop on her cheek, adding to that languorous effect. "This yours?" she repeated, her tone the same as before.

I didn't know what year she was, so I just nodded silently. 'Cause, you know, if she was older, I'd have to speak respectfully, and it would be pretty embarrassing if I was wrong, right? Silence is always best.

"Hold on a sec," she said with a sigh, putting her hands on the ladder and swiftly descending.

And then…the wind blew. Blew like it was casting aside some heavy, dangling blackout curtain—that kind of fateful wind. That single strip of cloth and the dreams entrusted to it fluttered in the divine breeze that the sight it revealed might be branded on my eyes forevermore.

I made it sound poetic, but basically, I saw her panties. *Hey, you pulled it off, wind! Nice job, seriously!*

She released the ladder's rungs halfway and hopped down. I got my glimpse of them just before she handed me my paper.

"You're an idiot," she said, brusquely shoving the form as me, just shy of throwing it. When I took it from her, she spun around on her heel and disappeared into the school.

I'd missed my chance to say *Thanks* or *What do you mean, "retard"?* or *Sorry for seeing your panties* and was left standing there. Holding the

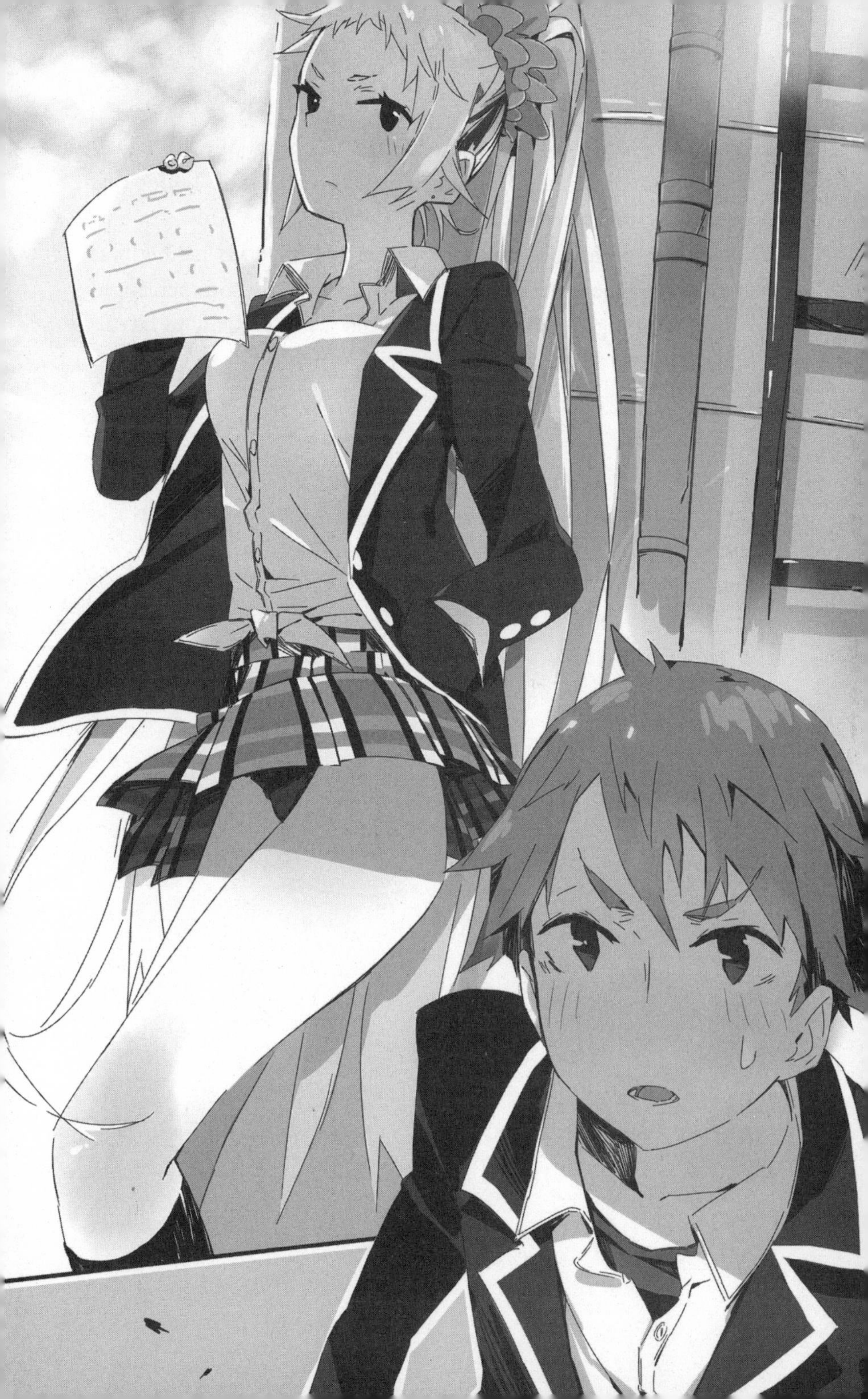

paper she'd returned in one hand, I scratched my head. The bell signaling the end of lunch sounded from the speakers on the roof. Taking that as my cue, I stepped toward the door.

"Black lace, huh…?" I muttered with a sigh that was neither blue nor off-color, and that exhalation was blown away on the summer-tinged wind and intermingled with the smell of the sea, eventually to be carried around the world.

Saki Kawasaki

Komachi Hikigaya

Birthday

October 26

Birthday

March 3

Special skills:

Karate

Special skills:

Flexibility, cooking,
taking care of brother

Hobbies:

Knitting stuffed toys

Hobbies:

Saving money,
teasing brother

How I spend my weekends:

Part-time job,
spending time with
younger siblings

How I spend my weekends:

Taking care of cat,
spending time with brother,
who spends all day at home

Workplace Tour Application Form

Soubu Secondary School   Grade: 2nd Year   Class: F

Name: **Hachiman Hikigaya**

1. Desired profession:

Househusband

2. Desired workplace:

At home

3. Write your reasons below:

As they said in ancient times, to get a job is to lose.
Labor is the practice of undertaking risk in order to attain
returns. Ultimately, it can be said that the primary goal of labor
is to maximize returns while minimizing risk. Little girls do not say,
"My dream for the future is to be a bride" because they are cute;
they are driven by biology.

Therefore, my choice of staying at home and not working is
appropriate and utterly justifiable. Consequently, regarding the
upcoming workplace tour, I request to be placed in my home,
the workplace of a househusband.

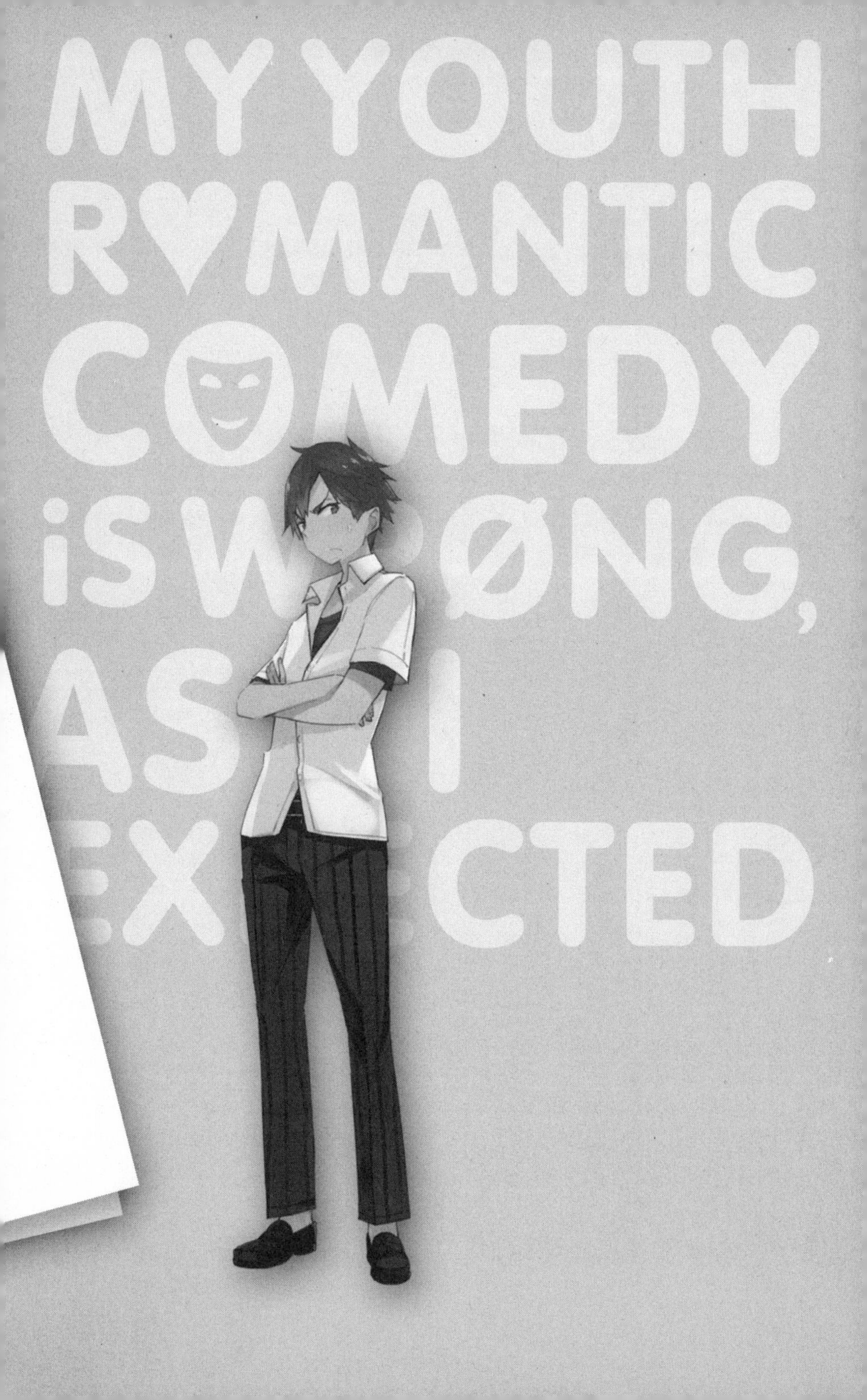
MY YOUTH
ROMANTIC
COMEDY
IS WRONG,
AS I
EXPECTED

And that's how **Yui Yuigahama** decided to study.

A corner of the faculty office was set up as a reception area. There was a glass-topped table by a black leather sofa, and the whole thing was set off by a partition. Immediately to one side was a window, and from it you could see out to the library. A mild early-summer breeze swept in through the open window, making a single piece of paper dance. Moved by the impressionistic scene, I followed the scrap of paper with my eyes to see where the wind was going. The paper fluttered gently, whisking toward the floor, fleeting as a falling tear.

And then, *BAM!* A stiletto heel stabbed it like an iron poker. Supple legs stretched up from those heels. It was quite apparent just how long and shapely those legs were, even sheathed in a tight pantsuit. It takes impeccable style to pull off a pantsuit. The bare legs and pantyhose that accompany a skirt can compensate for a lot when it comes to fulfilling the erotic component, but the pantsuit—which intentionally obscures that allure—is prone to leave an impression of lacking sophistication and elegance. Unless sported by a figure sufficiently slim but possessing legs of the proper curvaceousness, the pantsuit can lose its essential shape and even end up looking ugly.

However, the ensemble before me was different. These legs were of such balanced proportion that one might go so far as to call them an example of the golden ratio. And it wasn't just her legs. Her tight waist drew a gentle curve that eventually arrived at the superb mounds of her breasts. Oh-ho! Mount Fuji, here I come! The line from her feet to her chest was like a violin—nay, not just any violin. Like that famous instrument, the Stradivarius, it boasted a perfect shape.

The problem was the terrifying expression that topped it all off, like those on the Nio statues by Unkei and Kaikei. It was terrifying from an artistic, cultural, and historical perspective. Miss Hiratsuka, my Japanese teacher, chewed roughly on the filter of her cigarette and glared at me with an expression that bespoke the suppression of extreme rage. "Hikigaya. Do you understand what I want to talk to you about?"

"No…" Unable to take the glare from her wide, flashing eyes, I quietly played dumb and turned my head away.

Miss Hiratsuka began clenching each of the digits of her right hand, starting with her index finger. That alone was sufficient to squeeze a crack from her joints. "You didn't just tell me that you have no idea, now, did you?"

"No…no way I wouldn't understand! Is what I was going to say! I wasn't going to just say no! I understand! I'll write it over! Don't punch me!"

"Of course you will. Geez… Just when I think you've changed a little bit, you pull this."

"My motto is *Always stick to your guns*, so." I gave her a little *tee-hee*. ♪

I felt like I could hear the vein popping out of her temple. "So I have no choice but to fix you with a whack after all. It's always faster just to whack things—like you would a TV or anything else."

"H-hey, I'm a precision instrument, so that may not be the best idea. And by the way, TVs these days are thin, so you can't whack them like the old ones. You're really showing your age—"

"*Shocking First Bullet!*"

Thunk. The sound her fist made as it sank into my stomach was bland compared to her dramatic battle cry.

"Guh." I raised my head, desperately trying to reel in my departing consciousness, and saw Miss Hiratsuka giving me an unpleasant smirk.

"If you don't want to eat the Annihilating Second Bullet, you should stop talking."

"I-I apologize... Please spare me the Exterminating Last Bullet." I obediently apologized, and Miss Hiratsuka sat down on her chair with a creak, looking satisfied. Perhaps my immediate apology had borne fruit, because she was smiling and looking somehow refreshed. Most of the time her behavior was so cringeworthy that I'd forgotten for a moment, but she was actually quite beautiful.

"*S-CRY-ed* is a good show. I'm glad you caught on, Hikigaya."

Correction. She really was just a cringeworthy human being after all. Apparently, she was just happy I'd gotten her reference.

Lately, I had come to understand her tastes. Basically, she was into dramatic action manga and anime. I'd been learning more useless crap than I knew what to do with.

"Now, Hikigaya, I'll ask you just to be sure. What was your goal in writing that smart-ass application form? If you don't give me a satisfactory answer, you'd better prepare for trouble."

And make it double, I'm sure. "I don't know what to say..." I'd poured my entire heart out on that sheet of paper. I hadn't prepared a more in-depth response than that. If she'd read it but still didn't get it, what could I do about that?

As if she'd read my mind, Miss Hiratsuka flicked her gaze in my direction, exhaling cigarette smoke. "I understand your rotten, sordid personality. I just thought you'd grown a bit. Hasn't spending time in the Service Club influenced you at all?"

"Huh?" I replied, thinking back on my time with the Service Club of which she spoke. Simply put, members of the Service Club listen to students' problems and then help solve them. But in actuality, the club was just a bunch of kids who had a crappy time at school, all thrown together into an isolation ward. I had been forced into helping them, as that was somehow supposed to correct my deviant personality and do away with the rotten look in my eyes, but the club didn't do anything particularly worthy of mention, so I wasn't really attached to it. What would I even say about it?

Totsuka was cute. Yeah, that was about it.

"Hikigaya, that gleam in your eyes is rapidly devolving into something even more sordid. And wipe off that drool."

"Ah! Oh, crap, I was zoning out." I rubbed my mouth with my sleeve. That was close. I'd been inches from discovering my emerging sexuality.

"You're a sad sack, and you're not getting any better. You're getting worse."

"Compared to you, I don't think I'm so bad. Bringing up *S-CRY-ed*, at your age—"

"Annihilating…"

"—really is something a mature woman would do. I can really tell you feel a strong sense of duty to instruct me on the classics. Indeed. Honestly, truly." I somehow managed to rattle off something in an attempt to avoid getting punched, and Miss Hiratsuka sheathed her fist. But her eyes were sharp, as usual, reminding me of a wild beast.

"Geez… Anyway, redo your Workplace Tour Application Form. And you're going to help me sort the forms, too, as a punishment for hurting my feelings."

"Yes, ma'am."

There was a thick stack of papers before me. I was forced to sort through each and every one like I was a part-timer at a bread factory or something. Plus, I was being monitored.

Though I was alone with a female teacher, nothing exciting was going to happen here. Neither would the impact of her punch somehow result in me touching her chest, obviously, nor would there be any other convenient, accidental groping. Stuff like that is all total fabrication. You liars! All you dating sim and rom-com light-novel writers had better come and apologize to me.

×　×　×

Chiba City Municipal Soubu High School has a workplace tour event in second year. They gather applications from every student, and based on those applications, they decide which workplaces to tour and which students actually go there. It's a Yutori education–style program that just cuts into the curriculum and is supposed to give us experience interacting in society. That in itself wasn't a particularly big deal. Most schools probably have similar programs. The problem with this thing was that it fell immediately after midterms. I was being forced to waste part of my precious prep time on these frivolities.

"Man, why does the program have to be at this time of year?" I asked as I sorted the stack of papers by job type.

Miss Hiratsuka, who was sitting in an empty desk, replied with a cigarette in her mouth. "We're doing it precisely because it is this time of year, Hikigaya. You've heard that you have course selections for third year right after summer break, right?"

"We do?"

"I told you about it in homeroom."

"Oh, I feel like I'm less *home* and more *away* team there, so I wasn't listening." *No, seriously, why do you call it homeroom? I don't feel at home there at all. I hate it.*

Plus, the whole "day duty" system used to run homeroom is just terrible. Day duty is when you're forced to lead the morning greetings for the whole class. When I say, *Rise! Bow! Be seated!* things go deathly quiet, and I'd like it if people would stop being like that. When Hayama does it, fits of tittering flit through the class. He'll caution them with a smile, and they're all like one big, happy family, but when it's me—nothing. Come to think of it, they don't even boo me, so I'm even less than an away team.

"Anyway, we set the date for the work experience to fall between the midterms and summer vacation so students form a concrete plan for their future instead of just mindlessly taking their exams. I doubt it's very effective, though," she added, then blew out a smoke ring with a puff.

My school, Chiba City Municipal Soubu High School, is an academically oriented institution. The majority of the students here either hope to or actually are going on to university. Of course, I'd had university on my mind since first starting this school. Maybe it was because I'd already included a four-year postponement of adulthood in my calculations, but I wasn't that excited about my future. I'm the only one here who's actually been thinking properly about my future. I'm definitely not getting a job.

"You look like you've got nothing good on your mind. So which are you going with, arts or sciences?" Miss Hiratsuka inquired, exasperated.

"Me? I—"

"Oh! There you are!" The moment I opened my mouth, I was interrupted by a boisterous cry. Her bright hair, twisted into a bun, swung in displeasure. As usual, her skirt was on the short side, and there were two or three buttons undone over her open and breezy chest. It was Yui Yuigahama, with whom I'd only recently become acquainted. But we're in the same class, so the fact that I'd only just gotten to know her actually meant that my communication skills were impressive, in a way. Impressively bad.

"Oh, Yuigahama. Sorry, but I'm using Hikigaya right now."

"I-it's not like he's mine. I-it's totally okay," she stammered, denying her possession of me as she violently waved her hands back and forth. I couldn't help feeling like there was a nuance of *No, I don't need that thing!* in her expression. It kind of hurt watching someone rejecting me that hard.

"Did you need something?" The one posing the question wasn't Yuigahama, but rather the girl who'd popped up in front of her. Black pigtails bobbed as she stepped forward. "You never came to the clubroom even though it's long past time, so she came looking for you. Yuigahama did, that is."

"You don't have to add that last bit to emphasize that it wasn't you. I know."

The black-haired girl was Yukino Yukinoshita. Her face is the only nice thing about her. She looks as pretty as a porcelain doll, and her attitude is as chilly as ceramic to match. The first thing out of her mouth to me was a subtle dig, so you can infer from that what our relationship is like.

Yukinoshita and I are in the same club, more or less—the aforementioned Service Club. She's the captain. When we're together, we're constantly at each other's throats, retreating occasionally, and basically just digging at each other's open wounds and grinding salt into them. We spend day and night on our pointless disputes.

At Yukinoshita's remark, Yuigahama huffily put her hands on her hips, looking quite annoyed. "I went all over asking around, but everyone was like 'Hikigaya? Who?' It was horrible."

"I didn't need to know that." Had she come just to pierce my heart with pinpoint accuracy? She wasn't even aiming. What kind of natural sniper was she?

"It was really horrible!" For some reason she said it again, still looking put out and painfully reminding me once more that nobody at this school even knows I exist. *Oh well, I guess if everyone at school knows you, you're easy to find, huh? If I'm this socially invisible, maybe ninja would be the most appropriate career path.*

"Oh, um, sorry." This was the first time I'd ever apologized for the fact that no one knows me. Sad. Anyone of lesser mental fortitude would have bidets spraying from their eyes by now.

"It's...o-okay... U-um, so..." Yuigahama clasped her fingers together in front of her chest and began fidgeting as she wiggled them. "T-tell me your number? L-look! It's weird for me to go to all this trouble looking for you, and it's embarrassing... People asking me if we have a thing and stuff, and it's just...unbelievable." Unbearably embarrassed that she had been searching for me, she blushed at the memory. Averting her eyes, she squeezed her fidgety hands poised before her chest tighter and turned away before casting one more questioning look my way.

"Well, sure, why not...," I said, producing my cell phone. Yuigahama pulled out hers, all sparkly and jewel encrusted.

"What the heck is that? A phone or a disco monster truck?"

"Huh? Isn't it cute?" It looked like a cheap chandelier. Yuigahama shoved her cell phone in my face, a charm that looked like a strange plush mushroom dangling from it. It was superbly annoying.

"I dunno. I don't understand ho taste. Are you into glossy stuff? Are you a crow? Or do you just like technical literature?"

"What? Literature?! And don't call me a ho." Yuigahama looked at me like I was some kind of fantastic beast.

"Hikigaya. I don't think most high school students are going to get your gloss puns. That joke was outside her frame of *reference*... Get it, like reference material?" Miss Hiratsuka's eyes sparkled as she gave my humor a failing grade. Man, that expression on her face like *I'm so witty!* was so annoying...

"If you can't see this is cute, then your eyes are rotten," said Yuigahama.

I was on the road to being dubbed *Hikigaya of the Rotten Eye*. Yes, I happened to be the poster child of the affliction. Whatever. I'd already given up, anyway.

She shrugged. "Whatever. We can just bump it, right?"

"No, I don't have a smartphone, so it doesn't do that."

"Huh? Then you have to type numbers in by hand? What a pain."

"I don't need those kinds of functions. I hate phones, anyway. Here." I held out my cell, and Yuigahama timidly accepted it.

"I-I'll type it in... I don't mind. But wow, it's amazing that you don't even hesitate to hand me your cell phone."

"Well, there's nothing on it to embarrass me. I only get e-mails from my sister, Amazon, and McDonald's."

"Whoa! It's true! And they're almost all from Amazon?!"

Leave me alone.

Yuigahama took the phone and began typing something with incredible speed. She looked like a slow girl, but she sure could type fast. From now on, I'd call her the Ayrton Senna of fingertips.

"That's fast."

"Hmm? Isn't this normal? But, like, I guess you don't have anyone to e-mail, so your fingers must be degenerating, huh?"

"That's rude! I e-mailed girls in middle school, at least." I said, and Yuigahama dropped my cell phone with a *clack. Hey, that's my phone. My phone!*

"No way…"

"Hey, do you even realize how mean that reaction was? You don't, do you? Please do."

"Oh, like, I just couldn't imagine you talking to a girl." Yuigahama laughed to avoid the question, picking up the phone she had dropped.

"You idiot. I'm actually, like…when I feel like it, I can do all that stuff. I was popular enough with girls that when we were switching classes and everyone was exchanging e-mails, I took out my phone and glanced around, and this girl said to me, 'Oh…so I guess we could exchange e-mails?'"

"*'I guess'?* Kindness can be cruel, huh?" Yukinoshita smiled warmly.

"Don't you pity me! We actually e-mailed each other after that!"

"What was she like?" Yuigahama asked indifferently, dropping her gaze to her cell. But her previously swift fingers mysteriously ceased their clacking entirely, not even twitching.

"Hmm… She seemed health conscious and reserved. She was so health conscious that when I'd send her an e-mail at seven PM, she'd reply the next morning with something like 'Sorry, I fell asleep. See you at school.' But then after that, she'd be all shy in class. She was so introverted and quiet that she wouldn't talk to me."

"Erp, that's actually…" Yuigahama put her hand to her mouth like she was holding back a sob as tears poured from her eyes.

I didn't need to hear the rest of that sentence. I'd figured it out myself.

"She pretended to be asleep in order to ignore your message. Don't avert your eyes from the truth, Hikigaya. You need to confront reality."

How can you say such a thing, Yukinoshita? How can you say that with such a triumphant expression on your face, Yukinoshita? "I know all about reality. I know so much I could practically write a Hikipedia." *Ahhhh-ha-ha-ha-ha-ha,* this was all so nostalgic. I guess you could call it the folly of youth. I was so pure back then. I'd had no idea that she'd only asked for my e-mail to be nice and then only replied to my messages out of pity. In the end, after two weeks, I noticed that she hadn't sent me a single message even though I'd sent her several, so I stopped.

So, like, I keep getting these e-mails from Hikigaya... He's so creepy, it's, like, enough already!

He definitely has a crush on you, Kaori.

What? I would never—not ever!

Just imagining what sort of conversation had transpired between those girls made me want to die. I really had liked her!

I'd tried my best to use emotes and stuff; it was so sad. I'd thought that using hearts would be creepy, so I used sparkles and suns and music notes... Just remembering it was agonizing enough to make me faint, seriously.

"Hikigaya... Y-you could exchange e-mails with me. I'll actually return your messages, okay? I won't pretend to be asleep," Miss Hiratsuka said, taking my phone from Yuigahama's hand and typing in her e-mail. This was crashing waves of pity here.

"Uh, I don't need you to be nice to me..." E-mailing your teacher is just sad. It's about on par with my mom giving me chocolates on Valentine's Day every year. Where was this wave of pity coming from all of a sudden? At times like this, I was grateful for Yukinoshita's indifference.

In the end, my phone was returned with the addition of their numbers. Though merely adding data shouldn't have affected its weight, for some reason, it felt heavier. So this was the weight of human bonds, huh...? How light. So light that, looking back at how desperate I was—how I would beg for a few kilobytes of data—just made me laugh.

Thinking about how I'd never fill up the memory in this phone, I opened my address book. When I did, I saw...

☆★ Yui ★☆

...written on the screen. Hey, where is this supposed to go if the contacts are organized alphabetically? And no matter how you looked at it, this was like the sender line on spam. The ho-ishness of it was very Yuigahama. I pretended I hadn't seen it and stuffed away my phone.

I'd been brisk with my task, so I had only a few sheets of paper left. I sorted them quickly. Miss Hiratsuka glanced at my work from the corner of her eye and cleared her throat. "Hikigaya. That's enough. Thanks for helping me out. You may go," she said without turning toward me, lighting the cigarette in her lips with a sizzle. Perhaps the pity I'd inspired in her mere moments before still lingered, as she was being uncharacteristically kind. Wait, if *this* passed as kindness for her, then how mean was she most of the time?

"Yes'm. I'm going to my club, then." I picked up the bag that I'd left flopped over on the floor and pulled it over my right shoulder. Inside was the manga I'd brought to read during club time today and a few textbooks for studying for midterms. Club time was likely going to be another few hours of idleness with no one coming to seek our help, as usual.

I started walking, and Yuigahama followed me. If she hadn't come to get me, I would have just gone home. As I approached the door, I heard a voice at my back.

"Oh, yeah. Hikigaya. I forgot to tell you, but for the upcoming workplace tour, we're going in groups of three. You get to choose your own groups, so keep that in mind."

Wh-what did she just say...? As she spoke, my shoulders slumped. "Aw, man. I really don't want anyone from class coming over to my house..."

"You're still planning to do your workplace tour at home?" The determination Miss Hiratsuka saw in me turned her expression horrified. "I thought the 'form groups of three' part would turn you off that, though."

"What? What are you talking about?" I brushed my hair up as I turned, flared my eyes, and fixed Miss Hiratsuka with my most intense gaze. I also made my teeth sparkle. "The pain of loneliness is nothing to me at this point! I'm used to it!"

"Lame."

"D-don't be stupid. A hero is always alone, but he's still cool. In other words, alone equals cool!"

"Oh yeah, there is that hero who says that love and courage are his only friends, isn't there?"

"Exactly! Wait, I'm surprised you know about him."

"Yes, I find him quite interesting. I wonder when small children first recognize that love and courage are not friends."

"You have twisted interests." But it was just as Yukinoshita said; love and courage are not friends. That's nothing more than a sprinkling of powdered, sugary words over false pretenses. The essence of it is nothing more than greed and self-satisfaction. They're not friends. By the way, soccer balls aren't friends, either.

Kindness, pity, love, courage, friends, and also soccer balls... I don't need any of them.

X   X   X

The clubroom was on the fourth floor of the special-use building, on the east side, looking out over the grounds below. Through the open window wafted the music of youth. The calls of boys and girls avidly engaging in their after-school activities echoed among the trees, mixing with the sounds of metal bats ringing out and high-pitched whistles. Clarinets and trumpets from the brass band joined in to create a beauteous melody.

And what were we, the Service Club, doing with that wonderful youth BGM behind us? Well, nothing. I was reading a *shoujo* manga I'd borrowed from my sister, Yukinoshita's eyes were pointed down at a paperback with a leather book cover over it, and Yuigahama was idly clacking away on her cell phone. As usual, we were failing at youth.

Most clubs probably waste time like this. Our school's rugby team's clubroom had apparently been transformed into a mah-jongg parlor, and they usually played a half round before and a half round after practice. And then the next morning, you'd catch sight of the rugby club members arguing over rugby money. (This was the currency circulated solely among the rugby club. It was absolutely not cash. Its characteristic trait was that it looked very much like Japanese yen.) From what I could tell, they were just playing mah-jongg in the clubroom, but from their perspective it was a legitimate form of communication and an important part of their youth experience.

How many of them actually knew how to play mah-jongg in the first place, though? I was sure that few among them had endlessly played Shanghai and strip mah-jongg at the ACE by Tsudanuma like I had. They must have studied the game and learned the rules to fit in with the rest of the club. By the way, Shanghai is a game that uses mah-jongg tiles, but the rules are completely different from those of mah-jongg. In other words, strip mah-jongg is the only way to learn the rules. I can get serious about these things if it's for boobs.

Having a common language like that is essential for making friends. Yui Yuigahama used to be the archetype of this model. I considered this as I got to the "morning after" scene in my *shoujo* manga and closed the book, turning my attention to Yuigahama. I saw she had her cell phone in one hand and an ambiguous smile on her face. She was sighing so faintly no one could hear her, and yet I could see it was very deep. Though I couldn't hear the air coming out of her mouth, her chest rose and fell visibly.

"What's wrong?" The question came not from me but Yukinoshita. Though her gaze had not moved from her paperback, she had apparently noticed that Yuigahama was acting strangely. Or perhaps she'd heard the sigh. I'd expected no less from Devilman, whose devil ears could hear all the way to hell.

"Oh, uh…it's nothing. I just got a kinda weird text, so I was just like, *whoa!*"

"Hikigaya, if you don't want this to turn into a lawsuit, then stop sending her those obscene texts." She just assumed the content was some form of sexual harassment, plus she was treating *me* like the criminal.

"It wasn't me. Where's the proof that I did it? Give me proof. Proof!" I demanded.

Yukinoshita, looking triumphant, swept her hair off her shoulders. "Your statement is proof enough. Only the perpetrator would say something like that. 'Where's the proof it was me?' Or 'Amazing deduction. You should be a novelist.' Or 'I couldn't stay in the same room as a murderer.'"

"That last line is more like something a victim would say." That was an obvious signal that someone was going to die.

"Is that so?" Yukinoshita replied, tilting her head as she flipped through her paperback. Apparently, she was reading a mystery novel.

"I don't think Hikki's the culprit, though," Yuigahama offered belatedly.

Yukinoshita's hand ceased flipping through her paperback. Her eyes asked, *And where's your proof?* Come on, did she want me to be the perpetrator that badly?

"Hmm, I dunno, but, like…the e-mail is about our class. So…I don't think it's anything Hikki would be involved in."

"I'm in your class, though."

"I see. Then Hikigaya isn't the culprit."

"You're accepting that as proof?!" *Hello, I'm Hachiman Hikigaya, Class 2-F.* Yukinoshita hurt me so badly that I introduced myself in my head. But at least this way, she wouldn't be treating me like a criminal, so I figured I'd leave it at that.

"Well, this sort of thing happens sometimes. I'm not gonna let it bother me," Yuigahama said, snapping her phone shut. The way she did it made it seem like she was putting a lid over her heart. It had that sort of weight to it. She'd said, *This sort of thing happens sometimes*, but just so you know, I'd never gotten any messages like that. Isn't it great, having no friends? Seriously, though, people who have lots of friends always have to deal with that sort of sordid business. It seems really rough. When it came to our class, I wasn't bound by any of those hardships smeared in the disgraces of earthly life. From a Buddhist perspective, I'm a legit Siddhartha. I'm high up there.

Yuigahama didn't touch her phone after that. I could only guess as to the content of the message, but it probably wasn't anything pleasant. Plus, Yuigahama was an airhead, a guileless dork, and the kind of bleeding heart who'd waste concern on me and Yukinoshita, so she was probably tormenting herself over weird stuff, anyway.

Yuigahama leaned back in her chair and stretched up high as if she were trying to forcibly shake it off. "I'm bored." Her time-wasting item of choice, her cell phone, now stowed away, Yuigahama leisurely leaned way back in her chair. That really emphasized her chest, making me embarrassed to look at her, so I was forced to turn my attention to Yukinoshita's chest instead, as hers had nothing to be embarrassed over. Yukinoshita, with her safe-and-sound, flat-as-a-board chest, closed her book and admonished Yuigahama. "If you have nothing to do, then why don't you study? There's not much time until midterm exams."

Despite her warning, Yukinoshita didn't appear anxious about the deadline herself. She'd said it like it had absolutely nothing to do with her. But that was only natural; to Yukinoshita, midterms were mere routine. She was generally the kind of girl who would rank top in her year in any test worthy of the name. She wouldn't be rattled by a mere midterm at this point.

Yuigahama apparently knew that, as she averted her eyes petulantly and somewhat awkwardly, muttering through her barely open mouth: "What's the point of studying or whatever? We'll never use it after graduation, anyway."

"There it is—the dunce's cliché." Her reply had been so very, *very* predictable that it went the other way and ended up actually being surprising. *Is she seriously for real? Are there still high school students these days who say stuff like that?*

Even more petulant now having been called a dunce, Yuigahama leaped to a counterargument. "There really is no point, though! We won't be in high school for very long, so it's a waste to spend our time on that stuff! YOLO, right?!"

"Yeah, you only get one chance, and that's exactly why you're not allowed to fail."

"You're so negative!"

"I prefer to say I hedge my risks."

"You're failing in every aspect of your life in high school, though," Yukinoshita remarked.

That was true. I'd completely failed to hedge anything. Wait, seriously? Had this game of life come to an end, my king piece backed into a corner? In English, that's called *check out*, right? What was this, a hotel? "But, like, I'm not failing... My life is just a little different. I'm quirky! We're all different, and we're all good!"

"Y-yeah! Quirky! Being bad at studying is a quirk, too!" said Yuigahama.

There it was—the two of us had gotten together to bring up cliché of the dunces number two. Yeah, the word *quirky* really was convenient...

"Misuzu Kaneko would probably be angry to hear that." Yukinoshita put her hand to her forehead and sighed. "Yuigahama, you just said that there's no point in studying, but that's not true. Studying is about finding that meaning yourself. I'm sure everyone has his or her own reasons for studying, but nevertheless, you cannot deny the validity of all study."

Indubitably correct reasoning. Or perhaps I should say, the insincere rationale of an adult. That's why that reasoning only starts making sense to you once you're grown up. It's the kind of explanation that arises only when an adult is looking back on the past, wondering why on earth they had to study back then. And that's why people still in the process of becoming adults refuse to accept it. Yukinoshita was probably the only teenager who'd arrived at that conclusion on her own, sincerely believing what she'd just said with no affectation whatsoever.

"You're fine 'cause you're smart, Yukinon, but...I'm no good at studying, and no one else in class is doing it, either..." Yuigahama trailed off quietly.

Yukinoshita's eyes narrowed abruptly. There was a silence as if the temperature had suddenly plummeted, and Yuigahama, only just realizing what she'd said, snapped her mouth shut. Apparently, she remembered Yukinoshita being sharp with her about that sort of thing before.

She backpedaled with all her might. "B-but I *am* gonna study! Which reminds me! Are you studying, Hikki?!" Oh-ho! She deflected it before Yukinoshita got mad at her. It seemed she was plotting to escape Yukinoshita's ire by directing it my way instead. But too bad for her.

"I'm studying."

"This is betrayal! I thought you were my fellow dunce-in-arms!!"

"That's rude... I'm ranked third in our year in Japanese, you know. And I'm not bad in other humanities, either."

"No way... I had no idea..."

By the way, at our school, they didn't post test results for all to see. They just quietly handed back test results and rankings to each individual student. So student rankings circulated through hearsay, but having no one with whom to share my grades, nobody knew my ranking. Nobody even asked me about my ranking or whatever in the first place. Nobody asked me about anything else, either, of course.

"A-are you actually smart, Hikki?"

"Not very," said Yukinoshita.

"Why'd *you* answer that?" I complained. Well, maybe compared to Yukinoshita, my scores were a little lacking, but if you had to call them either good or bad, they were on the good side. That was why within this cluster, Yuigahama was far and away the dumbest.

"Ugh. I can't believe I've gotta play the dumb one of the group."

"Don't say that, Yuigahama." Though Yukinoshita's tone was cool, there was warmth in her expression and the clear color of conviction in her eyes.

Yuigahama immediately brightened. "Y-Yukinon!"

"You're not *playing* dumb. You're genuinely that stupid."

"*Wahhh!*" Yuigahama flailed her fists against Yukinoshita's chest.

Yukinoshita sighed as she sat there and took it with an expression that said she found all of this utterly irksome. "What I'm saying is that it's stupid to measure the value of an individual through things like exam scores or rankings. Some people with good grades are actually remarkably inferior human beings."

"Hey, why are you looking at me now?" They weren't just glancing at me. They were glaring hard. "For your information, I do it because I like studying, okay?"

"Oh?" Yuigahama was surprised.

"You've nothing to do except study, huh?" Yukinoshita added the self-evident commentary, as usual.

My face twitched involuntarily. "Well, yeah, just like you."

"I won't deny that."

"You should deny it! You're making me sad!" Though Yukinoshita was composed, Yuigahama's voice was full of heartrending empathy. Apparently, she'd given Yukinoshita's emotional wounds a lot of deep thought, because she flung her arms around her friend.

Yuigahama squeezed Yukinoshita tight, oblivious to her "This is stifling" remark and her put-upon expression.

Hey! Me too, me too! I don't have anything to do but study, either! Why don't I get any outflung arms or squeezes? Well, I'd feel uncomfortable if I did get any, though.

But that's the thing. I wonder why normies get so touchy-feely. It's like physical intimacy is natural for them, or like...*Are you American or what?* Whacking someone upside the head when you're fooling around or hugging them when something happens... I think that kind of

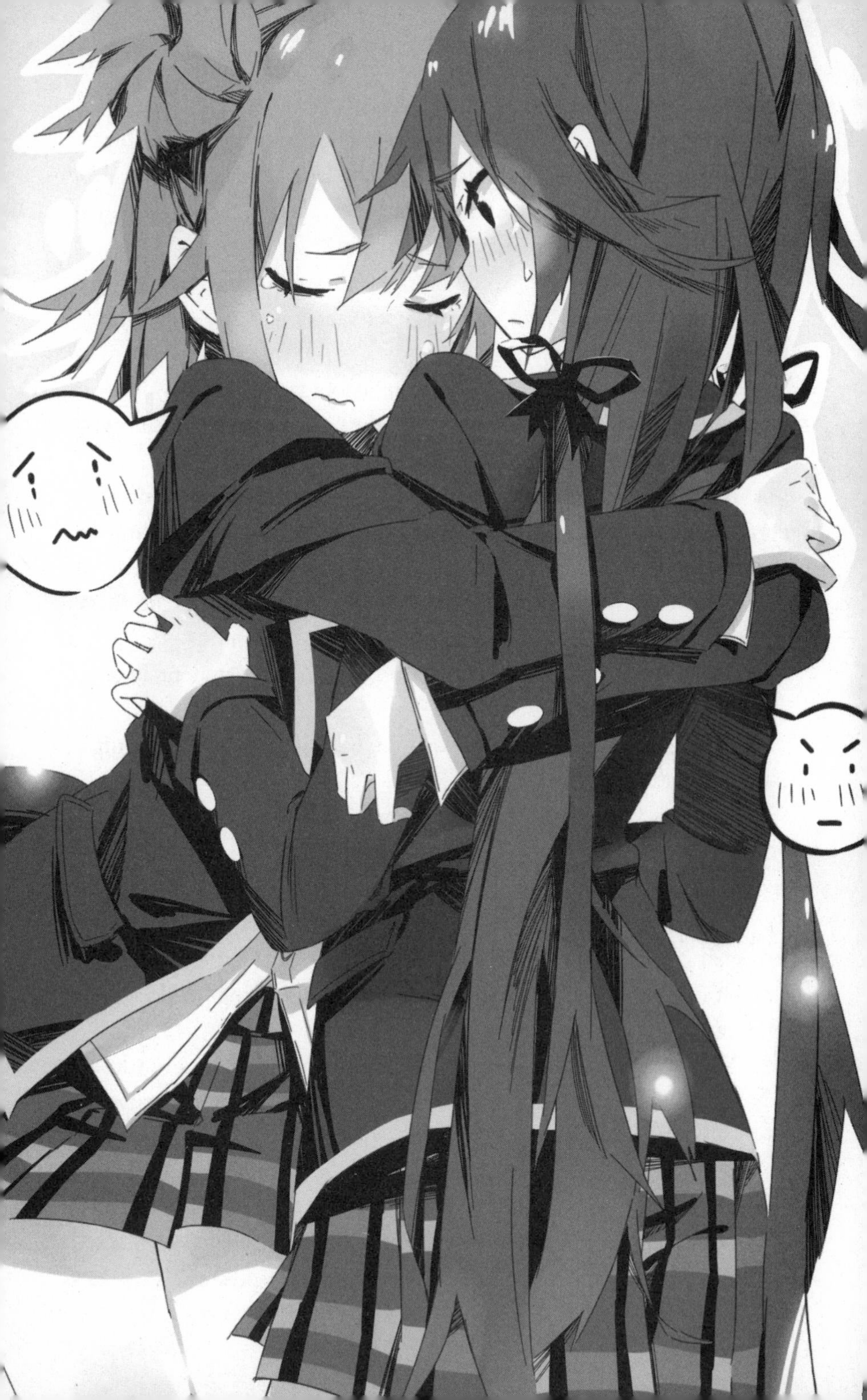

behavior is really cool. People like that are so emotionally open, if they were to pilot an Eva, they wouldn't even be able to activate an AT field.

Yuigahama held Yukinoshita's head and stroked it, casually remarking, "But, like, it's kind of surprising that you study so hard."

"Well, everyone else is studying right now, too, if they want to go on to university, right? And once summer vacation starts, some people will even take summer classes."

Chiba City Municipal Soubu High School was geared toward students who wanted to go to university, so the percentage of students who proceeded to post-secondary education was fairly high.

Those on the ball should already have been considering university entrance exams by the summer of their second year. This was around the time when they'd start working out whether to attend Sazemi in Tsudanuma, Kawai University Prep School, or Toushin on the Inage coast.

"Plus, you know. I'd like to be a *sukoraashippu* student in prep school, as they say in English."

"What? You want to be *sukurappu*? Like scrap material?" Yuigahama was baffled.

"If that's what you're aiming for, you don't have to work at it— you're doing fine right now," said Yukinoshita. "You're something like living industrial waste, aren't you?"

"Whoa, Yukinoshita. You're being so nice today. I would have expected you to deny that I'm even alive."

"It's refreshing to see you being so self-deprecating." Yukinoshita pressed her temple, her expression pained.

"Hey, hey, what's a *sukurappu*?" So Yuigahama didn't even know what *scrap* meant, and that was why she'd failed to follow the conversation. What, for real, Yuigahama-san?

"A *sukoraashippu* is like *shougakukin*—a scholarship," explained Yukinoshita.

"Prep schools these days waive tuition for students with good grades. In other words, I'd get a scholarship plus the tuition money from my parents, so I could just pocket all of the latter." I'd jumped for joy when I came up with that idea. I'd even started break-dancing in my room and weirded out my sister. I'm more motivated in my studies when I have a clear goal in mind, and my parents would rest easy if they got results appropriate to the sum they'd invested. Meanwhile, I'd have some money for myself. It was a brilliant plan.

Both girls seemed dubious about my plan.

"That's fraud…," said Yuigahama.

"At the end of the day, the studying still gets done, so you can't say that his parents are wasting their money. For the prep school, it's just another scholarship enrollment, so there's no problem for them, either. The fact that it can't definitively be categorized as fraud is what makes this boy so vicious."

I'm being totally slandered here. Wh-what's the problem? I'm just telling a victimless fib.

"University, huh…?" Yuigahama mumbled as she glanced in my direction, then grabbed Yukinoshita's sleeve as tightly as she could.

That strength of her grip must have surprised Yukinoshita, who peered at Yuigahama's face with mild concern. "What is it?"

"Oh, no. It's nothing… Or maybe it isn't… I was just sort of thinking, since the two of you are smart, once we graduate, we probably won't get to see each other." Yuigahama laughed as if to cover her unease.

"Indeed… I'll most certainly never see Hikigaya again."

Yukinoshita delivered this declaration with a slight smile, but I just shrugged my shoulders in silence. My lack of retort apparently inspiring suspicion in Yukinoshita, she flung her gaze at me askance.

I've got nothing. You're probably right, Yukinoshita.

There are people like that. They'll pick a high school that no one from their middle school is going to, study like mad, and then manage to pass the entrance exams to get into one of the leading academic high schools in the prefecture. They just throw away the past and decide never to see their classmates again. Some people really are like that, so Yuigahama's fears were undeniably legitimate.

Friendships can only be maintained when people are affiliated with the same group and in constant communication with one another. People are dependent upon situations like school to gradually fertilize their relationships. So when they're torn out of these scenarios, people always end up alone. Then your only means of contact become phone calls or e-mail—or you just lose touch altogether. And people call that friendship? I'm sure they do. That's why everyone leaves it all to their cell phones and takes the number of registered names in their contact lists to be equivalent to their number of friends.

Yuigahama squeezed her cell phone as she smiled at Yukinoshita. "But we have our phones, so that won't happen, right? We can contact each other anytime."

"I'd still like you to stop e-mailing me every day."

"Huh?! Y-you don't like it…?"

"It is occasionally extremely bothersome."

"Aw, you're always so honest!"

These two are sure close. But since when are they e-mailing each other? I just can't imagine Yukinoshita doing that. "You're e-mailing her every day? What do you even say to each other?"

"Um… Like, 'I had cream puffs today! ☆'"

"Like, 'Oh.'"

"Like, 'Can you make cream puffs, Yukinon?! I want to try some other sweets later!'"

"Like, 'Understood.'"

"Yukinoshita, your replies are offensively short."

"Adding any additional information would be unnecessary," Yukinoshita said in a dissatisfied tone, jerking her attention away. What was sad was that I got how she felt. No, really. How do you reply to that kind of small talk? They say the bedrock of conversation is talking about the weather, but then you just go, *It's sunny, huh?* and respond, *Yes, it is,* and then it ends. That's way worse than a mere *un ange passe, tee-hee,* when there's an awkward silence over the phone.

"Cell phones, huh…? They aren't that reliable. They're quite the imperfect method of communication, in my opinion," I said. I believe a cell phone is merely a device that allows you to lonerize yourself even faster. Even if someone does call you, you can just let it ring or refuse the call, and you can just ignore texts. You can decide to accept or reject relationships with no repercussions and are able to turn on or off interactions as you please.

"Indeed. It's all up to the receiver whether or not to return e-mails or answer calls." Yukinoshita nodded at my casual observation. This was Yukinoshita, whose looks were the only nice thing about her. I bet lots of people had asked for her e-mail or phone number.

Even I had screwed up my courage once and asked a cute girl for her number. It was back when I was an innocent boy in middle school. She told me, "Sorry, my battery's dead. I'll send you an e-mail later." As I hadn't given her my e-mail address, it was a mystery how she could message me. I'm still waiting for it even now…

"Not to mention that I just ignore unwanted messages, anyway," Yukinoshita added with a sigh.

"Hmm?" Yuigahama put her index finger to her chin, tilting her head. "So…that means my messages aren't unwanted?"

"I didn't say they're unwanted. They're just onerous." Yukinoshita flushed red and quietly turned away from Yuigahama, who was peering at her face intently. It was a rather cute reaction, but as I wasn't a part of any of that, I didn't give a damn.

When Yuigahama saw her blush, she screeched and glomped Yukinoshita. Captive to Yuigahama's tender mercies, Yukinoshita looked away, her expression a picture of sullen displeasure. But I wasn't a part of any of that, so I didn't give a damn.

"I get it—cell phones aren't perfect, are they?" Yuigahama clutched Yukinoshita tightly, as if fully realizing just how fragile that connection was. "Maybe…I'll study for real… It'd be great if we could go to the same university," she whispered quietly, dropping her gaze to the floor. "Have you decided on a school, Yukinon?"

"No, not a specific school yet. I'm aiming for a national public science university, though."

"Sounds like something a smart person would say! So…so wh-what about you, Hikki? J-just since we're talking about this."

"I'm going for private arts."

"That sounds like a place I might be able to get into!" The smile returned to Yuigahama's face. *Hey, what's with that reaction?*

"Just so you know, private arts doesn't mean *stupid*. Apologize to all the private arts students in the country. And you're way stupider than me, anyway."

"Ugh… I-I'm *gonna* try my best, okay?!" Releasing Yukinoshita, Yuigahama announced her resolution loudly. "So, anyway. That means we're gonna start studying together this week."

"How does it mean that?" Yukinoshita expressed her doubt.

"The week leading up to the test, there's no club time, and we're not doing anything in the afternoons, right? Oh, this week, Tuesday is a Pro-D, and there's no club time, so that might be good." Completely ignoring Yukinoshita, Yuigahama briskly set about planning their schedule.

But man, I hadn't heard the term *Pro-D* since middle school. Pro-D referred to Professional Development days, and because all the teachers had to participate, classes got shortened, and club time and stuff got canceled.

Well, it wasn't like I didn't understand her plan. It must have been quite reassuring for her, having the two of us around—Yukinoshita, ranked first in our grade and aiming for a public science institution, and me, boasting third in Japanese among our peers. Plus, I had a stupid little sister, so I thought I could teach pretty okay. My sister just didn't get results because she was stupid.

The only problem was that I had no desire to assist Yuigahama. What didn't I like about the idea? The part I disliked most was losing my personal time. I'm the kind of guy who even refuses to go to the athletic festival after party. I-it's not because I don't get invited! Time is a finite resource, and it pains me to spare any on someone else's behalf.

"Uh…" *How should I refuse?* As I pondered the question, the conversation proceeded without me.

"So are you okay with the Saize in Purena?" asked Yuigahama.

"I don't really care," Yukinoshita replied.

"Yuigahama, um, like…" If I didn't say something fast, it'd be a done deal! But the moment I decided on a flat refusal, that avenue was cut off.

"This is the first time the two of us have gone out together, Yukinon!"

"Is that so?"

Oh.

I hadn't been invited in the first place.

"Did you say something, Hikki?"

"No… You two study hard."

Studying alone is more efficient, anyway! …I'm not gonna let you guys beat me.

Hachiman's mobile

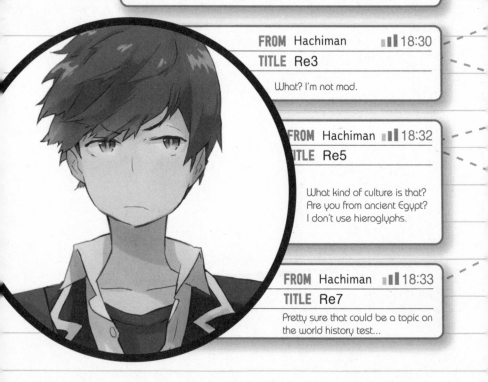

FROM	Hachiman	📶 18:29
TITLE	Re	

The curriculum is so broad for world history, if you try to guess what'll be on it, you'll be wrong, so there's no point. But because it's a big curriculum, there won't be essay-style answers. Just attempt to grasp the terms on the chronology tables and then start memorizing.

FROM	Hachiman	📶 18:30
TITLE	Re3	

What? I'm not mad.

FROM	Hachiman	📶 18:32
TITLE	Re5	

What kind of culture is that? Are you from ancient Egypt? I don't use hieroglyphs.

FROM	Hachiman	📶 18:33
TITLE	Re7	

Pretty sure that could be a topic on the world history test...

Yui's mobile

FROM ☆★ Yui ★☆:   📶 18:21
TITLE none

heya! 〜ヽ(*･ω･)ノ゜+.゜
have u already studied
4 world history?! im totally
screwed! (>_<)
what countries do u think
will be on it? im out of
time so all I can do is
study a couple topics
and hope I get lucky...
help me, plz ☆

FROM ☆★ Yui ★☆:   📶 18:
TITLE Re2

why are u mad, hikki (´･ω･`)?

FROM ☆★ Yui ★☆:   📶 18:31
TITLE Re4

if u don't use emotes or faces it looks
like ur mad (` ･ω･ ´)!

FROM ☆★ Yui ★☆:   📶 18:32
TITLE Re6

what r hieroglyphs (´･ω･`)?

Komachi Hikigaya is gonna marry her big brother when she grows up.

(says me)

It was two weeks before the midterm exams. Virtuous high school boys would stop by family restaurants to study on their way home from school. Classes ending early and clubs having been canceled due to the Pro-D made the situation ideal for studying.

I was focused intently on the simple task of transcribing English vocab. You could even have likened me to the great monk of old, Shinran. By the way, Shinran taught that one should *Let a higher power support you*, and he was a very important man. His philosophy left a deep impression on me, so I'm thinking I'll allow someone to support my lifestyle, too. From a Buddhist perspective, I'm practically Shinran.

I finished copying out a list of the test vocab. Thinking I might like a cup of cocoa while reviewing the words by hiding their definitions with a red sheet, I took my cup and stood. That's when it happened.

"Sorry this isn't Saize, Yukinon. We'll have Milan-style pilaf next time, okay? Oh, and I wanted to recommend the Diavola-style hamburg steak, but…"

"I don't particularly care where we go. We're going to be doing the same thing either way… Wait, is hamburg steak Italian food?"

Those voices sounded familiar.

"Ah!"

"Oh."

"Ugh."

Seeing each other, all three of us froze. Oh, so we're a snake, a frog, and a slug, then? For some reason, I felt like I was probably the slug in this scenario.

The pair who had just made their entrance was a uniform-clad Yukino Yukinoshita and Yui Yuigahama. Unfortunately, they were my fellow clubbians. By the way, *clubbian* refers to someone who is a member of an arts or a humanities club. This was my first time ever employing the word... It felt right.

"What're you doing here, Hikki?"

"Uh, studying..."

"Ooh, that's so funny. Like, me and Yukinon came around here to study, too... S-so...wanna study together?" Yuigahama asked as her eyes darted back and forth between my face and Yukinoshita's.

"If you want. I'd still be studying, anyway."

"Indeed. There would be no alteration to our agenda." Yukinoshita and I were in agreement for once.

"Hmm?" Yuigahama seemed puzzled for a moment to find us on the same page. Apparently, though, she decided to let it slide, because she cooed, "Okay, it's decided!" and trotted up to my table.

Each of them ordered a drink bar ticket. When Yukinoshita went to retrieve hers, she studied the machine intently. Her cup was poised in her right hand, and for some reason, she clutched change in her left. "Hey, Hikigaya. Where do you put in the money?"

"Huh?" *Seriously? You don't know what a drink bar is, Yukinoshita? What kind of extreme upper-class upbringing did you have?* "Uh, it doesn't cost money. Like, um...buffet style? It's like that, but with drinks."

"Japan is such a bountiful country," she said, a vaguely clouded smile flitting across her face. Her pontifications on beverage dispensers were baffling to me, but she let me go ahead of her. She watched rapt, her mien serious, as I poured myself a drink. Her eyes sparkled as I pressed the button, the machine whirred, and my cup filled with soda. Just in case, while I was at it, I put another cup under the espresso machine and pressed the button for cocoa, and she let out a quiet, "I see…" Though she seemed uncertain about it, Yukinoshita did get the drink she wanted, and the three of us sat down. We were finally ready to start this study thing.

"All right, let's get started." Yuigahama signaled the start of the study session, and Yukinoshita pulled out her headphones and put them on with a clack. Eyeing the others from the side, I put in my ear buds.

Watching us, Yuigahama's expression turned to shock. "What?! Why are you listening to music?!"

"Well, when you study, you listen to music, right? To block out noise."

"That's right. When you stop noticing the music, you know that you're concentrating. It's quite motivating."

"This isn't right! This isn't studying together!" Yuigahama objected, smacking the table.

Yukinoshita put her hand to her chin and adopted a thoughtful pose. "Then what *is* studying together?"

"Um…you check with each other what's going to be on the test, ask questions about stuff you don't understand… Oh, and you take some breaks, too, and then you ask for help with things, and after that, you exchange information. And sometimes…you chat, I guess?"

"That's all just talking." She called that *studying together*, but that wasn't actually getting any studying done. It was all just impeding studying.

"Studying is meant to be solitary, really," Yukinoshita said as if she knew all about it.

I agreed with her. Basically, she was saying that loners are good at studying. Hey, they should write that in those manga that advertise the Shinkan Seminar home learning courses.

At first, Yuigahama had this look on her face that said she really wasn't convinced, but with Yukinoshita and I silently and intently buried in our books, she surrendered with a sigh and began studying herself. This continued with five, ten minutes passing, and time went by.

When I happened to look up at them again, Yuigahama had a tortured look on her face, her hand still. Yukinoshita, on the other hand, continued quietly solving math problems. Perhaps Yuigahama was hesitant to interrupt Yukinoshita's concentration as she turned toward me.

"U-um...about this question...?" Yuigahama asked. Perhaps asking me offended her pride, as she looked extremely embarrassed.

"The Doppler effect, huh...? I'm not even bothering with math and science, so I dunno. I can explain *Grappler Baki* instead—how about that?"

"No way! The only thing they share in common is a *ppler!*"

No good after all, huh? I thought I could do a pretty good job explaining it, though.

Yuigahama closed her textbook and notebook as if she was giving up and slurped her iced tea through a straw. She took her emptied glass in hand and was about to stand when she gasped "Ah!" like she'd just noticed something.

Drawn by her exclamation, I turned in the direction she was looking and saw an amazingly cute, pretty girl in a sloppy sailor-style school uniform. "That's my sister." My little sister, Komachi, was standing in front of the register with a cheerful smile on her face. Beside her stood a boy wearing a *gakuran.* "Sorry, 'scuse me," I apologized, standing and immediately going after her, but by the time I got out of the restaurant, they were gone.

I reluctantly went back into the restaurant, and Yuigahama started interrogating me. "Uhh, um. Was that your sister?"

"Yeah. Why was she coming to a family restaurant with a boy...?" I was in shock. This was no time to be studying. My little sister had no business in a restaurant with some strange guy.

"She might have been on a date!"

"That's ridiculous...impossible..."

"I dunno. Wouldn't it be normal for Komachi-chan to have a cute boyfriend?"

"She can't have a boyfriend if her older brother doesn't have a girlfriend! No little sister can surpass her older brother!"

"Don't be so stupid at such a high volume. I could hear that even with headphones on." Yukinoshita removed said headphones and glared at me. The cord was taut in her hands. If I made any more of a scene, it seemed she would strangle me.

"I'm not being stupid. My little sister was abducted by an unidentified male—"

"He was obviously just a middle school student," said Yuigahama. "I get that you're worried about Komachi-chan, but she's not gonna like you anymore if you pry. Lately, my daddy has been pestering me with questions like 'Do you have a boyfriend?' It's so annoying."

"*Ha-ha-ha!* That's nothing. My dad is so firmly convinced that my sister doesn't have a boyfriend, he won't even ask the question. I feel bad just looking at him, frankly... Wait, how do you know my sister's name?" I didn't think I'd mentioned my sister's name to anyone. I doubted that anyone even knew *my* first name, so anyone knowing her name should have been out of the question.

"Huh?! Oh, uh, well, you know... I think it was...written in your cell phone?" For some reason, Yuigahama averted her eyes.

Oh. Now that I thought about it, I had handed her my cellphone once, huh? It might have been one of my texts. "Is that it? That's a relief. I thought maybe I'd turned into a poor bastard with such a severe sister complex that I unconsciously mutter her name."

"Uh, now you're sounding like you've got a sister complex," Yuigahama fretted, slightly weirded out.

"That's absurd! In no way do I have a sister complex. I don't even see her as my sister, but rather as a woman... Hey, I'm clearly joking—don't start pulling out weapons!"

Yukinoshita was glowering at me with a mix of shock and fear. I stopped talking when she picked up the knife and fork. Had I finished my sentence, there's no question she would have flayed me alive. "Coming from you, it doesn't sound like a joke. It's horrifying. But if this bothers you so much, why don't you ask her about it at home?" Yukinoshita put forward this conclusive suggestion, and she and Yuigahama went back to studying.

But I left my notes untouched after that. I reminisced about Komachi crying, *Bro!* and scampering after me, shouting, *I'm gonna marry you when I grow up, Bro!* and how my dad had gotten a lot harsher with me after that.

Whatever. Who cares about my sister?

And that was why even after I got home I didn't ask about that stuff. I-it wasn't like it was because I'd heard that prying would make her not like me anymore!

Yui's mobile

FROM Yui   ▮▮▮ 20:22

TITLE none

long day @ school today, huh~! ヾ(｡·ω·)ﾉﾞ° thanks 4 explaining the recurrence formula 2 me Yukinon ♪ let's go 2 Saize again sometime!! their milk Italian gelato is mad good °*｡(*´Д｀)｡*° woo!

FROM Yui   ▮▮▮ 21:37

TITLE Re2

but mebbe it'd be a good deal 2 order coffee jelly on top (>w<*) hey, u took 4ever 2 reply!

FROM Yui   ▮▮▮ 21:49

TITLE Re4

there it is again! hierowhatevrs. Σ(·□·) r those in right now (´·ω·`)?

Yukino's mobile

FROM Yukino ▮▮ 21:36
TITLE Re

Yes, I'm looking forward to it.

FROM Yukino ▮▮ 21:47
TITLE Re3

I'm not used to this.
Not that I care, but do you
type those hieroglyphic-esque
images by hand?

FROM Yukino ▮▮ 21:59
TITLE Re5

They went out of style
about 1,900 years ago.

Hayato Hayama's presence always shines.

There is nothing less relaxing to the soul than school recess.

The classroom was filled with chattering bustle. One and all were freed from the oppression that is class, and they were conversing intimately with friends about what to do after school or what they'd seen on TV the previous day. The conversations flying around the room might as well have been in a foreign language; even if they reached my ears, they held no meaning for me.

Things were even livelier than usual. This was because our homeroom teacher had dropped the bomb the day before that we'd be deciding on groups for the workplace tour at the end of the classes today. Though who'd be going where wouldn't be settled until long homeroom for a couple more days yet, everyone was already getting excited about it.

Though several of the conversations floating through room revolved around the question *Where are you going?* none of them seemed to be about *Who are you going with?* That was probably because nearly everyone in class had formed their particular cliques already. It was only natural. The institution known as "school" isn't just a facility for doing classwork. It's essentially a microcosm of society, all of humanity put together in a little diorama. Bullying exists in schools because war and conflict exist in the world, and school castes reflect our stratified, hierarchical society. Living in a democracy, the tyranny of the majority naturally applies at school, too. The majority—that is to say, the people with lots of friends—are superior.

My chin resting in my palms in a half-dozing posture, I hazily observed my classmates. I'd gotten plenty of sleep the night before and wasn't particularly tired, but having spent my breaks like this for so long, my body had been conditioned to fall asleep. As I was nodding off, a small hand flitted in a wave across my field of vision. I lifted my head, thinking, *Hmm? What?*

Saika Totsuka was sitting in the seat in front of me. "Morning!" he giggled with a smile, greeting me as I stirred.

"Make me my miso soup every morning."

"H…huh?! Wh-what do you…?"

"Oh, uh, nothing. I was just sleep-talking." *Oh man, I proposed to him. Damn, why was all this cuteness wasted on him? He's a guy! Or is it because he's a guy…? I guess he isn't gonna make me miso soup in the mornings…* "Did you need something?"

"Not really, but…I thought maybe you'd be around, so… Should I…not have come?"

"No, it's okay. It's actually so okay, I want you to come talk to me twenty-four-seven." More like I actually want him to come say he likes me 24/7.

"But then I'd have to be with you forever, wouldn't I?" Totsuka covered his mouth with his hand, grinning like he thought it was funny. Then, apparently realizing something, he brought his palms together in a tiny clap. "Have you already decided where you're doing your workplace tour, Hikigaya?"

"Well, I guess I've decided, but also kinda not," I admitted, but I suppose I failed to convey my point very well because Totsuka tilted his head, peering up at my face. The gesture revealed the collarbone peeking out from his gym clothes, and I averted my eyes automatically. *Why is his skin so pretty? What kind of body soap is he using?!* "Oh, what I'm saying is, I don't really care where I go. If it's not my house, it's all the same to me. Everywhere is equally pointless."

"Huh... You say such tough things sometimes, Hikigaya."

I don't remember having said anything particularly hard to follow, but Totsuka'd sounded impressed. I felt as if I could hear a *bading!* as my affection meter rose; though Totsuka was the kind of character who influenced your affecti-o-meter no matter what he said. It was actually scary. I felt at risk of going down a character route better left untraveled.

"So...then have you maybe...already decided who you're going with?" Totsuka was gazing into my eyes a little hesitantly, but I could feel his firm intentions. Why did he say it like that? He really made it sound like he actually meant *I want to go with you, but if you've already made up your mind, then that's too bad.* His attack caught me completely off guard. And that surprise attack was knocking on the door to my memories as vigorously as a newspaper salesman.

I feel like this has happened once before, long ago...

Yes, it was when I'd just started my second year of middle school. I'd drawn the short straw and ended up being picked as the boy class representative, and then a cute girl volunteered to be the girl class rep and told me shyly, *I'm looking forward to working with you this year.*

Yaagh! That was close! Once again, I'd been inches from being taken in by a line dripping with implications that I didn't remotely understand, leading to me getting seriously hurt. I'd already seen this play out once. An experienced loner does not fall for the same trick twice. Confessions of love as a part of a punishment game after losing rock-paper-scissors don't work on me, and neither do fake love letters from a girl written by boys in her name. I'm a hardened veteran schooled in a hundred battles. I am the best when it comes to losing.

Okay, I'd calmed down. In cases like this, the safest thing to do is just mirror the enemy's moves. In other words, Fearow is surely a master loner. That's why I decided to answer his question with a question. "Have you decided who you're going with?"

"M-me...? I've...already...decided." Bewildered at suddenly having this grenade suddenly thrown back at him, Totsuka's cheeks reddened.

He turned his eyes slightly downward, then glanced up again as if checking to see how I'd react.

Of course. Totsuka was in the tennis club, so in other words, there was a place for him there, a place in his own special community, and inevitable friendships he could derive from that. Of course he would have friends in class.

And then there was me. I was in a club, but it was really just an isolation ward gathering together kids who'd failed to conform to school expectations. I clearly wasn't gonna be making friends there. "Now that I think of it—actually, I don't even need to think about it—I don't have any guy friends."

"U-um…Hikigaya… I'm…a guy…though…" Totsuka muttered something very quietly, but he was so cute I couldn't hear him properly.

Anyway, conversing with another human being in class was an exceedingly odd feeling. Ever since the tennis incident a few days earlier, Totsuka and I had started exchanging what passed for something like small talk whenever we ran into each other. Was this really friendship? I had my doubts. You can share an exchange with a mere acquaintance—no, with someone who doesn't even rise to that level of distinction. For example, in line at Naritake Ramen, you might chat with someone next to you, like, *It sure is crowded, huh?* or *Long line again today—what a pain!* But you wouldn't call that person a friend. Friends are more like…

"So where've you decided to go, Hayato?"

"I'd like to go check out something related to mass media or maybe a foreign-owned company."

"Oh man, you've really got a focus on your future, Hayato. You totally have it together. But I guess we are at that age, huh? I have mad 'spect for my folks these days."

"It's all serious business from now on!"

"Whoa! But you don't wanna lose your boyish spirit!"

I guess friends are something like that. Maybe talking like they do—like every trivial conversation is the height of their youth—is what being friends is. There's no way I could do that; I'd burst into laughter halfway. And what did he mean, *mad 'spect*? Did he think he was some kind of rapper?

As usual and as always, Hayato Hayama had a charming smile on his face and was surrounded by three guys. Everyone was casually saying, *Hayato, Hayato*, calling him by his first name, and Hayama amicably returned the familiarity. I guess that display was something you could appropriately dub "friendship." But to me, it just looked like people posturing with first names to make them feel like they were friends. They're only doing it because that's what people categorized as "friends" do in TV shows, manga, and anime. How is doing that supposed to make you closer?

But hey, why not try it out? With anything, firsthand experience is a necessity. I'm the kind of guy who won't condemn any manga he hasn't actually read. I'll try reading it, but if it's a total mess, I'll slam it hard and fast.

Experiment: Does the usage of first names change human relationships?

"Saika."

When I called his name, Totsuka froze up. His big eyes blinked once, twice, three times, as his mouth gaped. See, it doesn't make you closer after all, huh? Well, it's normal for someone to be irritated if someone suddenly employs their first name. I mean, when Zaimokuza started calling me Hachiman, I ignored him hard. Basically, this first name business is just normies (LOL) lying to themselves, tamping down their anger, and pretending to get along.

Anyway, an apology to Totsuka was probably in order. "Oh, sorry, I just…"

"I'm so glad! This is the first time you've ever called me by my first name."

"Whaat…?"

Totsuka smiled sweetly, his eyes slightly moist.

Seriously? Does this mark the end of my time as a foreveralone? Am I transitioning from loner loser to just the normal kind of loser? Being a normie ('spect) is amazing. The scales have fallen from my eyes.

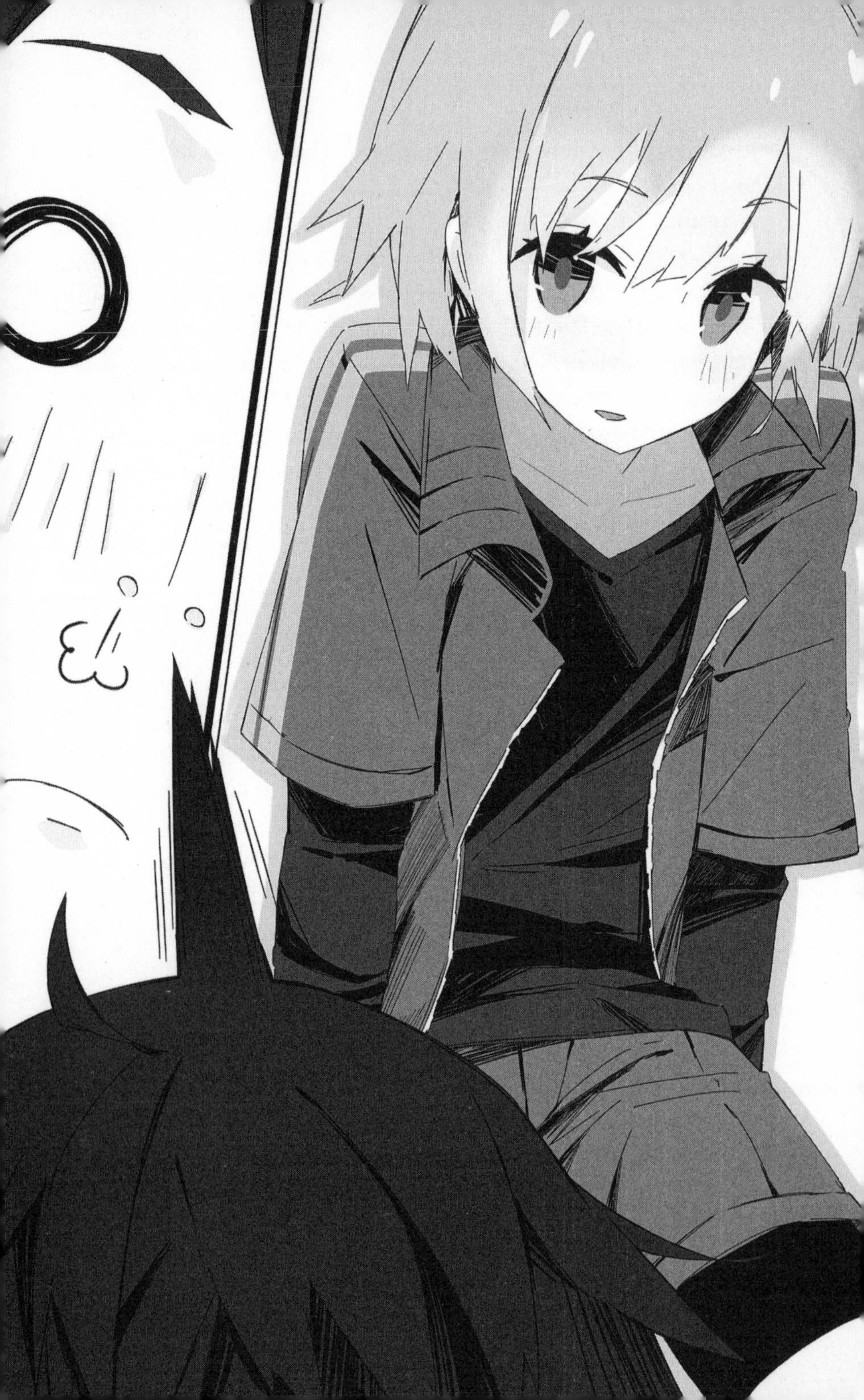

"So…," Totsuka began, fixing me with his puppy dog eyes. "C-can I…call you Hikki, too?"

"No." Why'd he have to go with *that* one, the one with all the shameful, shady implications? There was only one person on the list of individuals who addressed me by that name, and I didn't want to add another.

My flat refusal seemed to disappoint Totsuka somewhat, but he cleared his throat tentatively and tried again. "Then…Hachiman?"

Stab! There goes the arrow right through my heart. "S-say that three more times!"

Totsuka grinned sheepishly as if my crazed request confused him. He was so cute when he was embarrassed that it was embarrassing me. "Hachiman," he said, staring at me as if eager to quantify my reaction. "Hachiman?" He tilted his head to the side, expression quizzical. "Hachiman! Are you listening?!" He puffed his cheeks out in a bit of a pout.

His mild anger snapped me out of it. *Bad Hachiman, bad.* He was so cute, he'd entranced me completely for a moment there. "O-oh, sorry. What were we talking about?" I attempted to hide how I'd been zoning out as I mentally jotted down the results of the experiment in my head.

Conclusion: Totsuka is cute when you call him by his first name.

×　×　×

The din of the school grounds grew quiet, and the light of the setting sun shone into the clubroom. The glow of the sun's final rays as it set over Tokyo Bay began melting into the darkness of the far and distant sky.

"Hmm… And so the time of darkness begins…," the boy muttered, clenching his fists. The leather of his fingerless, faux-leather gloves creaked as he gazed fixedly at the one-kilogram weights peeking out of his sleeves and sighed. "It seems the time has come to remove these seals…"

No one replied to him…even though there were three other people in the room.

The guy glaring expectantly in our direction as if awaiting a reply was Yoshiteru Zaimokuza. The girl emanating silent contempt as she focused wholly on her book was Yukino Yukinoshita. The one stammering, "U-uh…," and turning to Yukinoshita and me for help was Yui Yuigahama.

"Zaimokuza… Do you…need something?" I asked.

Yukinoshita sighed deeply, then shot daggers at me as if to say, *And I was trying* so *hard to ignore him.*

Hey, I had a choice here. It's not like I actually wanted to talk to him, but this had been going on for about thirty minutes. It was as bad as the Haunted Housekeeper in Uptaten Towers in *Dragon Quest V.* If I didn't talk to him now, the situation will drag on interminably.

Zaimokuza rubbed the tip of his nose as if he was glad I'd asked and laughed, *Heh-heh.* How obnoxious. "Yes, my apologies. A good line just happened to arise in my mind, so I unconsciously gave voice to it that I might grasp its feel and the cadence of the words. *Heh…* It seems I am an author to the pith of my bones… I think of my novels, waking and sleeping. The pen is my fate…"

Unfortunately, Zaimokuza's talents were limited to talking big. Yuigahama and I exchanged exhausted looks.

Yukinoshita snapped her book shut, and Zaimokuza flinched. "I thought an author was someone who created things. Have you created anything?"

"Ngaaagh!" Zaimokuza threw his head back as if there were something stuck in his throat. His overreactions are so annoying. But he seemed unusually confident that day and recovered quickly, clearing his throat with a contrived *gahum, gahum.* "Ehem. You won't be able to say that for long. I finally have it in my grasp—the road to El Dorado!"

"What, have you won a prize?"

"N-no, not yet… H-however, once I finish my book, winning a prize is a mere matter of time!" For some reason, Zaimokuza was acting like he had it in the bag.

Come on. What part of that remark contained anything worth bragging about? If he's going to be like that, then when I'm done with the game I'm working on in RPG Maker, I'll change the course of Japanese gaming history.

Zaimokuza threw back his coat with a rustle and yelled loudly as if trying to steer the conversation back on course. *"Ha-ha!* Listen and be amazed! I have decided to go to a publishing house for the upcoming workplace tour! In other words…you get my gist, right?"

"No, I don't."

"Your wits are dull, Hachiman. What I'm saying is that my genius will finally be discovered. This means that I will have *connections!*"

"Come on, you're being ridiculously optimistic. You're worse than an eighth grader who brags about knowing some delinquent older kid."

But Zaimokuza wasn't paying attention to anything I said. He was staring in the opposite direction, smirking to himself, and mumbling: "And the studio will be…and the casting…" Creepy.

Anyway, even if he was going to a publisher, I figured quality varies. But if he believed that fervently that his future would be that bright, there was nothing I could say to him. Still, there was one thing that didn't make sense. "Zaimokuza, I'm surprised anyone would listen to what workplace you wanted."

"Why must you put it thus? You make me sound as lowly as an ant… But no matter. There happened to be two other so-called nerds in training for the forthcoming expedition. I said naught. Those two decided we would be sojourning to a publisher, going *eek-eek-eh-heh-heh* all the while. Those two are most certainly the BL that is all the rage these days. Even I was powerless before their love, so I kept silent so as not to interrupt them."

"You should have made nice with your kind…" Yukinoshita sighed, without so much as looking at Zaimokuza. But her suggestion would never come to pass. There are things some people cannot compromise on precisely because both parties are fixated on the same thing. It's kind of like a holy war.

"I see… The workplace tour, huh…?" Yuigahama mused, each word imbued with feeling. I peeked at her from the corner of my eye, and she turned away immediately. Her face was red, and her eyes were darting about so quickly I wanted to give her a board to use as a target. Did she have a cold or something? "Hey, where are you going, Hikki?"

"My house."

"Yeah, no. That's not gonna happen for you," Yuigahama said dismissively, waving her hand back and forth in the motion for *no*.

It's too early to surrender yet, I thought… But as I didn't want Miss Hiratsuka to punch me, I decided to give up. *I've surrendered, so the game's already over.* "Hmm… Well, I guess I'll go wherever the other people in my group want to go."

"Why so passive?"

"Well…it's always the same for me. I get stuck with whoever's left at the end, so I'll have no voting rights."

"Ohhhh—o-oh…uh, sorry." As usual, she was stepping all over my personal land mines. I bet she was bad at Minesweeper.

That particular land mine existed because, well, forming groups of three is unbelievably even more horrific than pairing off with one other person. If it's just two of you, you can both suck it up and simply accept the situation in grim silence, but in a trio, two of them will buddy up, consigning the third wheel to max heart alienation.

"So you never did decide where you'll go, then," Yuigahama muttered with a *hmm* and a faraway expression.

"Have you decided where you will go, Yuigahama?" asked Yukinoshita.

"Yeah. I'm going wherever's closest to school."

"Your ideas are as bad as Hikigaya's."

"Hey, don't lump me in with her," I protested. "My decision to apply to stay at home is based on high-minded ideals. And where are you going, anyway? The police station? A courtroom? Or a prison?"

"Wrong. Now I understand quite well what you think of me." Yukinoshita chuckled, the smirk on her face frigid.

That was what I'm talking about. *That. The way you smile is scary, seriously.* I'd thought up those potential destinations based on my impression of Yukinoshita as an intellectual person, but she apparently wasn't into any of them. How odd... It wasn't like I was saying that Yukinoshita was cold or cruel or callous or anything. *Eh-heh-heh.* Why was she giving me that weird smile in response?

"Perhaps...some think tank or a research facility. I'll make my choice later." Apparently, she hadn't decided yet, as she only briefly gave us an idea of the general field for which she was aiming. But anyway, judging from her calm and serious personality, I could easily imagine where she might go.

Just then, I felt someone plucking at the sleeve of my blazer. *What is this, some kind of sleeve-pulling imp?* I wondered, and when I turned, there was Yuigahama. She quietly pulled her face close to mine, drawing her lips to my ear. Her pointlessly sweet smell and her glossy hair touching the back of my neck made me shiver. This was the first time I'd ever felt her get this close. Blood rushed like mad to my heart so furiously it was deafening. "H-Hikki..." The sweet breath of her ticklish murmurs at my ear made me feel itchy. Now that she was close enough for me to feel her breath on my skin, I could almost hear both of our hearts beating.

What if...maybe...my heart is pounding like this because...?

"Wh-what's a *think tank*? A tank company?" She said *think tank* like an old lady would.

Nope. I guess it was just arrhythmia.

"Yuigahama." Yukinoshita sighed, looking exasperated, and Yuigahama peeled away from me. "Listen, a think tank is..." She began her explanation, and Yuigahama listened eagerly, *hmm*ing along. The two of them were in casual study mode.

Observing them with a sidelong glance, I refocused my attention on the important task of reading my *shoujo* manga.

About fifteen minutes passed after Yukinoshita finished explaining think tanks and related trivia to Yuigahama. The setting sun was nearing the sea. From the fourth-floor clubroom, you had a good view of the water shining and sparkling in the distance. If you looked below, you'd see the baseball team raking the diamond, the soccer team carrying away their nets, and the track team putting away their hurdles and mats. It seemed that club time was ending. I stole a gander at the clock on the wall, and Yukinoshita simultaneously snapped her book shut. When she did, Zaimokuza flinched. *Come on, you're way too jumpy around her.*

I can't say for sure when this rule was established, but Yukinoshita closing her book had become our signal that club time was over. Yuigahama and I quickly began readying for our departure.

In the end, nooobody had come that day to consult with us. Why was Zaimokuza the only one who'd shown up? Nobody wanted him there. I figured I'd have some ramen on the way back and then go home. Thinking about dinner, I decided on a light meal at Houraiken. It's a Niigata-style ramen shop, and their light and refreshing broth is first-rate. It's also a shop that Zaimokuza told me about. Oh, crap, my mouth is watering.

That was when it happened. There was a delightfully rhythmical *tap, tap* on the door.

"*Now?*" My blissful ramen time interrupted, I found myself in bad mood mode and glared at the clock. Had I been at home, I'd have reverted to my habit of pretending not to be there. I shot a look at Yukinoshita as if to ask, *So what do we do?* But...

"Come in." Yukinoshita reacted to the rap at the door without giving me so much as a glance. Though our visitor was clearly lacking in consideration, Yukinoshita was not to be outdone in this regard. No, she was probably winning there.

"Excuse me." It was a breezy, soothing voice; a boy.

Who the hell was this guy, barging in to deny me my ramen? I directed a resentful stare at the door and was surprised by who strode through. It was someone who shouldn't have even been there.

X X X

He was a rather handsome guy. So much so, I wouldn't know how to describe him other than handsome. His hair was styled into wavy points. Some sort of stylish frames fitted his trendy glasses, and the eyes behind them were direct. When they met mine, he grinned. Unwittingly, I returned a forced smile. He was so good-looking that I instinctively recognized my own inferiority.

"Sorry for coming at this hour. I wanted to ask for your help." He set his Umbro shoulder bag on the floor and asked, "Is here fine?" as if it were the most natural thing in the world, before proceeding to pull out a chair in front of Yukinoshita. Every single gesture just made him look that much more attractive. "I just haven't been able to slip away from practice. Club time is canceled for a week before exams, so they wanted to make sure we got through every drill today. Sorry."

I guess that was what it meant to be needed. If I were to bail on club early, not only would no one stop me, no one would even notice me leave. *Seriously, am I a ninja or what?*

Though he said he'd been busy with practice, I didn't smell a whiff of sweat on him. Quite the contrary, a refreshing citrus scent wafted off him.

"Enough with the humblebragging." Yukinoshita's words were like a smack in his cheerful face. For some reason, she seemed slightly brusquer than usual. "You came here because you want something. Is that right, Hayato Hayama?"

Though Yukinoshita's tone was icy, Hayato Hayama's smile didn't falter. "Oh, that's right. This is the Service Club, right? Miss Hiratsuka told me that if I needed help with any problems, I should come here." When he spoke, for some reason, a refreshing breeze blew in from the window. Did he have mystical wind powers or what? "Sorry for coming so late. If Yui and the rest of you have plans after this, I can come another time."

In response to his remark, Yuigahama smirked in her shallow, familiar way. Apparently, her defaults for interacting with the upper caste were not so easily abandoned:

"O-oh, no, you don't have to do that! You *are* the soon-to-be captain of the soccer team, after all. You couldn't help running late."

Yuigahama was probably the only one who felt that way, though. Yukinoshita looked tense, and Zaimokuza silently attempting to project an air both stern and tough.

"Hey, sorry to you, too, Zaimokuza."

"Eugh?! P-pfagh, uh, er, I-I'm done here now, um, I was just leaving..." The hostile vibe Zaimokuza had been attempting to emit dispersed the instant Hayama addressed him. Zaimokuza went so far the other way, he actually started acting like he was the one somehow in the wrong. *Koff, koff, koff.* "Hachiman! Farewell!" Zaimokuza split before the words were even out of this mouth. He seemed unusually giddy for a guy running away, though.

Zaimokuza, I understand that feeling so well it hurts. I don't really know why, but when dregs like us run into members of the elite, we shrivel up. We step aside for them in the hallways, and if one of them were to deign to talk to us, we'd have about an 80 percent stutter rate. You'd think that this would make us even more resentful and jealous of them, but that's isn't the case. We're actually a little happy if one of them even remembers our names.

A guy like Hayama knew my name—knew *me.* This recognition restored my sense of dignity.

"...and Hikitani, too. Sorry for coming so late."

"...No, it's fine." Mine was the only name he got wrong! Hey, my dignity was still gone. "Anyway, didn't you come here for a reason?" I wasn't unconsciously trying to hurry this along because I resented him for getting my name wrong or anything... Honest! I was deeply interested in Hayama's problems. I was honestly just baffled as to what sort of problems a person on the very highest rung of this school's social ladder might have. This was in no way motivated by a desire to discover his weaknesses or use that information for blackmail. I possessed none of those base feelings, none whatsoever.

"Oh yeah, about that," Hayama said, abruptly pulling out his phone. He swiftly *clack*ed away at the keys, opening up the e-mail window, and showed it to me.

Yukinoshita and Yuigahama leaned in for a peek from either side. Having three people in front of a palm-sized screen was crowded and smelled too nice and made me feel uncomfortable. I let the two of them take my place, and Yuigahama quietly exclaimed, "Oh..."

"What is it?" I asked, and Yuigahama withdrew her own phone and showed it to me. There was a message on it identical to Hayama's.

The e-mail was what you might call anonymous defamation. And it wasn't just one. Every time Yuigahama's finger moved, a litany of similar, hateful messages scrolled down the screen. All of them were probably sock accounts, as there were slanderous and defamatory messages from multiple senders. It was stuff like *Tobe is in a street gang in Inage and was targeting kids from Nishi High at an arcade.* Or *Yamato is a filthy, three-timing SOB.* Or *Ooka was deliberately playing dirty at a practice match with another school to take down their star player.* Basically stuff like that. There were tons and tons, and none of them could be verified. Though the majority came from socks, some were forwarded from people who appeared to be classmates.

"Hey, what the...?"

Yuigahama nodded silently. "I told you before, didn't I? About the stuff that's going around in our class."

"A chain e-mail, hmm?" Yukinoshita, who had been silent until then, spoke.

A chain e-mail, as the name suggests, circulates around and around like a chain. Usually, they come with directions at the end like *Please forward this to five people.* They're a lot like the 'chain letters' of yore, those old analog letters that read, *If you don't send this letter to five people within three days, you will be met with great misfortune.* You can think of chain e-mail as the digital iterations.

Looking at the message again, Hayama grimaced. "Ever since this started going around, things have been feeling nasty in class. It makes me angry seeing bad things written about my friends, too." Hayama was as vexed by this anonymous villain as Yuigahama had earlier.

There is nothing more terrifying than covert bile. If someone gets up in your face talking smack, you can punch them or insult them back to vent. There's also the option of holding on doggedly to your resentful feelings toward that person and sublimating that stress into something else. Those sorts of dark emotions are endowed with lots of energy you can channel into something positive. But when you don't have an enemy to make the recipient of all your hatred, jealousy, and thirst for vengeance, it all just feels vague and unclear.

"I want to put a stop to it, you know? This kind of thing just isn't nice," said Hayama asserted, cheerfully adding, "Oh, but I don't mean I want to bust whoever's doing it. I want to find a way to resolve this peacefully. Do you think you can help me?"

There it was. He'd just invoked his ultimate move: *the Zone*.

Let me explain. *The Zone* is a character skill that only true normies have, and its most prominent characteristic is how it sets everything up to go just right. Unlike regular normies (LOL) who expose their stupidity with little thought and waste all their time on shallow and idle amusements, true normies are fulfilled by real life in a real way. Because of that, they don't look down on anyone; in fact, they're kind to those whom others look down upon. The standard for telling these two apart is *Are they nice to Hachiman Hikigaya?* I think Hayama is pretty nice. I mean, he'll actually talk to me—though he gets my name wrong.

Basically, I guess you could call *the Zone* a unique air that nice, charismatic people have. To put it kindly, Hayama was nice and considerate. To put it normally, he was useless and full of flippant smiles. Put meanly, he was a cowardly piece of crap. I did think he was a good guy, though.

Confronted by Hayama's special powers, Yukinoshita seemed to ponder for a moment before opening her mouth. "In other words, you want us to come up with a plan to deal with this situation?"

"Yeah, well, that's the idea."

"Then we have to find the culprit."

"Okay, good…huh?! Wait, why do we have to do that?" Hayama had clearly not been paying attention to where the conversation was going. For an instant, he looked stunned, but he immediately composed himself as he calmly asked Yukinoshita to elaborate.

In contrast to Hayama, Yukinoshita's expression was glacial as she slowly began speaking, carefully selecting her words. "Passing around chain e-mails is the worst sort of human behavior: the kind that tramples human dignity. They spread their slander and libel purely for the sake of hurting others while concealing their own identities. The most vicious part is that those who spread this malice are not necessarily malicious themselves. Curiosity and sometimes even good intentions lead them to disseminate it further, and the web of malice expands. If you want it stopped, you must tear it up by the roots. Nothing less will have any effect. Source: me."

"So you're speaking from personal experience, huh?" I wished Yukinoshita would stop exposing her own personal minefields like that. Her tone was placid, but I could practically see dark flames wavering at her back. It felt like the kind of scene that deserved ominous sound effects.

"What on earth is so fun about propagating content that denigrates others? I don't see how it benefited Sagawa or Shimoda in any way."

"So you even figured out who did it." Yuigahama managed a stiff, awkward smile. This is exactly why making enemies of high-spec people is scary.

"Your school must have been pretty cutting edge, then," I said. "There wasn't any of that at my school."

"You just think that because no one asked you for your e-mail," Yukinoshita jabbed.

"What?! Hey! You jerk! I was just maintaining confidentiality! Haven't you ever heard of the Act on the Protection of Personal Information?!"

"That's a novel way to interpret the law." Rolling her eyes, Yukinoshita swished back the hair on her shoulders.

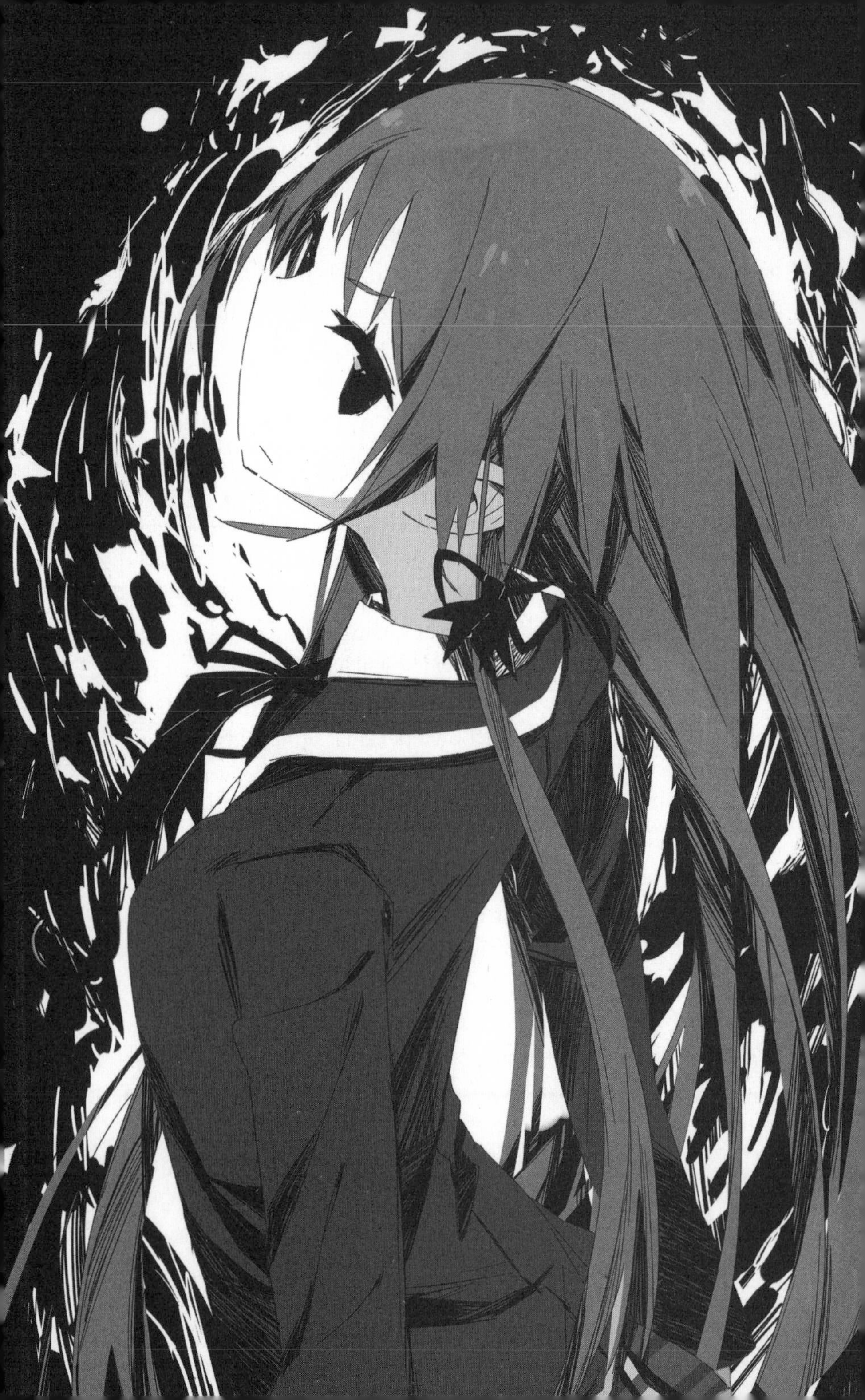

But that *was* probably the reason I'd never been caught up in that sort of chain e-mail imbroglio. Nobody would ever ask *me* for my e-mail address. This is the difference between Yukinoshita and me. She gets exposed to all this pernicious stuff, but I'm not worthy of even that. If something like that were to happen to me, not only would I never find the culprit, I'd probably just go home and moan to myself while soaking my pillow with tears.

"At any rate, anyone who would engage in such disgraceful behavior should certainly be led to ruin. An eye for an eye, a tooth for a tooth, and hostility in response to hostility is my philosophy."

Yuigahama perked up. Apparently, she recognized the saying from somewhere or other. "Oh! We learned that today in world history! That's the Magna Carta, right?"

"It's the Code of Hammurabi," Yukinoshita smoothly replied before turning to Hayama again. "I will search for the guilty party. I believe a few choice words will be sufficient to stop them in their tracks. What happens after that I will leave to your discretion. Is that fine with you?"

"Yeah, that's okay," Hayama said, as if resigned.

I was actually on the same page as Yukinoshita on this. This prick had deliberately used a bunch of different accounts to send that e-mail, which meant they were deliberately concealing their identity for fear of exposure. If they were dragged into the open, they'd probably stop. Basically, finding the transgressor would be the fastest way to fix this.

Yukinoshita stared hard at the cell phone Yuigahama had left on the desk, applying her hand to her chin in her pseudo-Thinker pose. "When were the e-mails first sent?"

"The end of last week. Right, Yui?" Hayama sought verification from Yuigahama, who nodded.

Wait a second… So Hayama calls Yuigahama by her first name, huh? I feel like…guys who are higher up in the school pecking order naturally take to using girls' first names. I'd stammer and choke for sure. Though I had to respect him a little for being able to pull off something that embarrassing while still looking cool, I was also kind of…annoyed. *Damn you—are you an American or what?!*

"So they suddenly started around the end of last week, hmm?" mused Yukinoshita. "Yuigahama, Hayama, what happened in class around then?"

"I don't think there was anything in particular," said Hayama.

"Yeah…it was the same as usual, right?" Yuigahama and Hayama exchanged puzzled looks.

"I might as well ask you, too, Hikigaya. What about you?"

"What do you mean 'might as well'?" I was in the same class as them! Well, I did see things from a different perspective than they would have, so there were probably some things only I would have noticed. Around the end of last week, huh…? In other words, it was something recent. I tried to think of things that'd happened recently… recently…but nothing quite came to mind. I guess if you considered stuff from *yesterday*, that's when I called Totsuka by his first name for the first time, but that was about it.

Finding the courage
to call you Saika, I found
you were very cute.
So yesterday is now the
Anniversary of You.

Now that I thought about it, why had I been talking to Totsuka again? As the thought crossed my mind, I suddenly remembered. "There was that one thing yesterday… Everybody was talking about forming groups for the workplace tour." Yup, Totsuka's cuteness had come out of that conversation.

This realization set something off in Yuigahama's brain. "Ack! That's it! It's because we're splitting into groups!"

"Huh? That's why?"

"Huh? That's why?"

Look at that, we were comment clones! Hayama grinned and said "jinx" or something or other I couldn't care less about.

All I could say was "Y-yeah…"

But if Hayama and I are clones, that means I'm also a fetching normie. QED. Or not.

Hayama fixed his attention on Yuigahama, and she tittered as she elaborated. "Well…because dividing into groups for a big field trip like this affects your relationships afterward. Some people get really anxious about it…" Yuigahama's expression turned dark, and Hayama and Yukinoshita looked at her as if confused.

It probably wasn't something Hayama had ever had to deal with, and as Yukinoshita didn't care about that stuff, she likely wouldn't get it. But I understood. This was Yuigahama, the girl who was always worried about what other people thought of her, the girl who'd survived the complicated and mysterious web that was human relationships, so her words carried weight.

Yukinoshita cleared her throat as if to redirect the conversation. "Hayama, you said these messages were about your friends, right? So who are you going with for the work visit?"

"O-oh, yeah… Now that you mention it, I haven't decided yet. I think I'll just end up with a couple of the guys from the usual threesome, though."

"I think I might have figured out who it is…," Yuigahama said, her expression somewhat downcast.

"Could you explain?" asked Yukinoshita.

"Yeah, well, like, basically, he's got this group of guys who are always with him, but one of them is gonna get left out, right? One guy out of their group of four won't get included. Being the one left hanging sucks." She said this as if speaking from personal experience. Everyone fell silent.

To find a criminal, it's best to start with the motive. If you can think of someone who would benefit from the act, there's your answer right there. In this situation, the motive was *not to be left out*. In our class, Hayama was part of a clique of four boys. It stood to reason, then, that if they had to form a group of three, one person wouldn't make it in. Anyone who didn't want to be the one on the outs would have no choice but to get someone else booted. That was probably how the cyber-assailant saw it.

"Then it would be correct to assume that the culprit is among those three?" Yukinoshita concluded.

Hayama, who so rarely raised his voice, did so now. "H-hold on a second! I don't want to think that one of them is doing this. Plus, these e-mails slammed everybody in the group, you know? How could one of them be doing it?"

"Ha! Are you stupid?" I asked. "How much of a wide-eyed innocent are you? Are you an anime character or what? The culprit would do it to deflect suspicion, duh. Though if it had been me, I'd have deliberately singled somebody out and said nothing just to make it look like they did it."

"You're a terrible person, Hikki."

Call me a smooth criminal, please.

Hayama bit his lips in frustration. He probably hadn't imagined something like this, that there was hate so close to home, that dark feelings surged beneath those ingratiating smiles.

"For now, could you just tell us about these people?" Yukinoshita requested.

Hayama lifted his head as if resolved. There was conviction in his eyes. It was probably motivated by some noble desire to clear his friends' names. "Tobe is in the soccer club, like me. He's got blond hair, and he comes off like a tough guy, but he's actually really good at setting an upbeat mood. He goes out of his way to help out with the cultural and the athletic festivals and stuff. He's a good guy."

"So he's a frivolous party type who has no talents aside from being loud?"

Yukinoshita's remark left Hayama speechless.

"Hmm? What's wrong? Continue." Yukinoshita prodded Hayama, perplexed by his sudden silence.

Hayama pulled himself together and proceeded to his next character profile. "Yamato's in the rugby club. He's levelheaded and a good listener. I guess you'd say he's the calm, easygoing, and quiet type, and that puts people at ease. He's shy and kinda cautious. He's a good guy."

"Dull-witted and indecisive…"

Hayama was silent and radiating disapproval. Then he sighed and continued. "Ooka is in the baseball club. He's nice, friendly, and always ready to help you out. He's polite and respectful, too. He's a good guy."

"Deferential and always worried about what others think, hmm?"

Hayama was not the only one at a loss for words. Yuigahama and I both watched agape. Yukinoshita, wow. I was starting to think her ideal job would be a prosecutor.

The scariest part was that her evaluations were not necessarily incorrect. Perspective can have a major impact on your impressions of a person. Hayama would always take the optimistic outlook, and that made him biased. On the other hand, Yukinoshita avoided all that when she could, so her impressions were naturally salty. Very salty. You could soak your feet in her opinions.

Yukinoshita *hmm*ed as she gazed at the notes she'd taken. "Any of them could be the culprit…"

"Well, you're the most likely culprit here. Or is that just my imagination?" I remarked. How dare she interpret people so harshly? In a way, she was even crueler than whoever wrote those e-mails.

Looking quite offended, Yukinoshita set her hands on her hips and glowered indignantly. "I would never do something like that. I would crush someone in person."

Did this girl not realize that while their methods were different, her goal of "crushing" was exactly the same as that of our mastermind? But this was Yukinoshita, so I wasn't surprised that the idea of making peace didn't even cross her mind.

After so many hits from Yukinoshita, Hayama had this awkward smile on his face like he didn't know if he should be angry or upset.

Yukinoshita was Yukinoshita, but Hayama was also Hayama. At the end of the day all he had was worthless and superficial information. I thought he was a good guy, but his perspective was so different from ours that he wasn't suited to looking for the culprit.

Perhaps Yukinoshita was thinking the same thing, as she turned around to ask our opinions. "I don't think Hayama's information is going to be very useful. Yuigahama, Hikigaya. What do you think of them?"

"Huh? I-I dunno how to answer that...," stuttered Yuigahama.

"I don't really know them." Actually, I didn't really know any of the students at this school. I had zero friends and only a few more acquaintances than that.

"Then could you look into it for me? The groups are going to be decided the day after tomorrow, right? You have a full day until then."

"O-okay." Yuigahama seemed rather hesitant about obeying. Well, she was trying to be friends with everyone in the class, so this was exactly the kind of thing she'd have been disinclined to do. Picking out other people's faults reveals your own. It's fairly risky social behavior.

Apparently, Yukinoshita understood that as well, as she quietly dropped her gaze. "I'm sorry. That wasn't a nice thing to ask. Forget about it."

I guess that means the task falls to me, but that's a given. "I'll do it. It's not like I care what our class thinks of me, anyway," I said.

Yukinoshita glanced at me, then smiled with a chuckle. "I'll be waiting, but I won't expect much."

"Leave it to me. Fault finding is included in my vast array of skills." What other talents might I have, do you ask? Cat's cradle and stuff. Yeah, I was basically Nobita.

"W-wait! I'll do it, too! U-um, I can't just leave it up to Hikki!" Red-faced, Yuigahama's voice faded to a mumble, but a moment later she clenched her fists tight. "P-plus! If you're the one asking, Yukinon, I can't say no!"

"I see," Yukinoshita replied, and then jerked her head away. Her cheeks seemed flushed. Perhaps she was embarrassed, or perhaps it was just the glow of the sunset.

Uh, but like I said, I'm doing it, too. Why does Yuigahama always get the special treatment?

Hayama had a wonderful, breezy smile on his face as he watched the two of them. "You're such good friends."

"Huh? Oh, yeah, they are," I replied.

"I mean you, too, Hikitani."

What was he talking about? There was no one named Hikitani in this club.

× × ×

In the classroom the next day, Yuigahama was on fire. It was lunch hour, and I was not going to my usual spot. As I reached out to grab the pastry and the Sportop I had bought, Yuigahama came over, and our meeting of careful planning began.

"I'll go ask around first... S-so you don't have to kill yourself trying, Hikki. Actually, you don't have to do anything!"

"O-okay. Thanks, I guess. You seem really into this..." Frankly, it was weirding me out.

"I-I'm just, like, y'know... It's because Yukinon asked me!"

"O-oh, really..." If she actually did worship Yukinoshita that hard, then I really was weirded out. But it was abundantly clear that for all Yuigahama's incentive, her pains weren't going to get her anywhere. It was deeply unnerving. "It's nice that you're so motivated, but what exactly are you going to do?"

"Hmm... I'm gonna try asking the girls about it. They're the ones who know the most about class relationships. Plus, sometimes when they're talking about people they don't like, they get carried away and tell you all sorts of stuff."

"Man, girl talk is scary. Whoa." So it was the enemy-of-my-enemy-is-my-friend idea. What advanced tactics...

"It's not that scary! It's just, like...complaining...or swapping information, I guess?"

"I guess it really depends on the way you put it."

"Anyway! You're bad at that stuff, right? I'll handle it, so don't worry."

Yuigahama was absolutely correct. Frankly, I wasn't suited to casual chitchat or investigative enquiry. Just me going up to talk might make people suspicious. I wouldn't be asking them questions; they'd probably end up asking *me* questions, questions like *Who are you?*

Yuigahama's position in the class was well suited for this task. She was also good at being social. She'd been polishing her fear of other people's opinions her entire life, and now it was time to put it to use.

"Yeah...sorry, I'll leave this to you. Go for it."

"Okay!" Yuigahama psyched herself up and cut into Miura's clique. These were the girls who were friends with Hayama and his guy friends.

"Sorry I took so long!"

"Oh, Yui. You took forever!" Miura and the other girls of the clique greeted her apathetically.

"So, like, Tobecchi and, like, Ooka and, like, Yamato have been acting kinda weird lately, huh? It kinda feels like...I dunno, you know?"

Pfft! I snorted as I overheard Yuigahama. Straight to the point like a baseball to the face. That was a 160 km/hr gyro ball! That would easily have been a rank S in *MLB Power Pros.* But her control scored a solid F.

"Huh? Since when have you been one to talk like that, Yui?" Ebina took a step back. I think her name was Ebina. Probably.

Miura's eyes glittered, and she wasted no time making her attack. "Look, Yui, that was uncalled for, you know? It's mean to gossip about your friends!" It was a lovely thing to say, and Miura's remarks put her in an overwhelmingly superior position.

Now Yuigahama was the one about to lose her place in the group. What the hell was she doing?

But Yuigahama was backpedaling with all she had. "No! That's not what I mean! Um, I'm just, like…kinda interested…"

"What, do you have a crush on one of them?"

"That's not what I mean at all! I mean, I am interested in someone, but he's, like…you know, so…," Yuigahama gasped, a look on her face that said, *Oh no!* Miura's lips twisted into a smirk.

"Ohh? Yui…do you have a crush on someone? Tell us! C'mon, c'mon. We'll help you out!"

"N-no, I said that's not what I mean! Those three have just kind of been on my mind lately…or their relationship? I guess? I just feel like it's been odd lately!"

"Oh, is that all? That's no fun." Miura had clearly lost interest. She opened her phone and began clacking away at it.

But Ebina bit. "I understand… So you've been thinking about it, too, Yui… Honestly, I have, too."

"Yeah, yeah! It's like things have gotten all tense between them or something!"

"Well, personally…" Ebina sighed, fixing her with a serious gaze. "I think Tobecchi is totally an *uke*! And Yamato is the arrogant *seme*. Oh, and Ooka is the seductive *uke*. There's definitely something going on with that threesome!"

"Yeah, I know…wha?"

"But, like, all of them are definitely after Hayato! Hnnng! It's like they're all holding back for the sake of their friendship! It's such a shiptease!"

Whoa, are you kidding me? Who knew Ebina was so intense? Like… her nose is bleeding.

"Uhh…" Yuigahama seemed at a loss, but Miura just breathed a weary sigh.

"There it is: Ebina's disease. Ebina, you're cute when you keep your mouth shut, so at least try to pretend to be normal. And wipe your nose."

"*Ah…ah-ha-ha!*" Yuigahama was so overwhelmed she laughed to avoid saying anything. When she noticed that I was watching, she quietly raised her hand in apology as if to say, *Sorry, I failed!*

Well, a lot of things had gone wrong from the start, anyway. Even without Ebina in the picture, it would have gone belly-up. So that meant it was my turn. But I couldn't just go around chatting up my classmates. So how should I go about performing recon on these people?

The answer was obvious. I'd just watch them intently. If I can't talk to people—no, precisely *because* I can't talk to people—I can gather information through other avenues. It is said that only around 30 percent of human communication is done through language. The other 60 percent is communicated through subtle gestures and movements of the eyes. It's so important there's a saying about it: *The eyes say more than the mouth.* It's a great paradox: loners who engage in no conversation at all can manage about 70 percent of all communication. Right?

Yeah, no, this is bull.

Now then, I shall exhibit another of my vast array of skills: human observation. I'm also a pretty good shot. Like I said, I was basically Nobita.

My method is incredibly simple.

1. Stick in ear buds but don't turn on any music. Just listen to the conversations around you.
2. Stare like you're zoning out, but actually be looking really hard at the guys in Hayama's clique to read their faces.

This concludes the explanation.

Hayama was encamped in a seat by the window. He was leaning against the wall, with Tobe, Yamato, and Ooka surrounding him. This told me something exceedingly simple: that Hayama was the highest-ranked person in the group. The wall is the ultimate backrest, the seat of a king. Though the four boys probably had no idea of this, their very ignorance proved it to be an instinctual, essential behavior.

It looked as if each of Hayama's three friends had their set roles.

"So yeah. Our coach started to hit balls for fielding practice right into the rugby club! It was rough, man. Those balls are hard!"

"Our advisor flipped over that, too."

"We were killing ourselves laughing, though! But, like, the rugby guys held their own. Not like the soccer team—we're a mess. Man, it was so crazy! Balls were just flying at us from the outfield! It was a war zone out there!"

Ooka started the conversation, Yamato *yes-man*ned it, and then Tobe got excited about it. It was like a well-organized play. Shakespeare said that all the world's a stage, but I think everyone just fulfills the roles that are given to them. And the director and audience of this performance was Hayama. He sometimes laughed, sometimes changed the subject, and sometimes joined in.

I observed a number of things in my surveillance.

Oh, that guy just clicked his tongue under his breath.

This one suddenly went quiet when the guy next to him started talking…

And the other one was fiddling with his phone like he was bored. He was really not into this.

The one who got this vague smile on his face whenever they talked about dirty stuff was a virgin. Definitely. Source: me. Seriously, I never know how to react when the conversation turns dirty. I'll just pause for a beat and then go, *I'm not horny at all lately!* like I'm trying to brag about it. I wonder why I do that?

I felt like all my intel was useless. Figuring I wouldn't be seeing any results, I sighed, and that was when it happened.

"Sorry, 'scuse me for a sec," Hayama said and stood, then headed toward me. Apparently, Hayama had noticed my staring. He was probably gonna be like, *What're you lookin' at, ya punk? What middle school do you go to?* My heart pounded with fear.

"What?" I said, hiding my trembling.

Hayama did not burst into a fit of rage or grab my collar and demand my allowance; he merely grinned brightly. "Oh, I was just wondering if you'd figured something out."

"Not really, uh…" About all I'd learned was that Ebina was a *fujoshi* and that Ooka was a virgin. As I reviewed my findings, I looked over at Ooka and the others, and what I saw caught me by surprise. The three guys were acting bored, fiddling with their phones, occasionally glancing over toward Hayama. And the answer suddenly came to me. It was a flash of insight like a tranquilizer bolt to the back of the neck.

"What is it?" Hayama asked, perplexed.

I grinned back at him. "This mystery is solved!"

Naturally, I will showcase my deductions after the commercial.

X   X   X

After school, Yukinoshita, Yuigahama, Hayama, and I all gathered in the clubroom.

"How did it go?" Yukinoshita asked for our findings.

Yuigahama tittered. "Sorry! I tried asking the girls, but they didn't know anything!" Her apology was sincere.

Well, there was no helping that. Afterward, Ebina had continued to babble on to Yuigahama about *semes* and *ukes* and division or some other nonsense, and there was no way Yuigahama could have discovered anything after that.

Head bowed, Yuigahama slowly peered up at Yukinoshita's face.

But Yukinoshita didn't seem particularly angry. "Oh, well, I don't really mind."

"Huh? You don't?"

"You could take it to mean that the girls are uninvolved and uninterested in this. The problem is between the boys in Hayama's clique. Yuigahama, good work."

"Y-Yukinon…" Yuigahama's eyes were brimming with tears of emotion. She tried to embrace the other girl, but Yukinoshita smoothly dodged, and Yuigahama's forehead smacked into the wall.

Yukinoshita, exasperated, patted the tearful Yuigahama's injured forehead as she looked at me. "So what about you?"

"Sorry, I didn't find any clues as to the culprit."

"I see." I was sure she was going to mock me, but Yukinoshita just sighed and cast a gaze of deep pity in my direction. "Nobody would talk to you, hmm?"

"That's not why." Though it was true that nobody would bite if I tried to start a conversation. I mean, just talking to someone and keeping the conversation going expended a lot of my mental energy. It used about as much MP as Magic Burst, seriously. "I don't know about the culprit, but I did figure one thing out," I said.

Yukinoshita, Yuigahama, and Hayama leaned forward to listen. Confronted with doubt, hope, and curiosity, I cleared my throat.

That was Yukinoshita's cue to ask, "What did you find out?"

"I found out that that clique is Hayama's clique."

"Huh? We already know that, duh," Yuigahama scoffed. It was as if her eyes were saying, *Is this guy a virgin or what? Like Ooka?*

Hey, you keep Ooka out of this.

"Um…what do you mean, Hikitani?"

"Oh, sorry I wasn't clear. Adding that *s* at the end denotes possessive case. In other words, it means 'belonging to Hayama, for Hayama.'"

"Uh, I don't feel like they're mine, though," Hayama said, but he was just ignorant of the situation. The other three might be, too.

But I was an outsider looking in, and to me it was clear as day. "Hayama, have you seen those three when you're not around?"

"No, I haven't."

"Of course he hasn't. How could he see them if he's not there?" Yukinoshita sneered and sighed.

I nodded. "That's why Hayama hasn't noticed. An outsider can see that when those three are alone together, they don't get along at all. To put it in a simpler way: They each see Hayama as their friend, but they only see each other as friends of a friend."

Yuigahama was the only one to react. "Oh, *ohhh*, I know that feeling… It's awkward when the person who keeps the conversation going leaves, you know? You don't know what to talk about, and you end up just messing around with your phone…" Her head drooped, apparently under the weight of a bad memory.

Yukinoshita tugged repeatedly at her sleeve, asking quietly, "I-is that how it is?"

Yuigahama folded her arms and nodded an affirmative.

It was no surprise Yukinoshita didn't know about this. She'd never had friends, so she'd never had friends of friends, either.

Hayama was silently considering what I'd said. But there was nothing he could have done. To Hayama, they were his friends, but their other relationships were their own business. To have friends is to accept the difficulties that come with them. Having a large cohort was not always advantageous, and Hayama was serving as a prime example. Put another way, lots of friends means lots of people surrounding you. You can't run away. In *Dragon Quest* terms, that means the entire party is going to die. But I knew a way out.

"Even if what you're saying is true, Hikigaya, that's only a corroboration of their motives. Isn't there a way to figure out which one of them is doing it? The situation will not be resolved until we take out the culprit. We have to hurry and get all three…" Yukinoshita put her hand to her jaw in thought.

Casually talking about taking people out, Yukinoshita, you're scaring me. Were the Sagawa and Shimoda you mentioned before *taken out*? The idea of people going missing at our school terrified me, so I suggested a different approach. "There's no need to take out the culprit. That's another matter entirely," I said, and Yukinoshita tilted her head with a question on her face as she looked at me.

Her reasoning was *To stop the crime you must stop the criminal*, and that wasn't wrong. But there's another way. A jewel heist could never be successful if there was no jewel to steal. So you just have to steal it before it's stolen. I had ninja skills, after all, so I was more suited to being a jewel thief than a detective, anyway.

"Hayama, I can resolve this problem, if you want. I can do it without exposing the thief and without any arguments. And they might become friends." I wonder what expression I was wearing. At the very least, I think it was a smile, and such a wonderful smile that Yuigahama went "E-eugh…" and shrank back.

I felt like a Zaimokuza-esque *heh-heh-heh* might slip out of my mouth. If there were demons that pressured humans into wicked bargains, they might have looked a little like me.

The pitiful lamb, Hayama, nodded in assent to the devil's proposition.

×　×　×

It was the day after Hayama made his fateful decision.

Our classmates' names were listed on the blackboard in the classroom. Each set of three names represented the groups for the work-experience event. The three girls who sat beside me chattered and smiled to each other. Apparently, they'd decided among themselves beforehand, as they went up to the blackboard and began to write down their names.

As for me, I didn't approach anyone. I just zoned out and watched. This was how I dealt with forming groups.

At times like these, it's important to do nothing. It was like Shingen Takeda said: *steadfast as a mountain.* He was exactly right. *Skipping out of class as swiftly as the wind, nodding off at your desk as quietly as the forest, jealousy raging hot as fire, steadfast as a mountain.* I would wait until the situation shifted and the homeroom teacher said, *Yes, yes, I get that you all hate Hikigaya, but it's not good to leave people out! You can't do that!*

You damn old bat Isehara, my homeroom teacher from fourth grade… I'll never forgive you.

Anyway, they say that all good things come to those who wait, so if I pretended to be asleep, then before you know it Hachiman the loner would join a pair who failed to find anyone else and took me as their compulsory third. And then we'd declare ourselves a group!

Agh, I'm going to sleep.

I made use of another of my vast array of skills: pretending to be asleep. By the way, one of my others was becoming one of the good guys during a long plot arc. I was basically Gian.

Then someone gently shook my shoulder. Even through my clothes I could feel a soft, delicate hand. A voice called my name, like music from the heavens. Still dozing, drifting above the clouds, I opened my eyes.

"Morning, Hachiman."

"An angel? Oh, it's Saika." Phew, that startled me. He was so cute I could have sworn he was an angel.

Totsuka giggled and plopped down beside me, replacing the girl who had been there until a moment ago.

"Is something wrong?" I asked, and Totsuka grasped the cuff of my gym uniform as he floundered, eyes upturned.

"W-we're…separating into groups…"

"Hmm? Oh, that's right. They should be about done figuring them out soon." I seem to remember that Totsuka had already decided his. That was too bad. I did a full-body stretch and looked around the classroom. Once most of the class was done picking out their groups, it was time for us loners to do our thing and steel ourselves to form temporary groups among ourselves. I would prefer to end up with other solitary types; if I took too long, I would get stuck with a pair who were already friends.

It happened while I was checking the names written on the blackboard, looking for other rejects. There was a group of three that was writing their names. A familiar-looking trio.

Tobe, the blond party-type.

Dull-witted and indecisive Yamato.

Assimilating virgin Ooka.

Three for the Kill: the Next Generation! I was witness to the formation of a new group. My favorite character in particular is *assimilating virgin Ooka.* After the three had made their group official, they looked at each other and smiled a little shyly. Hayato Hayama's name was not there.

As I watched, a voice from behind caught me unawares. "Mind if I sit here?" He sat beside Totsuka without waiting for my reply.

In the face of this sudden and unexpected guest, Totsuka mumbled, "U-um..." and sent me an anxious glance. Supercute.

"This all ended peacefully, thanks to you," Hayato Hayama said with his trademark grin. "Thanks."

"I didn't really do anything." Why was he coming to talk to me so casually? Was he just a good guy? Was that it?

"But you did. If you hadn't let me know what was going on, there would probably still be some bad blood between them," Hayama said.

I really was no saint, though. I had just wanted to try dragging Hayama down the path of the loner. The reason for the hostility in the first place was wanting to be with Hayama. So you just had to take away the cause of their conflict. In other words, you had to exclude him.

A loner is sort of like a permanently neutral country. Your absence prevents discord, and you don't get dragged into trouble. If everyone in the world just kept to themselves, there would most certainly be no war or discrimination. You know, I think it's about time I got a Nobel Peace Prize.

"I've always felt like I should be friends with everyone, but I guess sometimes I can be the cause of conflict, huh...?" Hayama mumbled, forlorn.

I had no words to offer him; all I could give him was a bored snort. Though Hayama had come to the Service Club in search of a solution, all I had been able to give him was the option to throw himself under the bus. Even though he was a good guy, the kind who would come and talk to me and remember Zaimokuza's name. Even though he was the best there was at living high school life to the fullest. But in spite of that—no, precisely because of that, Hayato Hayama said, "The three of them were taken aback when I said I wouldn't join any of them, though. I hope this will lead to them becoming real friends."

"Yeah…" Mildly disconcerted, I gave a noncommittal response to indicate that I was listening. Frankly, I thought that being this good of a guy was some kind of illness.

"Thanks. So then, since I don't have a group yet, how about we make one ourselves?" Hayama extended his right hand with a smile.

Huh? A handshake? *Why do normies always act so overfamiliar? Good grief, he's got to be kidding. He's practically an American.* "Oh, okkei!" He was so American, I ended up replying in English.

I gave his hand a firm smack, and Hayama said, "Ow!" and smiled yet again. Now that he was a fellow loner, perhaps he and I had come to understand each other. Now then, if we just got one more person, then the job would be done.

And right beside us was a cute creature going "Mnghh!"

"What's wrong, Totsuka?"

When I looked at him, I saw tears welling in his eyes as he puffed up his cheeks. It was ridiculously cute. "Hachiman…what about me?"

"Huh? Uh…what? Wait, didn't you say you already decided on a group?"

"Listen!" Totsuka braced himself and then squeezed the cuff of my blazer tight. "I decided from the start…that I'd be with you, Hachiman."

"That's what you meant?"

What a tricky way to put it. Loners are stupidly good at sniffing out hints that they're not wanted, so if you don't state yourself explicitly, we won't get these things.

I looked at Totsuka. He was red-faced and apparently sulking at the floor. Unwittingly, my face relaxed. When I smiled, Totsuka looked up through his lashes at me and giggled.

Hayama grinned at us, jumped to his feet, and turned to face me. "Then let's go write our names down. What about the workplace?"

"Up to you," I said, and Totsuka nodded his assent.

Hayama wrote our names on the blackboard. *Hayama, Totsuka, Hikigaya.* Oh-ho, he gets my name right when he's writing it down. Even a little thing like that made me rather happy. Maybe this was what they call "friendship"? Next, Hayama began to write where we wanted to go. But then...

"Oh, I'm gonna go with the same thing as Hayato!"

"No way, Hayama is going there? Oh, then I'm switching, I'm switching!"

"Maybe I'll go there, too..."

"Hayama's the best. He's so great!"

Everyone in the class gathered around Hayama all at once, and then while I was busy staring they all chose the same workplace as Hayama and wrote their names by his instead. Before I knew it, my name was erased, lost underneath all the names added by Hayama's. My presence disappeared along with it, and I faded into the background again. *What the hell, am I a ninja? Maybe I should go do this tour in Iga or Kouga or something.*

And then this humble ninja respectfully slipped away unnoticed from the schoolroom...

Needless to say, friendship is another thing that can slip away unnoticed, anytime, anywhere.

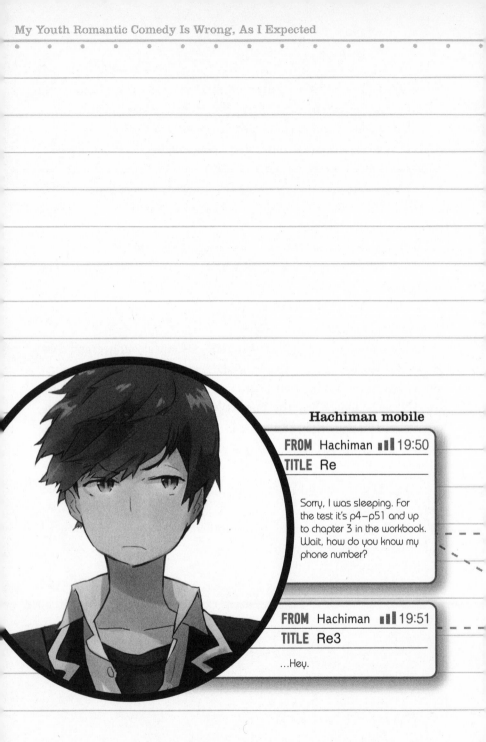

Hachiman mobile

FROM Hachiman ▪▍ 19:50

TITLE Re

Sorry, I was sleeping. For the test it's p4–p51 and up to chapter 3 in the workbook. Wait, how do you know my phone number?

FROM Hachiman ▪▍ 19:51

TITLE Re3

...Hey.

Zaimokuza's mobile

FROM Zaimokuza   ▮▮▮ 16:40
TITLE none

Hachiman, 'tis me, Zaimokuza.
Are ye endeavoring in your
studies? By the way, on a totally
unrelated subject, hast ye the
inclination to inscribe here, like
a revelation from the gods, what
will be on the math test?

FROM Zaimokuza ▮▮ 16:59
TITLE none

Hachiman, *crr crr*... Hachi...
crr *crr* *crrrrrr* Hngh, it seems
the Minovsky particles around here
are thick. Come in, Hachim... *crr*
crr ...an, come in. *crr* *crr*

FROM Zaimokuza
TITLE none
    ▮▮▮ 17:36

~~Beast~~ Hachiman, respond to my call! Ngh, so even this fails... Then
I have no choice but to recite that incantation... Darkness beyond
twilight, crimson beyond blood that flows...etc.

FROM Zaimokuza   ▮▮▮ 18:24
TITLE none

Sorry, I got a little carried away. Tell me what's going to be on the
math test.

FROM Zaimokuza   ▮▮▮ 19:51
TITLE Re2

Oh-ho... I shall not forget this boon for all eternity...... I pray
for your luck in battle. The next time we meet, it shall be on
the battlefield... ~< ` ·w· ´ > farewell!

Saki Kawasaki has some stuff going on,
so she's sulking.

Midterm exams were looming. While I usually studied at a family restaurant or at the library, high school students out and about after eleven PM were apt to get picked up by the police and taken home, and at ten PM family restaurants ask you to leave. So when I do nighttime studying, it ends up being entirely at home. By the way, when I say "nighttime studying," I don't mean night in the sense of *nighttime wrestling.*

The needle on the clock was pointing to just before twelve. I stretched with a groan. I felt like I could keep at it for about another hour or two. "I guess I'll have a coffee."

I went down the stairs with muted thumps and headed to the living room. Coffee is always the best thing for waking up. If you're going to abuse your brain with activities like studying, it's necessary to supply said brain with sugar. In other words, this is where the deathly sweet MAX Coffee comes in. MAX Coffee is sweet, it has caffeine, and it's full of cream, so I think an anthropomorphization of it would be pretty sexy. For starters, she'd definitely have a huge rack. And she'd say stuff like, *I won't let you sleep tonight ☆!* I wish someone on Pixiv would draw a MAX Coffee-tan...

As these trivial thoughts and feelings regarding MAX Coffee crossed my mind, I walked into the living room to see my sister, Komachi, fast asleep on the couch. She should have had midterms coming up, too, but as usual, she was unflappable.

I rummaged around for my stash of MAX Coffee before I remembered that I'd already opened a new package recently, and so there was nothing to do but boil water. I filled the T-Fal electric kettle with water and flipped up the switch on the rear. Not knowing what else to do while the water was boiling, I sat on one end of the couch my sister was passed out on and waited.

My sister left her stomach boldly exposed as she slept. Her white skin rose and fell rhythmically as she breathed softly in sleep, and with every breath her cute belly button moved. She was wearing my T-shirt, which she'd presumably stolen from me for herself, and when she stirred with a groan, it slowly rode up to let her bra peek out. I didn't notice before because she was curled up, but why wasn't she wearing any pants? She was gonna catch cold. There was a bath towel lying nearby, so I just draped it over her for the time being. Komachi mumbled something mumbly in response.

While I was occupied with my sister, the water began to burble and boil, and the electric kettle signaled it was done with a click. I tossed the instant coffee powder into a mug and poured in the hot water, and then the fine smell of coffee wafted up from it. This cup was on the strong side, so I added lots of milk and sugar and stirred it about four times with a teaspoon. My sweet coffee was done, and just how I like it. The rich aroma of the milk and the fragrant scent of coffee intermingling was quite pleasant.

Apparently, Komachi had gotten a whiff, too, as she leaped awake. First she jerked her head around to look at me, still for two seconds. Next she pulled open the curtains, still for three seconds. Then her eyes went wide, and she looked at the clock, still for five seconds. All told, it seemed to take her ten seconds to grasp the situation. She took a deep breath and then yelled in a stupidly loud voice, "Oh no! I overslept! I only meant to sleep an hour... I slept like a log for five hours!"

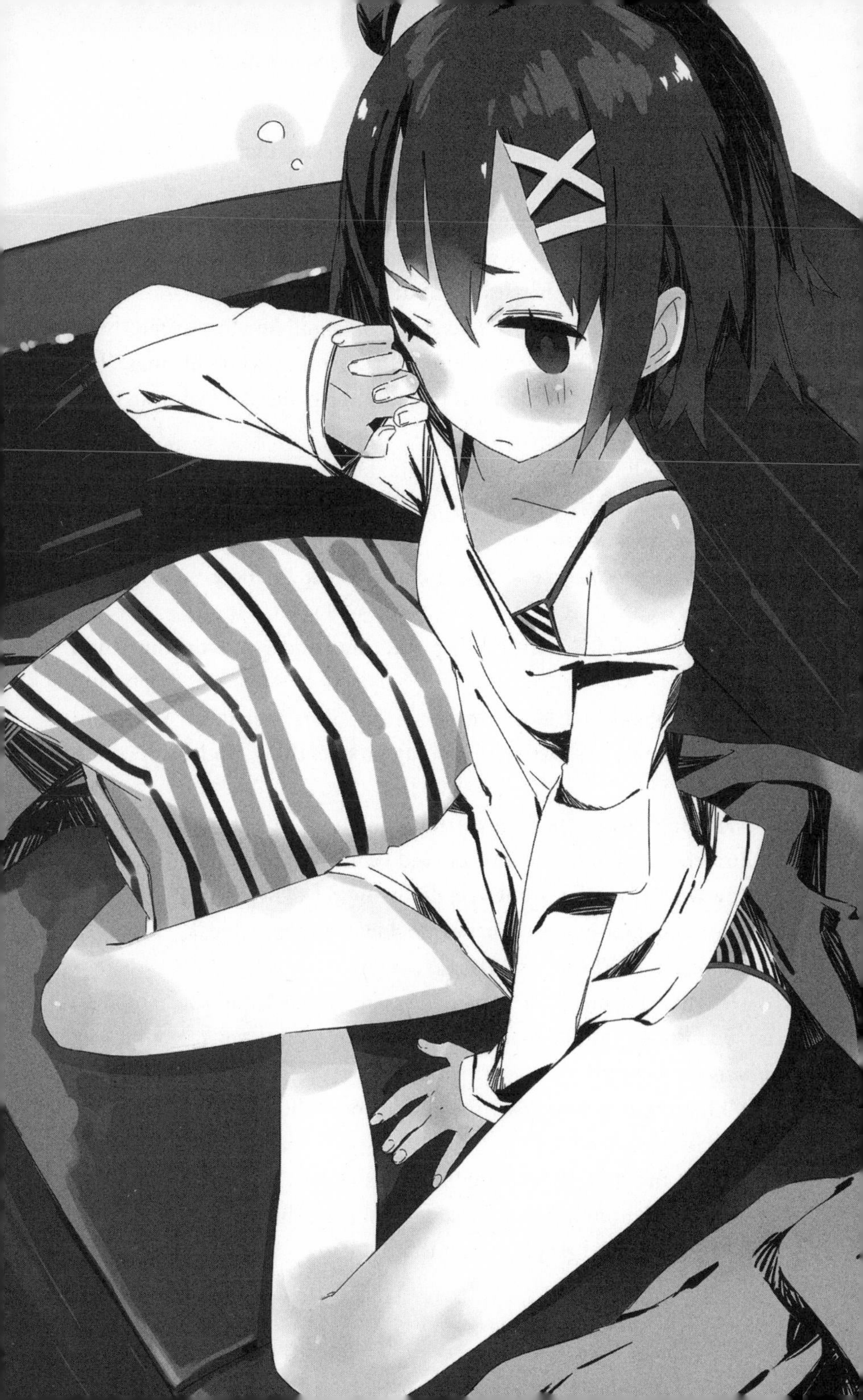

"Yeah, that happens sometimes… Wait, no, that's way too long! Did you go straight to sleep after you came home?!"

"Don't be rude! I did have a proper shower before I went to sleep!"

"I have no idea why you're getting mad at me right now."

"The real question here is why didn't you wake me up?!"

I don't know why Komachi was whining and howling at me about this. Speaking of sleeping like a log, that reminded me of dogs. The female kind. "Not like I care, but put on some pants! And you can't just take my clothes."

"Hmm? Oh, this. It's perfect as pj's. Don't you think it looks kinda like a nightgown?" she said, tugging the collar of the T-shirt out wide.

It really does stretch out. I can see your bra. Don't spin around like that; I can see your panties. "Well, I don't wear it anymore, so I'll give it to you."

"Oh-ho, thanks! Then I'll give you some underwear or something in exchange!"

"Yeah, thanks." I swore firmly in my heart that if she really did give some to me, I'd use them as a rag or something, and I sipped my coffee.

Tugging down the hem of the nightgown that was formerly my T-shirt, she came into the kitchen and went to warm some milk in the microwave. "Anyway, what're you doing up so late, Bro?"

"Studying for exams. I just came down here for a break," I replied, and Komachi went *ohhh* in surprise.

"If this is a break, that means you're gonna study some more… Bro, you know, I think that once you start working, you're gonna be a *bijinasu-raiku* guy."

"Hey, *businesslike* doesn't mean 'someone who likes business.' Your English is a disaster."

"Naw, Bro. I'm great at English. I'm a genius. *Ai amu peenasu.*"

I would definitely not call that level of English genius. Does she not even know the word *genius* in English?

The microwave went *ding*. Komachi took her mug in both hands, blowing away at it to cool it down as she walked up to me. "Maybe I'll study, too…"

"Yeah, you should. I'm gonna go back to studying. You study hard, too." I downed my coffee in one go and stood up. That's when I felt a tug at the back of my T-shirt, and I let out a croak like a bullfrog. When I turned around, Komachi was grinning ear to ear.

"You said 'you, too,' right? Normally, that means *Let's do it together*, you know. Bro, do you have a language disability?"

"You're the one with a language disability." I'd gotten a fair amount of studying done for the night, though, so it wouldn't kill me to help my stupid sister study.

And that's how I ended up *night-studying* with my sister.

× × ×

I brought a set of my study materials from my room and spread them out on the table in the living room. I'd decided to focus on Japanese history that day, so I had the *Yamagawa* workbook, the answer key, and a notebook. Komachi, perhaps unhappy about how bad she was at English, had *Middle School English Target 1800* out.

We both focused on our studies in silence. I solved the questions and then checked the answers, and when I got one wrong, I'd copy both the question and answer into my workbook. I repeated that over and over again. After I had done about one run-through of everything that would be on the test, I noticed that Komachi was staring at me. She seemed to be zoned out. "What?"

"Hmm? Oh, I was just thinking, you're such a serious boy."

"Wow, that doesn't sound condescending at all. Are you looking for a fight, you little brat? I'll pull out that stupid-looking cowlick of yours." I tried threatening her a bit, but Komachi just laughed.

"Sure, Bro, I know you'd never hit me or anything."

"What? That's because, like...'cause if I hit you, Dad would kick my ass. That's all. Don't get the wrong idea."

"Tee-hee! Aw, you're so shy! ♪"

"Ugh... Shut up...." For now I'd just settle for flicking her in the forehead in retaliation for how much she got on my nerves ☆. I flicked her like this was an eraser-flick match and her forehead was my opponent's eraser, steeling myself like a suicide bomber ready to obliterate his target. In other words, it was a real and genuine 100 percent all-out attack.

"Oww!" Komachi's forehead had let out a loud *plink*, and she pressed her hands against it as she moaned. Rubbing it, she glared at me with tear-filled eyes. "Nghh... I was being nice and talking about what a serious studier you are, and you flicked me!"

"Because you were being stupid. Just study, come on!"

"See, you're so serious about it! Man, there's so many different kinds of older brothers and sisters out there, huh? A friend of mine from my cram school, you know, has a sister who's going bad. Apparently, she doesn't come home at all in the evenings."

"Uh-huh."

It looked like Komachi had zero intention to study. At some point she'd closed *Target 1800*. She was trying to turn this into conversation time. Mostly ignoring her chatter, I continued studying Japanese history. Year 645, *picks your fries*, Taika Reforms.

"But like, but like, she goes to Soubu High and she used to be the serious type. I wonder what happened."

"Hmm, yeah." What Komachi was saying was going in one ear and out the other. Year 654, *licks live boar*, Fujiwara-kyo becomes capital. Hey, not *live* boar, it's *fine* boar.

But man, I was sleepy. Man is in possession of a will that is stronger than any drug. So what I'm saying is, no matter how much caffeine I have, I don't think the caffeine can triumph over my will to sleep.

"Well, it's not my family, so I can't talk, but since I got asked my advice about it, you know. Oh, so his name is Taishi Kawasaki, and he just started going to my cram school in April."

"Komachi." I lay my mechanical pencil down with a clack. My drowsiness instantly dissipated. "Just what is your relationship to this Taishi or whatever his name is? How friendly is this *friend*?"

"You're kinda giving me a scary look, Bro." Apparently, I'd gotten a very grave look in my eyes. Komachi was shrinking back a little.

But this was about my stupid sister. If I didn't watch out for her, anything could happen. Worrying was my prerogative as a family member. I didn't want her to get mixed up with some weirdo. *Your big bro won't let that happen, okay?* "Well, you know. If you have any problems, just let me know. I told you before that I'm in this Service Club thing that's apparently supposed to do stuff, so there might be some way I can help you out."

"You really are a serious guy, Bro."

✕ ✕ ✕

It was morning. The sparrows were cheeping. An archetypal *fade to black and morning after*. When I opened my eyes, I saw not my usual view but an unfamiliar ceiling. That is to say, the living room ceiling. Apparently, I had fallen asleep while studying. I remembered only as far as asking Komachi about her relationship with her "friend."

"Hey, Komachi. It's morning," I called out to her and then realized she wasn't anywhere to be seen. Looking around the area in search of her: approximately two seconds. Next I glanced out the window. The sun was pretty high up. Checking that: three seconds. Breaking into a cold sweat, I looked at the clock. Nine thirty. I read it backward, and I read it forward, and it was still nine thirty. For a full five seconds, the clock and I stared at each other. After ten seconds, I was faced with the shocking truth.

"I'm superlate..." My head slumped, and then I saw my morning toast, ham, and eggs on the table along with a note.

Dear Bro,
I don't wanna be late, so I'm going now, okay? Don't study too hard!
S.P. Don't skip your breakfast!

I guess the scribble there was supposed to be Komachi's self-portrait. A girl-like sketch was making a face at me.

"You moron… Are you security police?" The correct acronym is P.S., which stands for *PlayStation*.

Anyway, rushing wasn't going to do me any good, so I munched away at my breakfast and got ready to go to school. Apparently, my parents had already gone to work. Both my parents work, so mornings at the Hikigaya household are early. My mom makes breakfast, but Komachi usually takes care of dinner. The fact that no one had woken me up made me worry that no one loved me, though. I wanted to believe that they were just being nice, thinking like, *I'll just let him sleep for now.* I bussed my dish and changed into my uniform. I checked that the door was locked and then left the house.

Leisurely riding my bike along the river, I looked up to see some cumulonimbi in a hurry to stretch out across the sky. The road to school that day was very quiet and calming. Usually, when I cycled down this street, it was a road race of students from Soubu High and other schools. Passing them on my bike like *Gooo Magnum!* felt great. And when there was someone else on a bike, I could compete with them, like *Don't lose now, Sonic!* and I could get even more fired up about it.

But that day the only people on the road were middle-aged women trying to diet, middle-aged men walking their dogs, and fishermen. But it was nice to have a commute like this sometimes. Thinking about how I was actually cycling out here under the blue sky, it felt great. It was kind of like how *Iitomo* is over 50 percent funnier when you skip school to watch it. So then why was it that I suddenly got depressed when I got close to the school?

I didn't try to sneak around, though, I walked in boldly through the front gate and into the school. Indeed, during this time the teachers were in class, so I wouldn't be caught and yelled at for being late. There was no point in being fearful. I've learned that from being late a total of seventy-two times last year. I'd already been late eight times this year, so I might be able to improve on that record at this rate. I'd have liked to pull off 1,100 wins during my three years of high school.

Things were fine and dandy until I hit the school gates. The problem was getting into class. I parked my bike on the racks and walked briskly toward the entrance. When I stepped into the building, it felt like gravity had suddenly multiplied on me. Was this the planet Vegeta or what? I went up the stairs, walked through empty halls, and finally reached my classroom on the second floor. I took a deep breath before placing my hand on the door. The moment was electrified with tension. I slid the door open.

All at once, silent eyes turned toward me. A hush washed over the class. Whispered conversations, the teacher's lecture—all form of sound evaporated. I didn't mind being late. It was this atmosphere that I hated. If, by contrast, I'd been Hayama, I wonder how this would have gone down.

Hey, Hayato, why're you late?
Hayama, you're so slooow!
Ha-ha-ha! Hayama never learns.

I bet it'd be something like that. But when it's me, no one says a thing. In fact, they all give me this look like *Who's that?* My steps heavy, I trudged through the dead silence of the classroom. The moment I sat down at my desk, exhaustion hit me with a thud. "Agh…" I sighed.

Then someone just had to kick me while I was down. "Hikigaya. Come see me when class is over," Miss Hiratsuka demanded, tapping her podium repeatedly with her fist.

"Yes, ma'am," I replied, head drooping. That was checkmate for me.

Miss Hiratsuka nodded and, with a flutter of her white coat, resumed writing on the blackboard. *Wait, after class? There was only fifteen minutes left!* Cruelly, that time passed in a blink. While I ignored the lesson to itemize my top hundred excuses for being late, the bell rang.

"That's all for today, then. Hikigaya, come here." The teacher beckoned me with a wave. Resisting the urge to make a break for it, I presented myself at the front of the class. Miss Hiratsuka glared as I stood penitently before her.

"Now then, before I punch you, I might as well hear your excuse for being late for my class."

She's already made up her mind to punch me! "Hey, you've got the wrong idea. Hold on a second here. You know how they say 'fashionably late,' right? I've got serious ambitions to go into the fashion industry, and I'm practicing for when I become an elite fashion executive."

"I thought you wanted to be a househusband."

"Ngh! Oh, well, you know... Anyway, it's misguided to think that being late is wrong! Listen. Police arrive at the scene of a crime after the fact. The hero showing up late is the status quo. Basically, police and heroes are always the last ones to the party! But does anyone blame *them* for being late? Of course not! Paradoxically, lateness is justice!"

As Miss Hiratsuka listened to my soulful screams, for some reason, this faraway look crept into her eyes. "Hikigaya, let me tell you something. Justice without power is no different from evil."

"P-power without justice is way worse! Hey, hold on! Don't punch me!"

Swift death to evil. Miss Hiratsuka's fist connected with my liver precisely. The palpable impact reverberated through my body. I fell over coughing. While I writhed in agony, Miss Hiratsuka sighed, exasperated. "Geez... There're too many problem children in this class." But there was no loathing in those words. Actually, she seemed rather pleased. "And speak of the devil." Abandoning me where I lay floundering, the teacher headed toward the door at the rear of the classroom, heels clicking. Still rolling on the floor, I turned that way to see a female student with a bag stroll in as if she'd only just arrived at school. "Saki Kawasaki. Are you fashionably late, too?" Miss Hiratsuka acknowledged this new arrival with a smile, but the girl she called Kawasaki only paused for a moment to give the older woman a silent nod. She passed by where I was collapsed on the floor and headed straight for her desk.

She had bluish-black hair hanging all the way down her back, loosely tied front shirttails, and long, supple legs that looked capable of a swift kick. What left the greatest impression, though, were those listless eyes of hers that seemed to gaze into the horizon. Also, a peek of black lace with artisan-level embroidery.

I felt like I'd seen this girl before... Oh, wait, she was in my class, so of course I'd seen her before. I didn't want to be falsely suspected of peeking up girls' skirts from my ground-level vantage, so I hopped to my feet.

But I felt like I was missing something. "Black lace?" Then all the questions that had arisen in my mind instantly melted away.

I flashed back to the image that had burned itself onto my retinas just the other day. The girl I'd caught sight of on the roof who'd made fun of me out of the blue. Oh, so she was in my class. Having figured it out, I stole a second glance at her to confirm that she was indeed the student known as Saki Kawasaki. That was when it happened.

Kawasaki, who'd been heading for her desk, stopped in midstep to glare at me over her shoulder. "What an idiot." She didn't kick me or punch me. Just that. She wasn't blushing shyly or flushed in anger. She said it as if totally disinterested, like the whole situation was stupid.

If Yukino Yukinoshita was frozen, then Saki Kawasaki was cold. It was the difference between dry ice and the regular variety. Yukinoshita burned anyone who touched her. Kawasaki combed her hair back with a hand as if exasperated and headed for her desk again. Pulling out her chair and taking her seat, she proceeded to stare blankly out the window as if she was bored. It actually looked like a deliberate attempt to avoid the sight of the classroom.

No one tried to speak to her. She was emitting a *Don't talk to me*

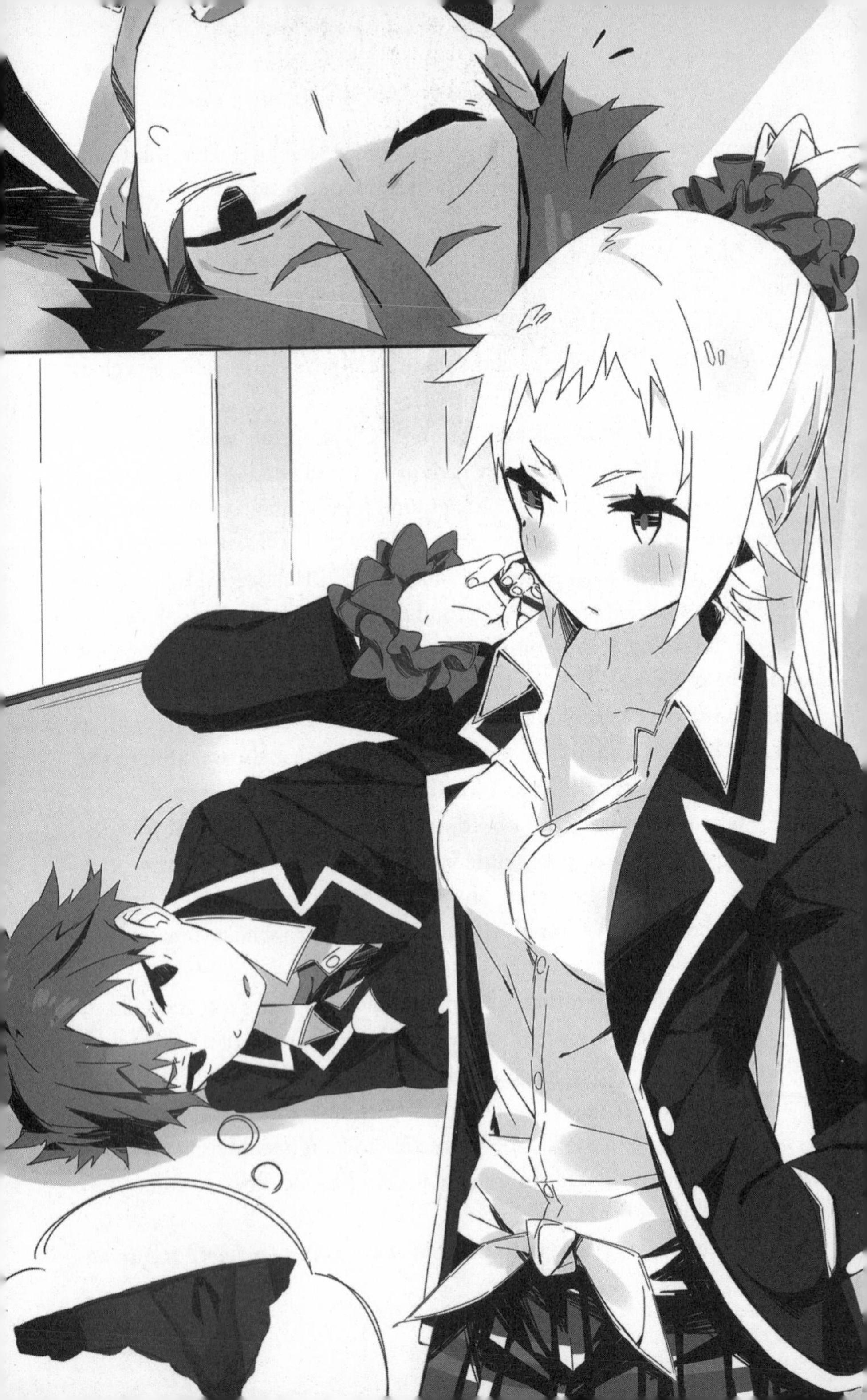

aura. But the fact that she'd turned on the *Don't talk to me* aura meant she was poorly informed. In our class, even if you emit a *Please talk to me* aura, no one will talk to you.

"Saki Kawasaki, huh…?"

"Hikigaya, don't use that deep, passionate tone to mutter the name of a girl whose skirt you just peeked up." Miss Hiratsuka put her hand on my shoulder. It was extremely cold. "Let's have a little chat about this incident. Come to the faculty office after class."

× × ×

I endured Miss Hiratsuka's lecture and chastisement for a little under an hour before being allowed to head home. On my way back, I stopped by the bookstore at the Marinpia shopping mall. After perusing the shelves, I bought one book. My thousand-yen bill disappeared, leaving some change jingling around in my wallet. After that, thinking I might study, I went to a café. But apparently, everyone else had had the same thought, and the place was packed with students. Right as I was considering bailing, I caught sight of a familiar face.

Totsuka, in his gym uniform, was staring down a cake in the display case. (On a side note, at our school, you're allowed to show up in either the regular uniform or the gym outfit.) This sight, sweeter than whipped cream, commanded my attention, and like ants swarming sugar, I was drawn toward him. It's like in that song, *the water over here is sweet!* ☆. No, wait, that was fireflies.

"Okay, it's your turn to give me a problem, Yukinon."

And then there were two more familiar faces. Yuigahama and Yukinoshita weren't wasting any time in the line for the cash register; they were studying hard. "Then I'll give you one from Japanese. Complete the following idiom: 'If the wind blows…'"

"'…the Keiou Line stops'?"

Correction. This was just the Trans-Chiba Ultra Quiz. Also,

Yuigahama's answer was wrong. The correct answer was "…lately it's been avoiding a full stop and just running slow."

Unsurprisingly, this mistake made Yukinoshita frown. "Incorrect. Next question. This one is from geography. 'Name two local products of Chiba prefecture.'"

The second hand of the clock prodded *ticktock, ticktock.* Yuigahama gulped, her expression serious. "Miso peanuts and…boiled peanuts?"

"Come on. Is this prefecture nothing but peanuts?"

"Ack! Oh, it's Hikki. I thought some weirdo had snuck up on me…"

Whoops. I'd been planning to come back another time, but jumping on Yuigahama's error had trapped me in this stupidly long line. Damn it! Curse my love for Chiba!

Yuigahama's dramatic reaction pulled Totsuka's attention toward us, and a sunny smile blossomed across his face. "Hachiman! So you were invited to study with us, too!" Beaming, he sidled up next to me. But of course, there was no way anyone would have invited me along, and Yuigahama had this awkward look on her face that said, *I knew it… he's come to crash our party.*

Hey, stop giving me that look. You're reminding me of my classmate's birthday party back in elementary school. Even though I brought a present, they'd had no chicken for me, and I almost cried.

"We didn't invite you to study with us, though. Did you want something?"

"Yukinoshita, you don't have to state facts just to hurt me." *Good grief, if I were a little more emotionally fragile, this could really go south. Specifically, I'd scream* Yaaaagh! *and hit you with a chair. I think I deserve a thank-you for being so exceptionally strong.*

"Uh, well…I thought about asking you to come, but the teacher called you to her office, so…"

"Whatever. I don't really care." I was used to this stuff now.

"Did you come to study for the test, too, Hikigaya?" asked Yukinoshita.

"Yeah, I guess. You guys?"

"Of course. It's less than two weeks until exams now."

"Hey, before you study, you need to brush up on Chiba prefecture again. Those questions you just gave her were freebies, weren't they?"

"I don't think they were freebies. Geography question: 'Name two local products of Chiba prefecture,'" Yukinoshita asked in the exact same tone as she'd used with Yuigahama, as if testing me.

"The correct answer is 'Chiba is famous for festivals and dancing.'"

"I said 'products,' didn't I?" And nobody knows the lyrics to 'Chiba Ondo.'" Yukinoshita shrank back, appalled.

Come on, you clearly know the lyrics. You're the appalling one. And by the way, 'Chiba Ondo' is the Bon Odori of Chiba. Around here, it's about as big a deal as 'Nanohana Taisou.' People from Chiba can sing and dance both. Also, there're no lyrics in 'Nanohana Taisou,' but for some reason, we can sing it.

Meanwhile, the line to the register was advancing, and I was next.

Yuigahama gave me a sly smile. "Hikki, treat me! ♪"

"Huh? Sure, I guess... What do you want to drink? Liquid sweetener?"

"Do you think I'm a beetle?! If you don't want to treat me, then just say it!"

So she figured it out. Why would I ever treat her in the first place?

Watching our exchange, Yukinoshita released a short sigh. "You're an embarrassment, so stop it. I don't appreciate that kind of behavior. People who sponge off others are trash."

Yukinoshita and I were on the same page, for once. "Yeah. I hate people like that, too."

"Huh?! Th-then I won't ask again!"

"I think it's fine as a joke between friends, though," I said. "Why don't you just stick to doing it with your clique?"

"Yes, that's true," Yukinoshita agreed. "It's not my clique, so I wouldn't mind."

"I can't believe you two don't consider me part of your clique!"

I watched from the side as Yuigahama tearfully clung to Yuki-noshita. Then it was my turn at the register. I ordered a coffee, which the cashier quickly poured for me.

"Three hundred ninety yen, please."

I stuck my hand in my pocket, and that was when it hit me. A recent memory suddenly bubbled up in my mind. I'd bought a light novel at the bookstore, and then what happened...? I'd had exactly one thousand yen and paid for the book, and the change was...

I didn't have enough money. But the coffee was already made, so I couldn't refuse it. Smiling, I appealed to the pair behind me. "Sorry. I didn't bring any money today. If you don't mind, can you treat me?"

"You're trash." Not missing a beat, Yukinoshita certified me as garbage, and Yuigahama sighed, exasperation etched on her face.

"Agh, I guess I've got no choice."

Y-Yuigahama! Yes! What a goddess! Yuigahama saves! But Yukinoshita takes full damage!

"I'll order that coffee as my drink and pay for it, so why don't you have some sweetener, Hikki?"

Who is this demon? This is less Ah! My Goddess *and more* Shin Megami Tensei.

"H-Hachiman, I'll pay! So don't worry about it, okay?" Totsuka smiled kindly at me. He was a goddamn angel. Just as I was about to embrace him, Yukinoshita's chilly voice cut between us.

"Nothing good will come of spoiling him."

"You've never spoiled me before! How would you know?"

In the end, Totsuka paid for me. I thanked him and looked for a seat. I figured I should do at least that much while the other three were waiting for their orders. There was a party of four leaving, so I quickly snatched their spot. I put my tray on the table, tossing my bag onto the seat. I flung it a little too hard, though, and it slid down the long padded bench.

A pretty girl in a school uniform one table over quietly pushed it back to me. As she performed this act of kindness without a single complaint, I bowed in deference to her refined and modest attitude.

"Oh! It's you, Bro!" That beautiful girl was my sister, Komachi Hikigaya. Still in her middle school uniform, a happy smile on her face, she waved at me.

"What're you doing here?"

"Oh, I was just listening to Taishi talk about his troubles," she said, turning back to the seat across from her. A middle school boy sat there in a *gakuran*. He bobbed his head at me in greeting.

I reflexively went on guard. Why? Why was Komachi with a boy...?

"This is Taishi Kawasaki. I told you about him yesterday, right? The guy whose sister's gone bad."

Now that she mentioned it, I seemed to remember her telling me something like that. I hadn't been listening to most of it, and all I could remember was 654, *licks live boar*. I wonder what the heck happened in 654...?

"So he was just asking me what he should do to get his sister back to normal. Oh, that's it! You help him, too, Bro. You told me to tell you if I had any problems."

Oh yeah. I seemed to remember running my mouth the day before and saying something like *Leave it to me and go ahead* on the spur of the moment. Of course, I had every intention of going out of my way for my sister, but I didn't have the slightest inclination to do anything for her friends, much less her male friends. "Oh, I see. You know, though, I think he should talk with his family first. I don't think it'd be too late if we regrouped after that. Yeah, in fact, it's probably premature now." Maybe that smart-sounding lip service would be enough to convince him. *And maybe he'll get away from Komachi and leave*, I thought, making a show as if I knew what I was talking about.

"Yeah, I know, but...lately she's always coming home late, and she doesn't listen to our parents at all. And if I say anything, she's just like, 'It's got nothing to do with you' and snaps at me...," Taishi said, head drooping. He seemed quite worried about her. "You're the only person I can rely on, Bro."

"You've got no business calling me 'Bro.'"

"You sound like a stubborn old man." A cold voice rained down on me from behind. I turned to find that Yukinoshita and the others had already arrived.

Komachi, judging that we were acquainted by the fact that we wore the same uniforms, quickly adopted a businesslike smile. "Hey, how are you! I'm Komachi Hikigaya. I'm so glad to meet my brother's friends," she declared, bobbing her head in greeting. She's always had a special knack for putting on a good "people face."

On the other hand, there was Taishi, who basically just lowered his head to a middling angle in a half-baked excuse for greeting before stating his name.

"You're Hachiman's sister? Nice to meet you. I'm his classmate, Saika Totsuka."

"Oh, nice to meet you! Wow, you're so cute! Right, Bro?"

"Hmm, yeah. But he's a guy."

"*Ha-ha!* You're so funny. Don't troll me, Bro."

"Oh, um… I'm…a boy…," Totsuka stammered, shyly blushing and averting his eyes.

Wait, was he really a boy at all?!

"Huh…? Really?" Komachi asked, poking her elbow into my side.

"Sorry, I'm not really sure anymore myself, but he's probably a guy. Though he is cute."

"O-oh…" Her expression still half-incredulous, Komachi intently scrutinized Totsuka's features. Every time she said, "Your eyelashes are soooo long! Your skin is sooo pretty!" Totsuka, red-faced, fidgeted, as if trying to escape her gaze.

He was so cute when he did that, I wanted nothing more than to watch him, but I caught the *S-save me!* plea he was giving me and peeled Komachi off him. "I think that's enough. And this is Yuigahama; that's

Yukinoshita." I briefly introduced them, and Komachi finally turned her attention to the girls.

When Komachi's eyes met hers, Yuigahama tittered and introduced herself. "N-nice to meet you... I'm Hikki's classmate, Yui Yuigahama."

"Oh, nice to m—huh? Hmm..." Komachi stopped. She stared at Yuigahama hard until sweat dribbled down Yuigahama's face, prompting her to avert her eyes. Were they a snake and a frog or what? After they'd been squaring off with each other for about three seconds, the silence was broken.

"Are you done?" Apparently, Yukinoshita was done dutifully waiting, as she now cut between Komachi and Yuigahama with a frigid voice. Her tone alone was enough to make them go quiet and acknowledge her. It was amazing. Her cool, clear voice was very soft and sedate. But even so, you could hear it distinctly. It was like trying to listen to the sound of fresh snow gently piling on the ground. I think it would be accurate to portray the two girls—rather than having fallen silent—as having had their collective breath stolen away. Komachi opened her eyes wide, unable to look away from Yukinoshita. From where I was sitting, for an instant, it looked as if she was mesmerized.

"Nice to meet you. I'm Yukino Yukinoshita. I'm Hikigaya's... Hikigaya's what, I wonder... We're neither classmates nor friends...so while it truly pains me...acquaintances?"

"Why'd you have to say it 'pains you' and phrase it as a question?"

"No, perhaps *acquaintance* is fine. Though all I'm really acquainted with is his name. To be precise, I don't want to be acquainted with any more than that. Can you still say that I'm acquainted with him?"

What cruel remarks. But when you think about it, the definition of *acquaintance* is vague. I get *friend* better, somehow. Can you call someone an acquaintance after only having met them once? Then if you see someone more than once, are they an acquaintance? How much information do you need about someone to call them an acquaintance?

I think it's a bad idea to use a designation with a vague definition.

In a case like this, I thought it preferable to adopt more concrete terminology. "Can't you just say we go to the same school or that we're schoolmates or something?"

"I see... I shall amend my statement, then. I am Yukino Yukinoshita, and while it pains me to say it, we attend the same school."

"So it still pains you, huh...?" *Yeah, well you're a pain in the butt.*

"But there's nothing else I could call you." Yukinoshita looked a little stumped.

"Oh, no, what you two just said told me all I need to know about your relationship, so it's okay," Komachi said kindly. It's nice that my sister catches on so quickly, but I think she's lacking in sisterly love.

"Um, so what should I do, then?" asked Taishi.

"Hmm? Oh, yeah." I turned to find the kid apparently near the end of his rope, his face troubled. Here I was feeling as if I'd been left out today, but it must have been even more uncomfortable for him. The only one he knew here was Komachi. It's really awkward getting dragged into some weird scenario by someone who's just an acquaintance of an acquaintance, to say nothing of the rest of us being older. You feel even more out of place and reserved. You get self-conscious and avoid saying anything that could be rude, and then everyone else is like, *What's wrong? You're so quiet,* and things end up going the other way entirely. They start tiptoeing around you, and you end up wanting to die. Then there's nothing you can do besides pretend to listen, say things like *Mm-hmm* and *Really?* with a vague smile tossed in every so often.

Taishi had actually tried his best to confide in us about something, though, so that meant he had fairly strong communication skills. He was a boy with a promising future. Not so promising that I'd let him have Komachi, though.

"Um...I'm Taishi Kawasaki. My older sister is a second-year at Soubu High. Oh, her name is Saki Kawasaki. She's, like...a delinquent now, or I guess you could say she's gone bad..."

I recalled hearing that name quite recently. Trying to remember when that had been, I put a drop of milk in my coffee, and that's when a deluge of memories assaulted me. The black-and-white contrast in my cup changed to gradations of brown, stimulating my vision.

That's it! The black lace girl! "Saki Kawasaki from our class, huh?"

"Saki Kawasaki..." Yukinoshita looked puzzled as the name came to her lips. Apparently, she didn't know her very well.

But Yuigahama was in our class, and so she clapped her hands. "Oh! Kawasaki, right? She's kind of...a bad girl? Like, sorta the scary type."

"You're not friends?"

"Well, I have talked to her before, but...I guess maybe we're not friends... And hey, don't ask girls questions like that. They're hard to answer." Yuigahama was obfuscating. I guess there's all sorts of groups and factions and associations and guilds and stuff between girls. Anyway, from the way she talked, Kawasaki and Yuigahama's relationship probably wasn't that close.

"I've never seen Kawasaki being friendly with anyone, though... I feel like she's always looking out the window and zoning out."

"Yeah, I get that impression, too," Totsuka said, reminding me of how I'd seen Kawasaki in the classroom. Her grayish eyes and how she watched the clouds, alone, as they flowed by. Her mind was indeed elsewhere, focused on something far away, someplace that wasn't there.

"When did your sister start turning into a delinquent?" asked Yukinoshita.

"Y-yes'm!" Taishi twitched at the unexpected question. Just so you know, I'll add that it wasn't just that Yukinoshita was scary. Taishi was nervous because a pretty older girl was talking to him. This is the correct response for a middle school boy. If I were in middle school, I'd probably have felt the same. Now that I'm in high school, though, she's just scary to me. "U-um...she was able to get into Soubu High, so when she was in middle school, she was a real serious student. Plus, she was pretty nice, and she cooked for me a lot. She didn't change much in the first year of high school, either... It's only been recently."

"So when she started second year?" I asked.

"Yes," Taishi confirmed.

Taking that in, Yukinoshita began pondering the question. "Can you think of anything that has changed since she started second year?"

"I guess the easy answer would be changing classes? Since she changed to Class F," I suggested.

"In other words, since she was put in your class."

"Hey, why are you saying it like I'm the cause? Am I a virus?"

"I'm not saying that. I think you have a persecution complex, Herpegaya."

"I heard that! I heard you call me a disease!"

"Slip of the tongue," Yukinoshita said, looking unconcerned.

Being treated like a disease unearthed some old trauma for me, so I really wished she would stop. Just one touch and they'd be going:

It's Herpegaya!

Tag!

I just put up a barrier!

Little kids can be too cruel, am I right? *Barriers don't work on Herpegaya!* they'd say... Just how powerful am I?

"But, like, when you say she comes home late and stuff, though, just how late is that?" Yuigahama asked. "Like, I stay out pretty late, too. It's not that weird for someone in high school."

"Oh, y-yes, I know, but..." Taishi turned away from her, flustered. This was because, well, he was shy having an incredibly sexy woman talk to him. This is a very middle school boy response. Now that I was in high school, I didn't give a damn what I said to hos like her.

"But she comes home at, like, after five."

"That's more like morning," I observed. That'd make you late all right. Even if you could get any sleep, you'd only manage about two hours.

"Y-your parents don't say anything...about her coming home that late?" Totsuka fretted, concerned.

"No...both our parents work, and we have a younger brother and sister, so they don't get on her case much. And because all three of them are out a lot, they don't see each other very often… Well, it's a big family, so my parents have their hands full just managing it all." Taishi answered Totsuka's question relatively normally. Hmm, so middle school boys don't get Totsuka's appeal yet. Now that I'm in high school, he's actually really cute. "Even when they do see each other, they just get into fights, but if I say anything, it's always just 'It's got nothing to do with you'…" Taishi's shoulders slumped, and he seemed quite distraught.

"Family issues, hmm… Any family has them," said Yukinoshita, her expression turning melancholy in a way I'd never seen before. It was as if she was on the verge of tears, just like Taishi when he came to talk to us about his problems… No, even moreso.

"Yukinoshita…," I started to say. Maybe a cloud had been hiding the sun, because suddenly a shadow fell over her downturned face. I couldn't make out her expression very well. All I could see were her shoulders sagging weakly, telling me she'd let out a short sigh.

"What is it?" she prodded, lifting her head, her cold expression unchanged from its usual posture.

The sun had been obscured by clouds for only an instant. I still don't know the meaning of that sigh. Perhaps I was the only one who'd noticed that she seemed different in that instant. Taishi and the others carried on as if nothing had happened.

"And that's not all… People from sort of…odd places keep calling her."

Taishi's statement prompted a question mark from Yuigahama. "Weird places?"

"Yeah. A place called Angel or something, I think it's a business… The manager calls her."

"What's weird about that?" Totsuka asked.

Taishi smacked the table. "I-I mean, it's called Angel! That's gotta be sketchy!"

"Huh? I don't get that impression at all…," Yuigahama said, slightly taken aback, but I understood perfectly.

Why, you ask? Because my eighth-grade-level naughty sensors were telling me so. For example, let's try adding 'Kabuki-cho' to the word *angel*. See, it sounds 50 percent sexier now. By the way, if you add *super* to it, too, it becomes another 40 percent sexier. This was definitely a sexy sort of business. This kid had potential, noticing something like that.

"Now, now, hold on and calm down, Taishi. I understand everything."

Taishi seemed happy that I got him. His eyes still fierce, he wiped them and enveloped me in a warm embrace. "B-bro!"

"Ha-ha-ha, don't call me 'Bro,' all right? I'll kill you, okay?"

While us men were busily erecting firm bonds over what is known as Eros, the girls, unperturbed, were settling on a proper course of action. "At any rate, if she's working, then first we must ascertain where," Yukinoshita strategized. "Even if it isn't some dubious establishment as those idiots suggest, it isn't good that she works there until dawn. We must find out where this place is and make her resign as soon as possible."

"Hmm... But if we force her to quit, she might just start working again somewhere else, you know?" Yuigahama said.

Komachi nodded. "It'd be like a viper and a mongoose, huh?"

"Are you trying to say whack-a-mole?" Yukinoshita corrected.

Oh, sister mine. Please refrain from shaming the Hikigaya name. Yukinoshita is rolling her eyes here.

"In other words, you're saying that we must treat both the symptoms and the root of the disease simultaneously." Yukinoshita drew her conclusion just as I was finally prying Taishi off me.

"Hey, hold on a second. Are you expecting us to do something?"

"Why not? Saki Kawasaki is a student at our school, and given that her younger brother's concern is related to her, I believe this falls within the scope of Service Club activity."

"Bro." I felt some tiny jabs in my back. I turned to find Komachi smiling sweetly. It was the smile she busted out when she wanted something. A long time ago, my sister had gotten that same look on her face when I had spent my Christmas wish on her. Why'd I have to ask Santa for *Love and Berry* cards?

I couldn't fight Komachi. She held the ultimate trump card, which was our parents' affection. Damn it, she was so uncute. "Fine," I conceded reluctantly.

Taishi erupted in joy and fired off some high-speed bows. "Th-thank you! Sorry, thank you so much!"

× × ×

The Saki Kawasaki correction program began the next day. When I went to the clubroom, Yukinoshita was holding a difficult-looking book in her hands. "Well then, let's get started."

Yuigahama and I nodded. For some reason, Totsuka was there, too.

"Totsuka, no one's forcing you to be here." Actually, I felt incredibly guilty for dragging him into Yukinoshita's ridiculous scheme. Most likely, the only thing he was going to get out of this was a bad end.

But Totsuka shook his head with a smile. "No, it's okay. I heard what's going on, too. Plus, I'm interested in finding out what you guys will do... If I'm not in the way, I'd...like to go with you."

"I-I see... Then...please go with me." I unconsciously tried to look cool while I said the 'go with me' part. I mean, like—look, he was looking up at me, saying he wanted to go out with me while squeezing the cuff of my jacket, you know? I'd have been a failure as a man if I hadn't take advantage!

But...he was a guy, though... *Sigh.*

Since club time was temporarily canceled, there weren't many people left in the building after school. Aside from us, there were pretty much just the students studying independently and Saki Kawasaki, who'd been called to the faculty office for counseling on account of being late. The policy was you got called to the faculty office for counseling if you were late more than five times in a month. Right about then, Miss Hiratsuka had probably caught Kawasaki and was lecturing her in earnest.

"I've considered the matter a bit, and I believe it's best for Kawasaki to resolve her issues herself. Recovering by means of her own efforts is less risky than forcing her into it, and she is less likely to rebound."

"Yeah, that's probably true." That assessment isn't just limited to juvenile delinquents. It's annoying when other people criticize your behavior. Criticism only makes you more resistant to change, even when it's someone close to you offering frank advice. Cast as a simple analogy, it's like your mom saying, *Why don't you stop lazing around and study?* before a test. Your natural reaction is like, *Agh, come on… I was just thinking about doing that! Man, now I don't want to anymore!* It's just like that.

"So what exactly are we going to do?"

"Have you heard of animal therapy?"

Animal therapy is, simply put, using interaction with animals as a sort of mental health treatment. It relieves stress and promotes positive emotional outcomes. Yukinoshita briefly explained it in similar terms, and Yuigahama listened, making *mm-hmm* noises.

Well, that probably wasn't a terrible idea. The way Taishi told it, Kawasaki had started out a serious and kind girl. A pet could trigger her kinder nature. But there was a problem. "So where are you gonna get this animal?"

"About that… Do any of you have a cat?" Yukinoshita asked.

Totsuka replied by shaking his head. How cute. Couldn't he pass as a therapy animal? I thought he was supereffective.

"I have a dog… Will that work?" Yuigahama stuck her index and pinky fingers in the air, bringing the other three fingers together to make a hand sign. Hey, wasn't that a fox?

"A cat is preferable."

"I don't really get the difference, though," I said. "Is there, like… some kind of scientific rationale for this?"

"Not especially, but… Anyway, no dogs." Yukinoshita insisted, jerking her gaze away.

"So you're just scared of dogs, huh?"

"When did I say anything like that? I'll thank you not to jump to conclusions." Yukinoshita pouted, her expression indignant.

Yuigahama leaped on that remark. "No way! Yukinon, you don't like dogs? Why not? Why not?! They're the cutest things!"

"You only feel that way because you like dogs." Yukinoshita's tone grew somewhat lower. What? Did she have some kind of dog-related trauma? Maybe she'd been bitten as a child. Well, if she hated them, we didn't have to force her. At the time, it was enough to have discovered one of her weaknesses.

"I have a cat. Will that work?"

"Yes." Once I got Yukinoshita's nod, I gave Komachi a call. I heard some weird music I didn't recognize ring like *doo dee dee doo*. What was that ringtone? Why was her phone singing?

"Hello, hellooo! This is Komachi!"

"Hey, Komachi. Are you at home now?"

"Yeah, I am! Why you asking?"

"The cat's there, right? Sorry, but can you bring him to my school?"

"Huh? Why? Kaa's heavy, and I don't wanna."

Kaa is the name of our cat. Originally, his name was Kamakura, which was too long, so at some point, it got shortened. We named him Kamakura because he's round like a *kamakura*, an igloo.

"Well, like, Yukinoshita is asking us to bring him."

"I'll come right away." The sudden *beep, beep, beep* of the disconnect tone blared in my ear after she hung up.

Huh? Why'd her attitude change the minute she found out it was Yukinoshita's request? She didn't want to do it when it was me asking! Still irked, I put away my phone. Our school was well known in the area, so she probably wouldn't get lost on the way.

"She said she's coming right away. Mind if I wait outside?" I asked to Yukinoshita. I waited by the school gates for twenty minutes, and then Komachi appeared gallantly with a cat carrier in one hand. "Sorry for making you come all the way here."

"It's okay! Yukino asked, after all!" Komachi replied with a grin, opening the top of the carrier.

Kamakura was inside, enshrined in the box like a rare item. He glared back at me with a brazen expression that said, *Oi. What're you lookin' at?* He was distinctly lacking in cuteness as a cat.

"Wow! He's so cute!" Totsuka exclaimed, petting him.

Kamakura twisted himself around like *Hey, hey, are you serious? Wait! Not the tummy, not the tummy! Don't fluff it up!* He was utterly at Totsuka's mercy.

"So what're we gonna do with him?" I took Kamakura from Totsuka, grabbing him by the scruff of the neck and just letting him dangle. By the way, this is the wrong way to hold a cat. The right way is to cradle it in your arms.

"We'll put it in a cardboard box and place it where Kawasaki will find it," Yukinoshita said. "If she's touched by the sight of it, she'll surely pick it up to take home."

"She's not some 1980s street gang leader." *Juvenile delinquent = stray cat? Your ideas are two generations behind.* But still, we weren't really friends with Kawasaki, so this sort of roundabout approach was necessary in order to pull off this animal therapy thing.

"I'll go get a cardboard box, then," Yukinoshita informed us.

I tried handing the cat over to Yuigahama, who was standing nearby, but she took a quick step back. *Hey, c'mon, take it.* I tried one more time, calling "Yuigahama!" as I held out Kamakura. She avoided him again. "What?"

"Oh, uh, i-i-i-i-it's nothing!" Yuigahama stammered nervously as she reached for the cat. When he saw her hands, Kamakura meowed. Yuigahama flinched and snatched them back.

"Wait... Do you not like cats?"

"Wh-what?! O-of course not! I love them, in fact! W-wow, s-so cute! M-meow!" Her voice quivered. This weird pretense that she liked them was wholly unnecessary, though.

"You take him, Komachi." I handed Kamakura to Komachi, and he suddenly started purring comfortably. Damn, even the cat hated me.

"I'll be back in a sec." If I asked at some office building, they'd probably have cardboard boxes. Every cat has specific tastes when it comes to boxes, but ours isn't very picky. Also, for some reason he likes plastic and tends to lick the shrink-wrap on comics and stuff. Did that taste good?! I walked along, considering getting him a plastic bag. As I mulled on that and other ways I might increase the cat's affection for me, Yuigahama caught up to me.

"S-so, like, I don't actually hate cats, okay?"

"Hmm? Oh, well, you don't have to like them. Yukinoshita apparently doesn't like dogs, and I didn't like bugs and stuff." Also, while I'm at it, I'm not fond of people, either.

"No, but I really don't hate them. I think they're cute and stuff."

"So are you allergic or something?"

"No, that's not the problem... Um, cats can disappear, you know? So, they make me kind of sad," she confessed, very unlike her usual chipper self. Her eyes were timid and sad. Her pace slowed, and I naturally slowed to match her. "I used to live in an apartment complex. Back then, there was a fad for secretly keeping a pet cat."

"First I've heard of a fad like that."

"Kids living in apartments go through phases! You can't keep pets in an apartment, you know? So you take in a stray cat and hide it from your parents. But at some point, it disappeared..." She giggled evasively.

So that's why she didn't like them. I wonder how losing that cat had affected her at that age. She'd treasured it so much, bonded with it and gotten close, but even so, it had disappeared. Maybe wondering why it had run off had made her resent it. She might even have felt betrayed. But she probably knew by now that cats leave their owners when they sense they're about to die. Now that she was older, I wondered how Yuigahama looked back on that parting. Maybe she regretted it.

This was all just my speculation, and I might've been totally off the mark. Even so, I thought Yuigahama's grief and kindness were real.

Silently, without exchanging a single word, the two of us carried the admittedly light cardboard box together.

X   X   X

When we put Kamakura in the box, he tested its texture with his front paws. He kneaded it about three times, and then, apparently satisfied—as if thinking, *Hmm, not bad*—he began to purr.

Now all that was left was to wait for Saki Kawasaki to make her entrance. The problem was we didn't know when she might show up. Miss Hiratsuka's lectures varied in length depending on her mood.

"Just in case, let's designate different roles for everyone," Yukinoshita suggested.

And so Yukinoshita became our self-appointed leader, Totsuka the lookout in front of the faculty office, and Yuigahama was stationed by the parking lot. Komachi was the switchboard keeping us all in contact, and my orders were to hold the box and dash into position when the time came.

I don't know what the others were up to, but I had nothing to do pending my signal. With a mind to restoring some of my flagging energy, I went to a vending machine nearby to buy a Sportop while I waited. I stabbed a straw into the Tetra Pak and took a sip or two, and on my way back, something happened.

"Meow!" I heard Kamakura's familiar refrain.

"Meow!" Answered by the unfamiliar mimicry of a girl's voice.

Unable to help myself, I scanned the area but didn't see any other girls around besides Yukinoshita. So I called from behind her, inquiring, "What're you doing?"

"What?" Yukinoshita replied nonchalantly.

"Uh, you were talking to the c—"

"More importantly, I thought I ordered you to stand by. But you're incapable of even something that simple, aren't you? I thought I'd sufficiently accounted for your incompetence, but frankly, I didn't think you were this bad. How do you supervise someone with an intellect inferior to an elementary schooler?" Yukinoshita's merciless frigidity was amped up about 50 percent greater than usual. But most notably, her eyes warned, *If you talk anymore, I'll kill you.*

"S-sir, yes, sir. Returning to standby." As I trudged back to the bench that served as my post, I felt my cell phone vibrate. It was an unknown number. Given the timing, it could only be Komachi, Yuigahama, Totsuka, or possibly Yukinoshita. I knew Komachi's and Yuigahama's numbers, and since I'd spoken to Yukinoshita just a moment ago, she probably wouldn't call me... So that meant Totsuka?! "H-hello?!"

"Oh, is that you, Bro? I got your number from your sister."

"I have no brothers or stepbrothers." I hung up and instantly got another call. I ignored it at first, but as he refused to give up, I decided I'd be the one to surrender.

"Hey, why did you hang up?!"

"What is it?"

"Well, I just heard you have some kind of plan with a cat, but my sister is allergic."

Huh? Was our operation compromised? "Hey, why didn't you tell me that earlier?"

"Sorry, I only just found out what you were doing now."

"Oh, fine. I get it. Thanks for letting me know. Bye."

This time I hung up on him for good and quickly headed over to Yukinoshita. She was crouched in front of Kamakura, scratching his chin and smooshing the pads of his paws.

"Yukinoshita." Hearing my call, she yanked her hands away from the cat, glaring at me as if to say, *Now what?* I thought, *Look, I already forgot what happened before. If you keep eyeing me like that, you're just gonna make me remember.* "I just got a call from Taishi, and he says

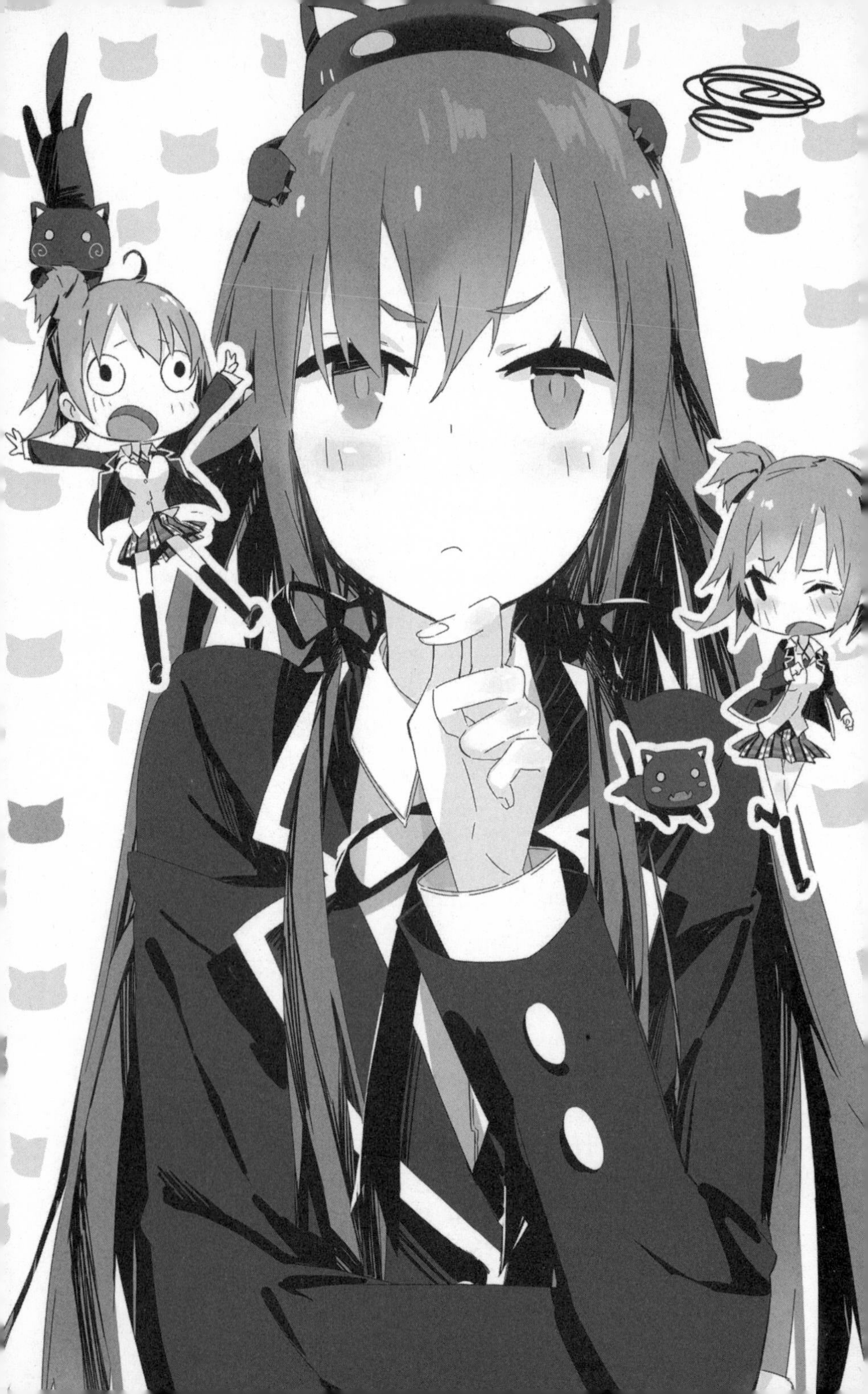

Kawasaki's allergic to cats. So even if we leave him somewhere, I don't think she's gonna pick him up."

"Sigh. Abort, then," Yukinoshita said, patting Kamakura's head as if she didn't want to see him go. Meow.

We called everyone to inform them of our retreat, and Yuigahama, Totsuka, and Komachi all came back.

"Bro, did you get Taishi's call?"

"Yeah, I did. But, like...don't go giving out phone numbers randomly. What if something bad happens? You've gotta be careful handling personal info."

"Your personal information isn't worth all that much, though," Yukinoshita teased in a slightly humorous tone.

"Not mine. I'm talking about Komachi's. Don't give it out so casually. Especially not to boys."

"Come on. I'm always careful with this stuff!" Komachi ignored my warning with a smile. Well, she was good at dealing with things, if nothing else. Probably better than me.

In fact, I was the one who had to pull it together. Now that our animal therapy gambit had fallen apart, we had to come up with a new plan. I turned back toward Yukinoshita, figuring she might know what to do.

Yukinoshita looked from Komachi to me and then back again and sighed. "You two sure are close... I'm a little envious," she said.

"Huh? Oh, most only children say stuff like that, but it's not that great."

"No, I'm... Oh, never mind." Oddly, she didn't finish her thought. Usually, she never held back. She'd say anything loud and clear. Maybe she'd eaten something bad, like Yuigahama's cookies or something.

"Anyway, what're we doing?" I asked. "We've gotta come up with something."

"U-um..." Totsuka timidly raised his hand. His eyes darted back and forth between Yukinoshita and Yuigahama, his anxious gaze pleading, *I-is it okay for me to say something...?*

Of course it's okay! Even if everyone else forbids it, I won't! Even if it's a forbidden love!

"Go ahead. You may speak freely. We'll help out, too," said Yukinoshita.

"Then, well…why don't we have Miss Hiratsuka talk to her? I think there might be some things she can't tell her parents… They're just too close. But maybe she can confide in another adult?"

Oh-ho, that was a respectable idea. Indeed, there are things you can't say to your parents precisely because they're your parents. For example, I'd definitely never want to talk to my parents about anything having to do with porno mags or relationships. Also, I can't tell them about the time I went to school and my desk was on the balcony, or that time my shoe cubby was stuffed with garbage, or when I got all excited about getting a love letter only to find my classmates were pranking me.

So consulting a third party was the way to go. Having a dependable adult with a lot of life experience help us out might be just the thing. "But Miss Hiratsuka…" That was the part that made me uneasy. Could you really call a cringeworthy person like that an adult? I think the only adult part about her was her boobs.

"I believe that Miss Hiratsuka is very concerned about her students' welfare in comparison to other teachers. I don't think we could make a better choice."

"Yeah, I guess." Yukinoshita was right: Miss Hiratsuka was serious about her job as a guidance counselor. She was always sending kids off to the Service Club with their problems, but she could only do that because she was in constant contact with her students and spent a lot of time watching them. "Then I'll try contacting her." I summed up everything going on with Saki Kawasaki in an e-mail. I never would have guessed I'd need Miss Hiratsuka's e-mail address, but here it was proving unexpectedly useful. "'Details on the above matter at the entrance.' Okay, now she should come." I finished off the e-mail and waited. Five minutes later, I could hear the hard *click, click, click* of her heels.

"Hikigaya, I understand the situation. Give me the specifics."

Miss Hiratsuka appeared, her expression serious. She crushed the cigarette that had been perched between her lips in a portable ashtray. I explained everything we knew about Saki Kawasaki and what we had surmised about her. Miss Hiratsuka listened patiently and, at the end of our explanation, let out a short sigh. "A student at our school working late at night is concerning. Urgently so. I'll take care of this personally, *heh-heh-heh.*" Miss Hiratsuka laughed fearlessly. "Come on. You kids just watch. Right before I came down, I dismissed Kawasaki. She should be here in about two minutes."

What was this indescribable foreboding? A scent lingering in the air told me she was about to have her bubble burst. "Um, you're not allowed to punch or kick her or anything, okay?"

"Come on… I-I only do that kind of thing to you, okay?"

"Was that supposed to sound cute?"

Meanwhile, Saki Kawasaki showed up at the school entrance. Her pace was sluggish, and occasionally, she'd let out a wide yawn. The bag dangling off her lazy, drooping shoulders was sliding down her arm, but she showed no sign of caring. It swung back and forth, caught on her elbow.

"Kawasaki, wait." Miss Hiratsuka called out behind her, adopting a dramatic stance.

Kawasaki turned to look, her eyes narrowed, half-lidded like she was glaring. When she turned around, her posture smoothly straightened. Miss Hiratsuka was tall, but Kawasaki had her beat in that capacity. The loosely tied boots on her long legs kicked a pebble with a rattle. "Did you want something?" Her listless, husky voice was sharp. Frankly, she was scary. It wasn't the come-at-me-ya-punk style scariness of a juvenile delinquent or a gang member. It was more the brazen scary of a bartender in the sketchy end of town, the type who'd be leaning alone on the bar smoking a cigarette with a whiskey in hand.

And then there was Miss Hiratsuka. Scary vibes were rolling off her body in waves. Hers was the intimidation factor of an office lady who acted like an old man eating *gomoku soba* in a Chinese restaurant by the station in a commuter city, tossing back a bottle of beer in one go, and yelling *Get off the field, you lousy pitcher!* at the baseball game on TV.

What the hell? Is this some kind of epic *kaijuu* battle?

"I heard you've been getting home late recently, Kawasaki. Apparently, you're not going back until morning. What on earth are you doing and where?"

"Who told you that?"

"I can't divulge my source, obviously. Just answer my question." Miss Hiratsuka's confident smile didn't break.

Kawasaki heaved a languid sigh. Depending on how you saw it, it could have been interpreted as scoffing at the teacher. "Nothing. What does it matter where I was? I'm not bothering anyone."

"Your activities could start causing trouble at any time. Even if you hardly come, you're still in high school. See what happens when you get picked up by the cops. Both your parents and I will get a call from the police."

But Kawasaki just scowled vacantly.

Unable to tolerate the look, Miss Hiratsuka grabbed her arm. "Have you never considered your parents' feelings?" The teacher's gaze was intense. She'd seized her student's arm with no intention of letting go, and undoubtedly, her hand was warm. Perhaps that warmth would reach Kawasaki's frigid heart…

"Miss Hiratsuka…," Kawasaki mumbled, touching the older woman's arm and meeting her eyes. But then… "I don't care about my parents' feelings. And you don't even have kids, so how would you know? Why don't you get married and have children before lecturing me?"

"Gagh!"

Kawasaki casually shook free of Miss Hiratsuka's grasp. The educator lost her balance as if she'd been struck by a hard right. She'd taken quite a bit of damage. Apparently, those warm feelings had missed their mark.

"Miss Hiratsuka, you need to worry about your own future, not mine. Like finding a husband."

That final blow sent Miss Hiratsuka jerking forward where she'd previously been pitching back. Her knees shook wildly. So the damage went to her legs, huh? The trembling shot up through her waist to her shoulders, reaching even her voice. "...Ngh...guh..." Her eyes held a tinge of moistures, and her reply was caught in her throat.

Kawasaki callously ignored her and disappeared into the parking lot.

At a loss for words, we exchanged glances. Yuigahama and Komachi awkwardly fixed their vision on the pavement, and Totsuka muttered, "Poor Miss Hiratsuka..."

Then Yukinoshita prodded me in the back. Apparently, she expected me to do something.

Wait, why me? Despite my misgivings, seeing our teacher's pitiable state, I felt obligated to say something to her. Was this feeling... perhaps...sympathy? "U-um...Miss Hiratsuka?" I began, trying to come up with something comforting.

She turned, hunched over like a zombie. *Sniff.* "I'm going home now," she said in a thin, wavering voice, rubbing the tears from the corners of her eyes with a knuckle. And then, without waiting for my reply, she began staggering unsteadily toward the parking lot.

"G-good-bye!" I watched her back as she trudged along, all alone in the dusk. The sun got in my eyes, almost making them water.

Seriously, someone needed to marry that woman.

X X X

An hour after Miss Hiratsuka disappeared into the sunset, becoming a single star shining in the night sky, we were at Chiba station.

Komachi had gone home with the cat, Kamakura. My little sister was still in middle school and too young to be going into central

Chiba. Eating chips at the Food Court in Yokado by Highway 14 with her friends suited her better. Seriously, why did middle schoolers like Yokado so much? I couldn't stand running into her and her friends when I went shopping with our mom. *Cut it out, Komachi. Go to Mother Farm or something.*

Anyway, it was almost seven thirty, the perfect time for the city to show off its vibrant night scene. "Apparently, there are only two establishments with *angel* in their name open until morning," I said.

"So this is one of those places?" Yukinoshita gave the neon sign flashing Maid Café Angel Tale a dubious look. There was even a sandwich board to the side that said, *WELCOMEOW BACK—WOOF!* ♪ with a picture of a beckoning girl with animal ears. Yukinoshita's attitude blatantly conveyed her impression of *What the hell?*

I felt the same way. *What the hell. "Welcomeow back—woof!"? Are you a dog or a cat?*

"So there's a maid café in Chiba, huh…?" Yuigahama made interested noises and gazed at it curiously.

"You have no idea, Yuigahama," I said. "Chiba has everything. Getting a mistaken impression of some fad from somewhere or other and then adopting it is what Chiba does. Feel this sad, disappointing vibe. This is Chiba quality." Indeed, you could even say that Chiba prefecture has mastered the art of disappointment. Be it the New Tokyo International Airport, the Tokyo Game Show, the Tokyo German Village or the "Shibuya of Chiba," Kashiwa…despite Tokyo's constant influence, it's Chiba's thing to obsess over being Chiba-ish in weird ways and to rework things in its own fashion. And when you consider the existence of the high-class residential area Chibarly Hills, it's apparent that this fixation has led Chiba to take on the entire world.

And so in Chiba city, Animate and Tora no Ana and their ilk have crowded together close to Chiba Central Station on the Keisei Line, becoming the center of a certain type of Chiba subculture. *Chiba's* reaction to *Akiba*. And so it was only natural that a maid café would pop up around here.

"I don't really know much about this sort of thing, but…um, what's a maid café like?" Totsuka had been reading the signboard over and over, but apparently, it was over his head. Well yeah, the sign said, WHY DON'T WE SPEND SOME MOE MOE MAID TIME TOGETHER? Nobody would get that. What the heck was "moe moe maid time"? Was I gonna be a maid, too?

"Well, I've never actually gone to one myself, so I don't really know… So I called up someone who does know a lot about this stuff."

"Oh-ho-hem! Thou hast summoned me, Hachiman?" That was when Yoshiteru Zaimokuza emerged from the ticket gate of Keisei Chiba Central Station. Though it was early summer, he was sweating like a pig in his trench coat, chuckling to himself. There were salt crystals forming on his collar. *Hey, if this were ancient China, you'd be executed for the illicit manufacture of salt.*

"Eugh…" Yuigahama's face twisted. It would have been harsh of me to blame her for it, though. Why? Because my expression was even more disgusted.

"Why do you look at me thusly? You're the one who asked me to come."

"Oh, I had to invite you, but dealing with you is kind of a pain in the ass."

"I am shocked. Indeed I am. But as your abilities rival mine, I find it difficult to restrain my might when dealing with you. So I well understand how you might be loathe to deal with me."

"Yeah, yeah, that. That's the part that's a pain in the ass," I said, but Zaimokuza just burst into a weird, loud *gwaba-ha-ha-ha!* Get lost.

I didn't actually want to invite him, but the only people I knew well versed in this stuff were Zaimokuza and Miss Hiratsuka. Plus, Miss Hiratsuka's predilections were *shonen* manga and such, so naturally, my options were reduced to one. I'd already let Zaimokuza know what was going on via e-mail. I'd told him what time Kawasaki went home, that the place we thought she worked at had *angel* in the name, and stuff about Kawasaki herself. From those details, one of the shops Zaimokuza had come up with was this *Angel Tale.*

"Zaimokuza, are you sure this is the place?"

"Yes, there's no question about it." Zaimokuza's fingers danced across his phone to bring up the information Professor Google had taught him. These things are convenient, but I worry that using cell phones or smartphones too much just wears out your fingers, and then you'll really have a problem on your hands. "As you see here, there are two such shops in this city. And my ghost is whispering to me that Saki Kawasaki would most certainly pick this one."

"How do you know?"

Zaimokuza's reply was so abundantly ripe with confidence that my breath caught in my throat. Perhaps he'd grasped something that eluded us. He gave a throaty laugh.

I see... What he's got isn't confidence... It's conviction.

"Just keep your mouths shut and follow me... The maids will lavish you with affection," he declared, making his coat flutter and rustle. It looked as if a wind was rising from his feet.

Zaimokuza...

With those words, there was nothing for it but to follow him...to the promised land, the golden world overflowing with ambrosia, the holy kingdom where all men are loved. Feeling my heart throb as I wondered what the maids would do, I took one small step for mankind but one large step for me, and then it happened.

A tug on the bottom hem of my blazer. When I turned, there stood Yuigahama pouting.

"What?"

"Nothing. I was just thinking, *Oh, so Hikki goes to places like this, too. It's kinda gross.*" Yuigahama kneaded my jacket with her fingertips, grinding away at it, her expression sullen. *Stop it. You're gonna give it lint balls.*

"Uh, I don't know what you mean. I need a full subject, verb, and object, okay?"

"I mean, like, isn't this a café for guys? What about us?"

Hmm? Oh. Now that she mentioned it, I wondered if girls did go to maid cafés. Thinking, *Teach me, O wise Zaimokuza*, I cast him a glance, and reliable old Zaimokuza positioned himself on a slightly raised bit of pavement, crossed his arms, and spoke.

"Worry not, broad."

"Are you calling me fat?"

Well, I think you do have certain large and round parts. I won't say where, though.

"I thought perchance this might occur, so I brought maid outfits for infiltration and investigation," he said, smoothly producing two maid uniforms from behind his back. They were even in plastic clothing covers from the cleaners and in perfect condition. Seriously, did he have a metal bat or a frying pan hidden back there, too, or what? "Ga-hum, ga-hum. Now then, Master Totsuka, shall we proceed…?"

Oh, so he was going for that one. Nice.

"Huh? Wh-why me…?"

Zaimokuza inched forward. Totsuka took one step back, then another in an attempt to run. What was this, a Godzilla movie? Usually, I'd play the hero and save Totsuka, even if it meant punching Zaimokuza in the gut, but this time, I couldn't move at all.

I-I want to see it…

Finally, Totsuka was backed against a wall. Lit from behind as Zaimokuza was at that moment, he really seemed like a monster. "Come, Master Totsuka… Come on, come on, come on, come on, *come on!*"

A creature with a maid uniform in one hand looming before him, Totsuka shook his head vigorously, tears in his eyes. "N-no…no…" Though he knew resistance was futile, Totsuka squeezed those large eyes brimming with tears shut in an attempt to deny the reality before him. And then…

"Sure, sure, sure! I'd love to try one on! They're cute!" Yuigahama squealed, yanking the costumes from Zaimokuza's hands.

Ptoo. Zaimokuza spat.

The gesture apparently annoyed Yuigahama, as she gave Zaimokuza a look that said, *What an obnoxious virgin.* "Huh? What's with that attitude? You're kinda pissing me off."

Normally, Zaimokuza'd have fled a situation like this by bursting into a coughing fit, but ensnared in a maid transfixion now, he was bolder. "Hmph, that is not what a maid is. The maid you speak of is just maid cosplay. It has no soul."

"I have no idea what you're talking about." Yuigahama looked to me for assistance, but this was something I couldn't help her with. As for why? Because I got it.

"You know, I get it. It's like, you can put on a maid outfit, but it's not gonna be right. You'll just look like some irritating college student wearing it on a whim." Seriously, most of the time, people like that look down on *otaku*, maids, and people into that sort of thing, but then they'll turn around and worship maid outfits just for some party. What's with that? It's not a pleasant sight to see.

"When you cosplay, you must costume your soul as well! Come back once you've read *Shirley*! People like you do Miku cosplay at Comiket and then see nothing wrong with lighting up in the smoking area!" Zaimokuza's fervent tirade drove Yuigahama back about three steps. Moaning as if pained, she looked for an ally, eyes darting to and fro before taking cover behind reliable Yukinoshita's back.

Yukinoshita, now a shield, huffed and pointed to the ANGEL TALE sign. "It looks like this place welcomes women, too."

I looked at the line where Yukinoshita was pointing, and she was right. It said, WOMEN ARE ALSO WELCOME! YOU CAN BE A MAID!

Hey, so the sign hadn't been lying. They really did have "maid time."

X   X   X

Anyway, so the five of us, boys and girls together, went into Angel Tale.

"Welcome back, Masters, my ladies!" We were given the standard greeting and led to a table. Yuigahama and Yukinoshita went to that maid dress-up thing or whatever, leaving just myself, Totsuka, and Zaimokuza at the table.

"I await your orders, Masters," A girl wearing a cat-ear headband and red-framed glasses offered us menus. There were various dishes, like *om nom nomlette rice* and *fluffy white curry* ☆ and *cutie cutie ♪ cake*. Aside from the default menu, there were also several options like *moe moe rock-paper-scissors* or a photo session or the Sobu Line game. Hey, why'd they charge just for playing rock-paper-scissors? Was there some kind of hand-game bubble market?

Well, I didn't really understand those kinds of choices, so I turned to Zaimokuza, who was sitting beside me, figuring I'd leave that stuff to him. Zaimokuza was looking right and left, all hunched up in his seat, quickly drinking his water. He hadn't said a single word since we came in.

"Hey, what's gotten into you?"

"Ngh... Though I am fond of places such as this, when I go in, I get so nervous... It's hard for me to talk to the maids."

"Oh." I decided to ignore him.

Hands trembling, he continued wielding the glass in his hand like a vibroweapon.

The third person at the table wasn't saying anything at all, so this time I tried talking to him. "Totsuka, so about this maid café..."

No reply.

"T-Totsuka?"

Once again, nothing. My sun, who always smiled brightly at me whenever I spoke to him, was ignoring me! Totsuka stubbornly stared in the opposite direction without saying a single word.

"Are you mad?" I asked. Ready to die if he kept up the cold shoulder, I picked up a fork as I spoke, ready to drive it into my own throat.

Finally, Totsuka broke the silence. "You didn't save me out there."

"Huh? Uh, well, that was because, like…"

"You tried to make me wear those cutesy clothes, even though I'm a boy." Totsuka looked at me huffily.

He's so cute even when he's angry… Whoops. Bad. Stop right there. Totsuka's a guy. Plus, the fact that he was mad probably meant he didn't like being considered girlish. So if I said anything else along those lines, he'd probably feel awkward. "That was, um, like…you know…a joke between men. Like two wolves play-fighting. Sorta like that."

"Really?"

"Really. A real man never lies." Anyway, I had to emphasize the word *man* here. I'd draw attention to his intense manliness by saying *man* over and over.

"Th-then…okay…," Totsuka said, blushing and finally forgiving me.

"Sorry. Let me apologize by buying you a cappuccino. In Italy, all men drink cappuccinos."

"Yeah, thanks." Perhaps my persistent *man* emphasis had paid off, as Totsuka cheered up. As he showed me the greatest smile, I cheerfully rang the bell on the table.

"I apologize for keeping you waiting, Masters."

"Yeah, two cappuccinos, please."

"If you would please, Master, we could put some art on your cappuccinos, like a kitty. Would that be to your liking?"

"No, we're good."

The maid showed no signs of displeasure at my refusal. "Very well, Master. Please wait just a bit ♪," she said, a brilliant grin on her face.

I guess that was something like the *Sure, with pleasure!* they say in an *izakaya*. As expected of a pro. Her service was lively, brisk, and quite delightful.

I don't think maid cafés are popular merely because of the superficial pleasantness of words like *moe moe* or *Master*. They're popular because they're overflowing with this sort of passion for service. They hew to the principle of doing whatever it takes for the customer's enjoyment. Rock-paper-scissors and drawing pictures on omelette rice in ketchup are merely expressions that spirit of hospitality can take. Customers come precisely because they can sense that enthusiasm in the maids.

Among these maids there was one who seemed particularly awkward. The tray in her hand trembled, and her eyes were constantly fixed on the cups on her tray, making her footsteps unsteady. She was bound to trip and show us her panties... Just as that thought crossed my mind, I realized it was Yuigahama.

"Th-thank you for waiting...M-Master." Embarrassed, Yuigahama put the cups on the table, her face red. She was wearing a relatively plain, mainstream maid outfit. It was the kind with a black-and-white theme and frilly lace, and though the skirt was short, the outfit mainly emphasized her chest.

Silence.

"D-do I look okay?"

Yuigahama laid the tray on the table and spun around slowly. The decorative ribbons and frills fluttered.

"Wow, you look so cute, Yuigahama! Doesn't she, Hachiman?"

"Hmm? Oh, yeah. I guess." My reply to Totsuka was halfhearted.

Apparently, though, that qualified as praise to Yuigahama, and she smiled happily. "Really? That's a relief... Hee-hee... Thanks."

Frankly, I was surprised. Yuigahama looked ditzy, as usual, but her meek attitude and mildly embarrassed expression combined to give her a different impression than she usually made.

"Man, but, like, this outfit has such a short skirt, and the knee-highs are so tight! The people who wore this working back in the day must have had a rough time. If you had to wear this cleaning, you'd get as dusty as an old Swiffer."

I retract my previous remarks. Yup, this was Yui Yuigahama. "It's better when you keep your mouth shut."

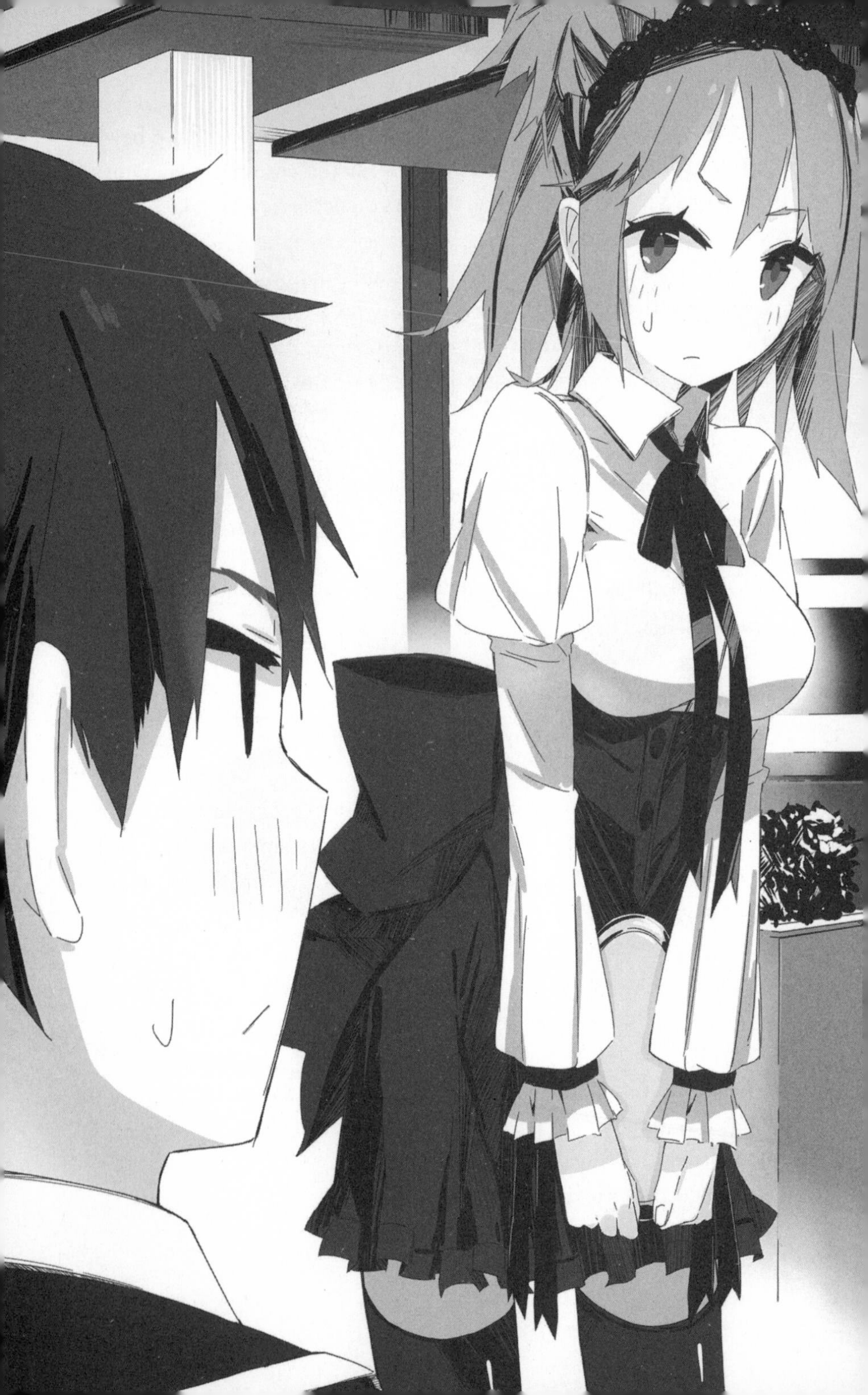

"What?! What's that supposed to mean?!" She clonked me on the head with a tray. To think she'd raise a hand against her master...

"Enough fooling around." I heard a cold voice and turned. There stood a maid from the era of the British Empire. Long skirt, long sleeves, dark moss green and embroidered black ribbon. Her stately image gave the plain garb a sort of extravagant air.

"Wow, Yukinon! Oh my gosh! It looks so good on you! You're so pretty..." Yuigahama sighed in admiration.

Indeed, she was right. It really suited Yukinoshita. "You seem less like a maid and more like Rottenmeier, though..."

Personally, I felt like that was an understandable reference, but apparently, neither of the girls got it. Both of them looked puzzled, gaping at me quizzically.

"I'm saying it suits you."

"Oh? Not that it's important, though," Yukinoshita replied as if she cared not in the slightest.

By the way, Rottenmeier was the older housekeeper from *Heidi*. Was she technically a maid? I suppose she was. A similar example would be the female cast at the Haunted Mansion in Disney parks.

"It seems Kawasaki does not work at this cafe."

"So you were actually investigating..."

"Of course. That's why I'm wearing this outfit." Yukinoshita had been following through with this undercover investigation by her lonesome. A maid detective had been born.

And I'd had nothing on my mind beyond cheering up Totsuka...

"She's not just off today?" Yuigahama asked, but Yukinoshita shook her head.

"Her name wasn't on the shift schedule. And since they've been calling her at her house, I don't think she could be using a fake name, either."

To have deduced this much, she was less a maid and more a housekeeper. And *The Housekeeper Saw It!*

"Then that means that we've just been manipulated by fake information." I gave Zaimokuza next to me a long, hard look.

He tilted his head and began groaning. "This is strange... It cannot be possible..."

"What can't be possible?"

"Ah-hum! It's simply preordained that a prickly girl should be secretly working at a maid café! And then when you walk in, she greets you with 'Meow meow! ♪ Welcome back, Master... Wait, why are you here?!'"

"You're not making sense." I didn't give a damn about Zaimokuza's fetishes. This guy had cost us an entire day. It was getting pretty late, so going to another place probably wasn't gonna happen.

But, well, Yuigahama seemed happy about trying on the maid outfit, and we'd found a nice café. So I was fine with just letting it go.

$$\times \quad \times \quad \times$$

The day after we went to the maid café, there were more people in the clubroom than there had ever been in its history. We'd been brought together by Yukinoshita's assertion that if treating the symptoms failed, we should try another tack and aim to treat the source of the problem.

Yukinoshita, Yuigahama, and I were basically members, so I got why we were there. And Totsuka and Zaimokuza visited us regularly, so there wasn't anything odd about their presence, either. Though anyone else being there should have seemed unnatural, oddly enough, the last guy fit right in.

"Why are you here?" I asked Hayama. He was reading a book by the window. *Hey, you're supposed to be the sunny sports type. You can't be reading books. Are you Perfect Cell?*

"Hey." Hayama closed his book and waved. "Well, Yui invited me, too..."

"She did?"

I turned to see Yuigahama proudly puffing out her chest for some reason. "Well, I've been thinking that there's a reason Kawasaki changed, right? So I think taking away whatever made her change is a good idea, too, but that'll be hard if she won't listen to anybody, right?"

"Hmm, well, that's true." Miraculously, Yuigahama was attempting to employ logic. Impressed by this tiny miracle, I commented to indicate I was listening.

Perhaps this flattered her, because she threw her chest out even more, leaning so far back she was practically looking at the ceiling. "Right?! So we need an idea to turn things around. Since she changed and went bad, if she changes again, she should go back to good."

I guess this is what they mean by "The opposite of approval is approval." Man, Fujio Akatsuki is so great.

"So why was it necessary to invite Hayama?" Perhaps Yukinoshita wasn't so fond of him, as her tone was sharp. Hayama didn't seem to be particularly bothered. His attention was focused on Yuigahama.

"Come on, Yukinon. There's only one reason a girl would change."

"The reason a girl would change… Do you mean the depreciation of her assets?" ·

"You mean like getting old?! N-no! At the end of the day, a girl is always a girl! Yukinon, you don't get the importance of thinking with your *smexy* bits!"

"That again…" Yukinoshita sighed, exasperated.

But you know…I think girls who fail to notice that girls who use the word *smexy* aren't overly smexy themselves lack smexiness.

"A girl would change because of…l-love." What an embarrassing thing to blurt out. Plus, Yuigahama was more shamed for having said it than we were for hearing it. "A-anyway! Lots of things change when you have a crush! So I think maybe if we could just trigger that… And that's why I invited Hayato."

"U-um, but, I'm still not really following…," Hayama confessed with a strained smile.

Come on, you jerk! If you really don't get it, I'm gonna lose it, I thought, flaring my eyes wide and glaring at Hayama. At almost exactly the same moment, Zaimokuza did the same.

"There's lots of other guys girls'd go for. Like, look at the guys here... Lots of girls like Totsuka, right?"

Phew... So Hayama is aware he's a chick magnet... Wait, no—this is absolutely unforgivable! My eyes popped, and I doubled down with the glaring. Perfectly in sync, Zaimokuza did the same.

"I-I don't really understand that stuff, though..." Totsuka looked down, blushing.

Seeing Totsuka like that, Yuigahama crossed her arms pensively. "Hmm, I agree that lots of girls like him, too, but I don't think he's Kawasaki's type. And the rest of these guys are like...well, Special Snowflake is a special snowflake, so Hayato's the only one left."

"Hey, you can't just casually leave me out."

"Y-you're out of the question, Hikki!"

Hey, no need to turn beet red and get all mad about it... But still, it was a bit of a shock that I was even more out of the question than Zaimokuza... And was "Special Snowflake" his nickname?

"Yuigahama's assessment is sound," said Yukinoshita. "Do you think anyone in our class who got to know you would be swayed?"

"You have a point." Well, I was convinced. I mean, if I were a girl, I wouldn't be interested in a loner like me. It's because, you know, loners have ninja talents. Ninjas can't afford to have people noticing them, so we can't help but be ignored. Seriously, my ninja skills are awesome. Believe it.

"Oh, um, but I didn't go that far, like...you're not actually that bad, and, uh...there's lots of reasons, so unfortunately...um, I want to ask Hayato to do this." While I'd been busy wondering how best to make use of my ninja skills and considering becoming Hokage, Yuigahama had been attempting to move the conversation forward. "Could you do this for us?" Yuigahama pleaded, putting her palms together as she bowed her head.

No boy could refuse after being asked like that. Boys are complicated creatures. A boy is happy when someone relies on him, gets distracted by the boob jiggle when a girl smacks her hands together, and this sort of request stimulates his desire to save someone—to be a hero—that's he's fostered since he was small. You know, so complicated.

Apparently, Hayama was no exception to this rule, as he gave a tiny shrug and replied, "I understand. If that's the reason, then I have no choice. Though I have my reservations, I'll give it a shot. You give it your best shot, too, Yui," he said, and he patted Yuigahama on the head.

No, you're the one who's going to be giving it your best shot.

"Th-thanks…," said Yuigahama, rubbing the spot where he'd patted her.

And thus, the curtain rose on Yuigahama's proposal: the *Gigolo Hayama's Rom-Com Pitter-Patter Heart-Pounding Operation!* Hey, what's with this Showa-esque naming affinity?

The gist of the plan was simple. Hayama would muster all his strength to HeartCatch Kawasaki, no keyblade required. See what I did there?

We readied ourselves to head home and then went to the parking lot to wait for Kawasaki to show up. Of course, it'd be weird for Hayama to be seen with the rest of us, so we decided to keep an eye on the two of them from a distance.

And then, finally, the time came. Just as she had the day before, Kawasaki walked listlessly, sluggishly, as if dragging her feet. She swallowed a yawn, and just as she unlocked her bike, Hayama appeared as if on cue.

"What's up? You look pretty tired." He greeted her casually. It was supposedly acting, but he seemed so natural, just eavesdropping I felt the urge to give him a *Wh-what's up?* in reply. "Do you have a job or something? Don't work too hard, okay?"

What an amazing display of casual concern… Man, seriously, Hayama was such a great guy.

While I was halfway to falling for him myself, Kawasaki just sighed in annoyance. "Thanks for your concern. I'm going now. Bye," she said brusquely, pushing her bicycle as if to leave.

But then, a kind, warm, heart-melting voice called out behind her. "Hey…"

This was enough to bring even Kawasaki up short. She stopped in her tracks and turned to face Hayama. The fresh early-summer wind blew between the couple. The suddenly blossoming rom-com atmosphere prompted Yuigahama to lean forward, rapt, as she clenched her sweaty palms. Zaimokuza burned with jealousy, hatred, and murderous rage, also clenching his fists.

The invigorating wind stopped, and Hayama's voice rang out. He seemed to be sparkling. It was as if he were radiating negative air ions or something. "You don't have to put on that tough act, you know?"

"Yeah, whatever."

The wheels of her bicycle rattled as they spun out, but for Hayato Hayama, time had stopped. He stood there for a full ten seconds, left in the dust with a rather embarrassed smile on his face, before he returning to our vantage from the shadows. "I think…I just got rejected."

Silence.

"Oh, well, thanks for…" I'd thought to thank him for his trouble, but the rest of the words refused to come out. A strange feeling cascaded through the muscles in my stomach. *Damn it! Calm down, abs!* I tried to suppress the mounting pressure somehow, but my sides split before I could manage it.

"Pft…pfffft! GWA-HA-HA-HA-HA-HA-HA-HA! Th-thou has been SPURNED! She rejected you! You were trying so hard to look cool, and she still rejected you! Pfffft-ha-ha-ha!"

"Stop that, Za…ah-ha-ha-ha…"

"B-both of you! Stop laughing!" Totsuka scolded, and I tried to restrain myself. Zaimokuza's bellowing made it even funnier, though, and I couldn't help it.

"O-oh, well, it doesn't really bother me. It's okay, Totsuka," Hayama reassured, the awkward purse of his lips looking wry.

He was a good guy. He helped us out even though he wasn't into it, and he got hurt doing it.

Perhaps even Zaimokuza was affected by Hayama's gentlemanly attitude. He sucked in his laughter, coughed, and composed himself. "Whatever-your-name-is...Hayama...you don't have to put on that... pfft...tough act, you know! Ha-ha-ha!"

"You jerk! Stop that, Zaimokuza! Don't laugh at him!" Zaimokuza and I were cracking up, but Yuigahama's face was twitching. "You guys are so horrible."

"So this strategy has failed, too," Yukinoshita noted. "Oh well. Let's go to that other place tonight."

"Yeah."

Phew, that was fun.

This was the first time I'd ever been glad I joined the Service Club. Period.

× × ×

The arms on my watch showed the time to be 8:20 PM. We were meeting up in front of Kaihin-Makuhari Station, so there I was leaning against a sculpture that, for some reason, was big, long, and pointy. Nickname: weird pointy thing. The place we were heading was on the top floor of the Hotel Royal Okura: the bar Angel's Ladder. It was the only other business in Chiba that operated until morning and had a name starting with *angel*. This was probably the first and last time I'd ever go to such a fancy place.

I had a thin jacket with me that still felt unfamiliar, and I put it on again to get used to it. I'd liberated this gem from my father's closet without asking, and I guess we had roughly the same build, because it fit me perfectly. With the jacket, I wore a black shirt with a collar, jeans, and long-nose leather shoes on my feet. Usually, I'd never dress up like this. I just didn't really care about clothes and stuff in general. All of it aside from the jeans was my dad's. I'd even gelled up my hair.

Outfit coordinated by: Komachi Hikigaya. I'd asked Komachi to pick out some stuff for me to try and make me look older, so she'd ransacked the house and pulled together this outfit. "You've got this exhausted look in your eyes like a salaryman who's tired of life, Bro, so if you just do something about your clothes and hair, you'll look like a grown-up."

How was I supposed to react to a remark like that? Come on... Are my eyes that bad?

The first one to show up at our rendezvous point was Saika Totsuka. "Sorry, did I keep you waiting?"

"No, I just got here."

Totsuka's outfit was slightly sporty in a unisex sort of way. His cargo pants were on the loose side, and his T-shirt was slightly on the tight side. He had a fine-threaded beanie pulled back on his head, and there were headphones around his neck. The dully shining wallet chain at his hip swung every time his sneaker-clad feet moved. This was the first time I'd ever seen Totsuka out of uniform, so I stared at him, dazed.

Totsuka pulled down the beanie as if he was embarrassed for some reason in an attempt to hide his eyes. "D-don't stare at me like that... D-do I look weird?"

"N-no, not at all! It suits you."

It kind of felt like we were on a date, somehow, but unfortunately, we weren't. As proof of that, Zaimokuza materialized. For some reason, he was wearing *samue* and had a white towel wrapped around his head like a bandanna. I ignored him.

"Hmph. I believe this was where our party was supposed to meet... Oh-ho! Is that not Hachiman?"

His obnoxious little act got on my nerves, but now that he'd found me, there was nothing I could do. "What's with that outfit? Why are you wearing a towel on your head? Are you gonna run a ramen shop?"

He sighed. "Oh, Hachiman. Was it not you who said we should dress like adults? And so I chose the style of a working man: a *samue* and a towel."

Oh, so that's what he'd been thinking. Well, he already had it on, so there was nothing that could be done about it now. Actually, we could just leave him behind, so whatever.

I think I'd reached that conclusion right around the time I heard the *click, click* of Yuigahama approaching. Her eyes darting about, she pulled out her phone. Oh, so she hadn't noticed us.

"Yuigahama." I called out to her, and she twitched before turning timidly in my direction. *Hey, wait. You were just looking at me a second ago, though.*

"H-Hikki? Oh, it's you! I didn't recognize you for a second... Th-that outfit..."

"What? Don't laugh."

"N-no, that's not it at all! Um, it's so different from what you usually wear, it just startled me..." She ogled me, going "Whoa!" and "Ooh!" and "Ahh!" before giving me a vigorous nod. "Komachi picked this out, didn't she?"

"Oh, so you could tell."

"I knew it." Yuigahama came off as if she'd somehow been convinced of something...but what? She was giving me a Piiko-esque fashion evaluation for some reason, so I decided to do the same like Don Konishi.

Yuigahama wore a tube top with a plastic bra strap over the right side; the left was off the shoulder. Apparently, she liked her heart-charm necklace a lot, as she still had it dangling from her neck. Over her top, she sported a short-sleeved denim jacket, and down below, she had on a pair of black short shorts with metal buttons. Her feet were covered by some fairly high-heeled mules with a bit that wrapped around her ankles like a vine. With every step, her anklet rattled.

"You're kinda...not very adult-looking."

"What? Howso?!" Yuighama seemed flustered as she scrutinized her arms and her legs. That made her look even more like a college student than her style already did.

That accounted for almost our entire party. Now just one more...and with that thought, a voice called out from behind us. "I apologize. Am I late?" Her white summer dress was vivid in the darkness. The black leggings beneath it made her slim legs look supple. Her utterly simple, tiny mules complimented her slender ankles. When she turned her wrist up to check the time, the pink face of her smallish wristwatch shone cutely against her white skin. The metal strap wrapped around that smooth wrist looked like silverwork. "So I'm right on time." Like edelweiss blooming at night, Yukino Yukinoshita radiated a composed charm.

"Y-yeah…" Nothing else came out of me. I remembered that first time I stepped into the Service Club clubroom and how she'd overwhelmed me.

If only she had a decent personality…

"Have you ever heard of the no-waste ghost?"

"What nonsense. There's no such thing as ghosts." Yukinoshita immediately waved my comment aside and looked our entire entourage up and down. "Hmm…" Then, starting with Zaimokuza, she pointed to each of us in order. "Fail."

"Muh?"

"Fail."

"Huh?"

"Fail."

"What?"

"Disqualified."

"Hey…" For some reason, she was grading pass/fail, and I'd gotten a different mark from everybody else.

"I told you to wear mature clothing, didn't I?"

"Not to dress up like adults?"

"You can't get into the establishment we're visiting without appropriate attire. It's common sense that a man would wear a collared shirt and a formal jacket."

"R-really…?" Totsuka asked, and Yukinoshita nodded.

"It's a fairly standard policy at some of the more upscale restaurants and hotels. You should keep that in mind."

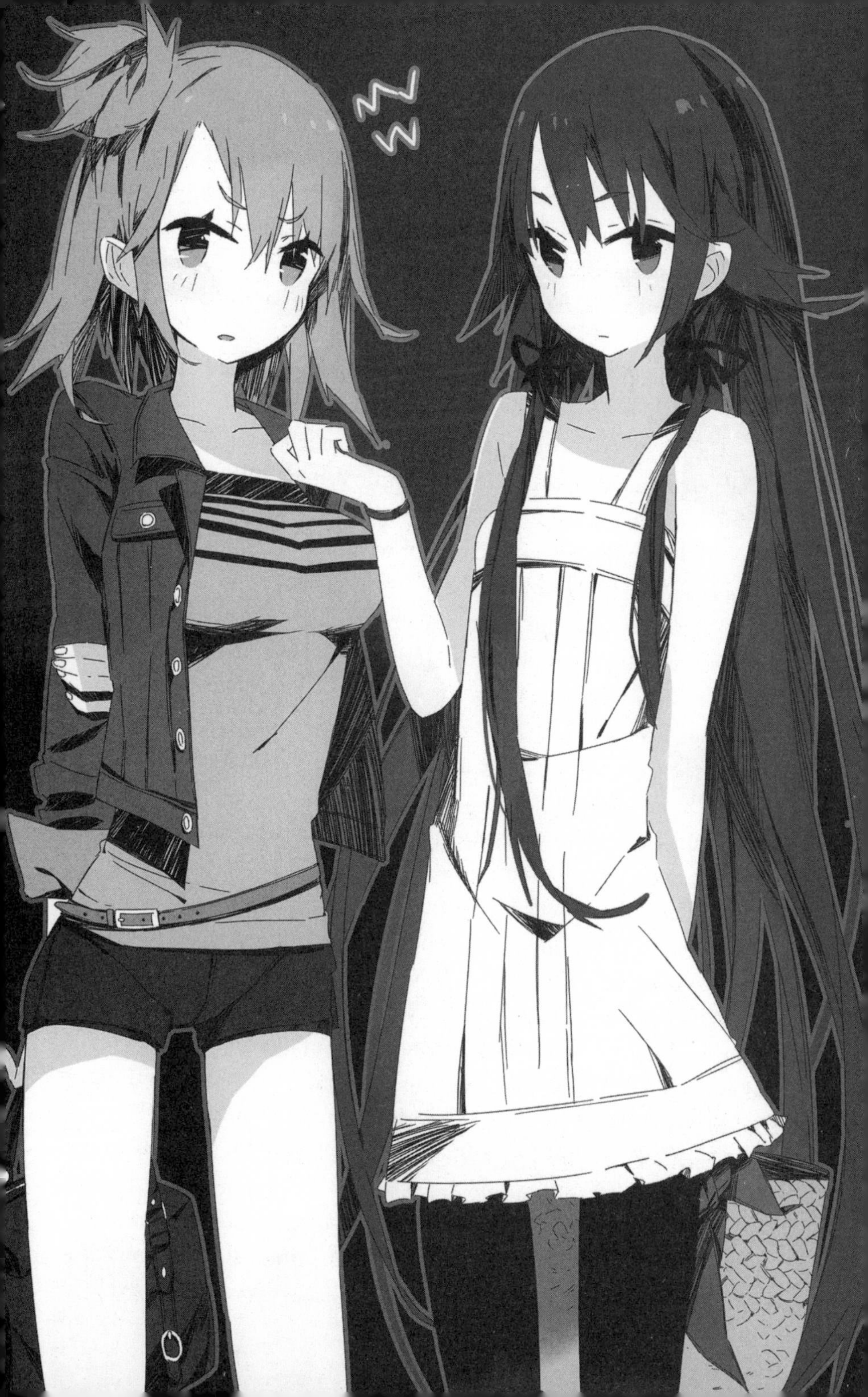

"You sure know a lot about this." This didn't sound like the sort of intel your average high schooler would have at their fingertips. I mean, the only restaurants we went to were Saize and Bamiyan. The fanciest it got was Roiyaho. Anyway, the only one of us wearing a formal jacket was me. Totsuka was fairly casual, and Zaimokuza was dressed up like a ramen chef.

"M-my clothes are no good?" Yuigahama fretted, and Yukinoshita looked slightly troubled.

"The dress code isn't so particular for women, but…if Hikigaya is the one escorting you, that might be a little sketchy."

"Come on, come on! Lookit the jacket, the jacket!" I fluttered my jacket like Hiromi Gou in an attempt to call attention to it, but Yukinoshita only chuckled derisively.

"No matter how much you attempt to divert attention from them with your clothing, your eyes are so rotten, I doubt your ability to get in."

Were they really that bad?

"I don't want to have to come back a second time because we were refused service, so it might be a good idea for Yuigahama to come get changed at my place."

"Huh? I can go to your place, Yukinon?! Let's go, let's go! Oh, but I'm not being a bother, coming over this late?"

"You don't have to worry about it. I live alone."

"You're such a strong, independent woman!" Yuigahama's astonishment was overdone.

Was that her standard, really? Was every woman who lived alone strong and independent? But hearing that Yukinoshita lived alone, it did make sense. She was an amazing cook, but more than anything, I couldn't imagine her living with another human being.

"Then let's go. It's just over that way." Yukinoshita turned to the skyline behind her, indicating an apartment building known for being expensive, even within the region. Since I didn't watch TV much, I didn't really know, but apparently, they sometimes shot commercials or TV shows there. (Fun fact: Kaihin-Makuhari was often used as a location for superhero shows, too.) Yukinoshita's gaze was fixed near the top of the skyscraper distinguished by a pale orange light. It seemed her apartment was on one of the higher floors. *Wh-whoa, is she actually bourgeoisie?* I guess if she wasn't, her parents probably wouldn't have let their high school daughter live alone.

"I'm sorry you came all this way, Totsuka, but—"

"No, it's okay. I got to see everyone out of uniform, and that was fun," Totsuka said, smiling brightly. He was so cute, I didn't want him to go yet.

"Hey, so, Yuigahama, while you're getting changed, the three of us will go get something to eat," I said. "When it's over, just give me a call whenever."

"Yeah, I will!"

We split with the pair, and the three of us guys fell silent as if gauging how hungry we were.

"So on what shall we dine?" Zaimokuza asked, rubbing his belly.

Totsuka and I looked at each other.

"Ramen, I guess."

"Yeah, ramen."

× × ×

I parted ways with Totsuka and Zaimokuza at the ticket gates. At the ramen shop, Zaimokuza had been mistaken for staff, and people kept trying to give him orders, but he and Totsuka appeared satisfied at having been able to eat delicious ramen.

I left the station and headed for the Hotel Royal Okura. This time, I was supposed to just meet Yukinoshita and Yuigahama there.

As I approached the entrance of the hotel for a second time, its size made me hesitate. Even the pale light illuminating the building had this high-class air. It clearly wasn't the kind of building a mere high school student could enter. But even so, heart pounding in my chest, I stepped inside. An unfamiliar feeling greeted my feet as my shoes sank into the plush, wall-to-wall carpet. *Am I getting an Academy Award now or what?* All the madames and dandies scattered throughout the lounge seemed somehow classy, and I also caught glimpses of a few foreigners here and there. Oh man, Makuhari was so metropolitan.

The place Yuigahama had designated in her e-mail for us to meet was in front of the elevator hall. Unlike the elevators with which I was familiar, these doors sparkled. Also, the sofa where I'd deposited myself felt rather nice. *Hey, is this memory foam?* And there were, like, vases and crap on display, too. As I messed around and contemplated the delightful *smoosh* sensation beneath me, my phone rang.

"We're just walking in now. Are you there already?"

She said they were here, but… I glanced around.

"S-sorry to keep you waiting!" A girl who smelled kinda nice called out to me. Her crimson dress had a wide, plunging neckline that flowed down in a sort of mermaid shape. The whiteness of the back of her neck peeking from underneath her updo took my breath away. "Th-this feels like I'm dressed up for a piano recital…"

"Oh, Yuigahama. I was wondering who it was." Her remark was so pedestrian, it finally clued me in to the fact that this was Yuigahama. Had she been breezily composed, I probably wouldn't have recognized her.

"Couldn't you at least say it's like you're dressed up for a wedding? I have mixed feelings about you comparing this to something you'd wear to a piano recital," chastised a second voice attached to a beauty in a black dress just making her entrance. The fabric of her gown had a smooth, obsidian luster that emphasized the beauty of her pale skin like virgin snow, and the flared skirt ending above her knees showed off her long legs. Her luxurious, flowing, silken black hair was even glossier than the dress. It was tied up and loosely twisted, left to fall over her chest like jewelry. It couldn't have been anyone but Yukino Yukinoshita.

"B-but this is the first time I've ever worn anything like this. And, like, seriously, Yukinon, who are you?!"

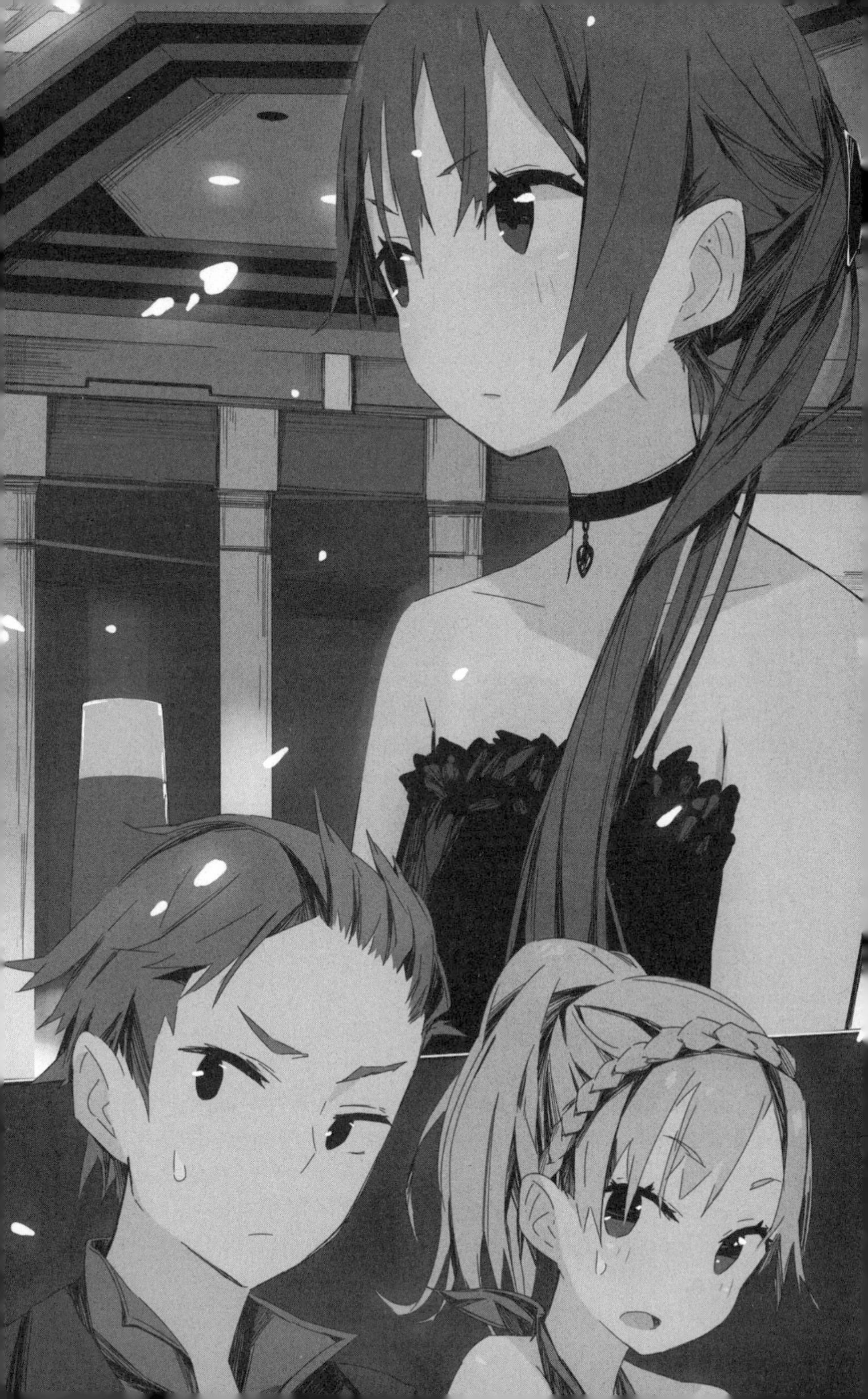

"Don't be so dramatic. I have occasion to wear dresses from time to time, so I happen to have a few."

"Most people wouldn't have those sorts of occasions in the first place," I remarked. "And, like, where do they sell stuff like that? Shimamura?"

"Shimamura? I'm unfamiliar with that brand," she replied in all sincerity.

She doesn't know Shimamura. I bet she doesn't know Uniqlo, either.

"Come on, let's go." Yukinoshita pressed the elevator button. With a *ping*, the button lit up, and the doors silently opened. The car was glass-walled, and as it climbed, we could see over Tokyo Bay. The lights of cruising boats, the taillights of cars driving along the coastline, and the dazzling illumination of the high-rises colored the night view of Makuhari.

When we arrived at the top floor, the doors opened again. There was a calm, gentle light ahead of us. Splayed out in a glow so soft it was almost like candlelight, the bar lounge almost felt dark.

"Whoa...whoa, is this for real?" The scene unfolding before me clearly wasn't meant for my eyes. On a stage, a spotlight shone down on a white woman playing jazz music. She was probably American. Foreigner = American. I made eye contact with Yuigahama as if to say, *Maybe we should go back after all?* She nodded swiftly and vigorously. Just having a plebe like Yuigahama here with us calmed my nerves.

But high-society Yukinoshita wouldn't allow that. "Stop gawking." She ground her heel into my foot.

"Ow!" I nearly cried out: *What's with those stiletto heels? Is that Ray Stinger?*

"Stand up straight and push our your chest. Pull back your jaw." Yukinoshita whispered into my ear, quietly grabbing my right elbow. Her slender, well-shaped fingers clasped my arm.

"U-um... Wh-whatever is the matter, Miss Yukinoshita?"

"Don't get flustered over every little thing. Yuigahama, do the same thing."

"Wh-whaa?" Yuigahama's expression said, *I don't get this!*, but she obediently followed Yukinoshita's instructions.

"Now then, let's go."

Doing as I was told, I matched my pace to the girls' and slowly began walking. We passed through the heavy-looking open wooden doors, and immediately, a male server appeared by our side, quietly bowing his head. He didn't say a word—no *How many guests?* or *Smoking or nonsmoking?* He just took a step and a half forward to show us the bar counter at the end of the room, in front of a floor-to-ceiling window. At the bar, a female bartender was polishing glasses squeaky clean. She was slender and tall with fine facial features. She had a teardrop mole, and her expression seemed vaguely sorrowful. It suited the faintly lit establishment's ambiance.

Wait, that's Kawasaki.

She seemed different from how she normally was at school. Her hair was tied up in a ponytail, and she was dressed professionally in a black vest and white-collared shirt. Her movements were graceful and silent, not sluggish in the slightest. She didn't seem to recognize us as she quietly set out coasters and then waited silently. I would have thought she'd be handing out menus and asking *So what'll it be?* But I guess not. Duh.

"Kawasaki," I called out to her softly, and she seemed rather confused.

"I apologize. To whom am I speaking?"

"She doesn't remember you, even though you're in the same class. Impressive, Hikigaya," Yukinoshita said admiringly, seating herself on a stool.

"Well, you know. Our clothes are way different today. Of course she wouldn't recognize us." Yuigahama defended me as she sat down as well. The empty seat was the one right in between the two of them. If this were Othello, this would be my losing move. If it were Go... Well, I don't actually know how to play Go.

"We've been looking for you, Kawasaki," Yukinoshita began, and Kawasaki's face changed color.

"Yukinoshita..." Kawasaki scrutinized her as if she were the man who'd killed her father: Her eyes filled with distinct enmity. I'd been under the impression they'd never met before, but Yukinoshita was famous at our school, after all. And with her looks and personality, it was no surprise that some people found her disagreeable.

"Good evening." Whether she knew how Kawasaki felt about her or not, Yukinoshita gave her a composed salutation.

The pair locked eyes. Perhaps it was the light, but I felt like I could see sparks flying between them. Scary. Kawasaki's lids suddenly narrowed, focusing their attention on Yuigahama. It was as if she was probing her, thinking, *Since Yukinoshita's from school, oh my, that means this girl must be, too, huh?*

"H-hi..." Yuigahama gave a non-committal greeting after Kawasaki's optic drubbing.

"Yuigahama, huh? I didn't recognize you for a second there. Then is he from Soubu High, too?"

"Oh, yeah. Hikki is in our class. Hachiman Hikigaya."

Kawasaki gave a faint bow and then smiled as if somehow resigned. "I see. So I've been found out." She shrugged her shoulders, seemingly unconcerned, then leaned against the wall folding her arms. Perhaps she realized the end was nigh, so none of it mattered anymore. Reassuming the languid manner she bore at school, she heaved a shallow sigh and considered us. "Want something to drink?"

"I'll have a Perrier," Yukinoshita said. *What? Perry? Did she just order something?*

"I-I'll have what she's having!"

"Uh..." I'd just been thinking I'd say that...but Yuigahama got in ahead of me, and now the timing was off. *Nngh.* What, what should I say? Should I say Dom Perignon or Don Penguin? By the way, Don Penguin is the mascot for the palace of low, low prices. So even if I did order Don Pen, he probably wouldn't show up.

"Hikigaya, right? What about you?"

So that Perry guy Yukinoshita mentioned was a drink, huh...? I don't have to say Harris or Earnest Satow here, right? Then I guess I'll go with a drink name. "I'll have MAX Coff—"

"Get him a dry ginger ale," Yukinoshita interrupted.

"Right away," said Kawasaki with a wry smile as she set out three champagne glasses and poured into them with practiced hands before softly placing them on our coasters.

The three of us then silently contended with our glasses for some reason, bringing them to our lips.

"Of course they wouldn't have MAX Coffee," Yukinoshita said, as if she'd just remembered it.

"Seriously?! But this is Chiba!" *A Chiba with no MAX Coffee is no Chiba at all, come on! It was like Yamanashi having mountains.*

"We do have it, though," Kawasaki muttered, and Yukinoshita shot her a glance. *Hey, guys, seriously, why does it seem like you have some bad blood going on? You're acting scary.* "So what did you come here for? You're not on a date with *that*, are you?"

"Of course not. If you're saying that in reference to *this* right here, that's in poor taste, even as a joke."

"Um, hey, this fight is between you two, so can you not make indiscriminate digs at me while you're at it?" *"That"? "This"? Stop calling me by demonstratives.* It looked like we were never gonna get anywhere if left to their own devices, so I decided to get the ball rolling. "I hear you haven't been getting home until late recently. It's because of this job, isn't it? Your brother's worried about you," I said.

Kawasaki smiled in her usual irritating way as if scoffing at me. "You came all this way just to say that? Well, good job. Come on, did you think I'd quit because some total stranger told me to?"

"Wow, Hikki...you're getting treated like a total stranger even though you're in the same class..." Yuigahama picked a weird time to be impressed. But I hadn't recognized Kawasaki, either, so we were probably even on that count.

"Oh, I've been wondering why everyone's been getting on my case lately. So it was you, huh? Did Taishi say something to you? I don't know how you know him, but I'll talk to him myself, so you don't have to worry about it. Stay away from him from now on." Kawasaki was glowering at me. I guess her point was *It's none of your business, so get lost.*

But something like that wasn't enough to make Yukinoshita back down. "If you need a reason to quit, here's a good one." Yukinoshita's gaze shifted from Kawasaki to the watch on her left wrist. "Ten forty... Cinderella would have a little over an hour left, but it seems your magic spell has already worn off."

"If my spell's worn off, doesn't that mean there's a happy ending waiting for me?"

"I don't know about that, little mermaid. I think what's waiting for you is a bad ending."

The way the two of them sniped back and forth was much like the atmosphere of the bar: It made you hesitant to step in. Their exchange of sarcastic quips and snide remarks came off like some high society pastime. Seriously, what was with all this nastiness between them? I thought this was the first time they'd ever spoken. The whole situation terrified me.

As these thoughts crossed my mind, I felt a tap on my shoulder and a whisper at my ear. "Hey, Hikki. What are they talking about?"

Oh, Yuigahama. Having a plebe like you here really does make me feel better...

Minors working past ten PM was a violation of labor laws. If she was still working at this hour, it meant that she'd been weaving the magic that is age misrepresentation. And that spell had been undone at Yukinoshita's hands. But even so, Kawasaki didn't seem particularly anxious.

"You have no intention of quitting?"

"Hmm? No. And even if I did quit this place, I could just work somewhere else." Kawasaki said nonchalantly as she polished a sake bottle with a cloth.

Perhaps that attitude irritated Yukinoshita a little, as she lightly tossed back her Perry. Or was it Harris?

The atmosphere tense and foreboding, Yuigahama timidly interjected. "U-um…Kawasaki, why are you working here? Um, like, 'cause
I work when I'm broke, but I wouldn't work so late I'd have to lie about
my age…"

"No reason. I just need the money." She put the sake bottle down
with a quiet clink.

Well, of course. Most everyone works because they want the money.
I'm sure there are some who work because the job is worthwhile or gives
their lives meaning or whatever, but I don't know much about that.
"Oh, you know, I get that," I said innocently, and Kawasaki's expression
turned hard.

"There's no way you could understand. Nobody who'd write down
such a bullshit career choice would." At some point, Kawasaki and I had
met on the school rooftop, and that was when she'd seen my workplace
tour application form. So she did remember.

"I was serious, though."

"Yeah, you were serious, and that means you're still just a kid. You
don't know anything about life." Kawasaki tossed the cloth she'd been
using on the counter and leaned against the wall. "You…no, not just
you—Yukinoshita and Yuigahama wouldn't get it, either. I'm not working because I want money to party with. Don't lump me together with
those idiots." Kawasaki's glare was intense. It was if her eyes were roar-
ing, saying, *Don't get in my way.* But they were moist, too. Was that
actually strength, though? I can't help thinking that people who yell,
No one understands me! actually do want to be understood. That cry is
their lament, a sign that they're giving up.

But look at Yukino Yukinoshita. Though no one understood her,
she didn't bemoan it; she didn't give up. That was because, despite it all,
she had this conviction that sticking to her principles is strength.

And Yui Yuigahama. She never gave up on trying to understand
people. She didn't run away from that because she hoped that maintaining contact—even superficial contact—could be a trigger for change.

"Well, but, like, sometimes people don't understand until you talk to them about it, you know? We might be able to help you somehow… like… just talking might make you feel better…" Halfway in, Yuigahama's voice started to falter. Kawasaki's cold stare ripped her words apart.

"The fact that you said that only proves you guys will definitely never get it. Help me? Make me feel better? Okay then, can you get me some money? Can you take over the responsibilities my parents can't manage?"

"W-well…" Yuigahama looked down as if embarrassed. Kawasaki was too scary!

"Just stop right there. If you keep howling at us like that…," Yukinoshita snapped, her tone ice-cold. The way she'd trailed off just made the implied threat that much more frightening. *What? What are you planning to do?*

Kawasaki faltered for a moment, too, but then she clicked her tongue quietly and turned back to Yukinoshita. "Hey, your dad's a member of the prefectural assembly, isn't he? Someone that loaded could never understand my position." Her voice was subdued, almost a whisper, as if resigned.

Just as those words crossed Kawasaki's lips, I heard a glass topple over with a clatter and turned to find a champagne glass on its side with Perrier spilling out to form a puddle. Yukinoshita bit her lip, her gaze downcast and fixed to the counter. It was a look I'd hardly have expected to see on her.

Surprised, I studied her face. "Yukinoshita?"

"Huh? O-oh, sorry," she stammered, reverting to normal—no, now she was even more frigid and expressionless than usual as she calmly wiped the table with her moistened hand towel. This peculiar insight led me to infer that this subject was taboo for her. Now that I thought about it, she'd had that same expression not so long before… When I tried to remember when that was, though, a loud slap on the counter snapped me back into the moment.

"Hey! Yukinon's family is none of your business!" Yuigahama's tone was unusually assertive, and she had Kawasaki in her sights. She wasn't joking or fooling around; Yuigahama was pissed. *So this is what she looks like mad...*

Perhaps Yuigahama's sudden transformation from her usual breezy, ebullient self startled Kawasaki. Or maybe she just realized she'd crossed a line, but the edge in her voice softened a bit. "Then my family is none of your business, either."

Once she'd dropped that line, that was the end of it.

It was neither mine nor Yuigahama's business, and it was clearly none of Yukinoshita's. Even if Kawasaki was breaking the law, the ones who would take her to task for that would be her teachers and parents, and it was the law that would be judging her. We weren't even her friends. We couldn't do a single thing for her.

"You might be right, but that's not right! Not to Yukinon."

"Yuigahama. Calm down. I just knocked over a glass. It's nothing. Don't worry about it."

Yuigahama was leaning over the counter while Yukinoshita gently restrained her. Yukinoshita's voice was calmer than usual which just made it sound that much colder. Though it was already summer, the air felt chilly.

Well, that was it, then. It didn't look like Yukinoshita, Yuigahama, or Kawasaki could carry on a civil conversation. But we had learned a few things. Now we just had to do something about it. "Let's call it a day. I'm sleepy, frankly. Once I'm done with my drink, I'm gonna go." I still had over half my ginger ale left, though.

"You're such a—"

"C-come on, Yukinon. Let's go home for today?"

Yukinoshita sighed in exasperation and seemed like she wanted to say something, but Yuigahama stopped her. Yuigahama and I exchanged glances, and then she gave me a slight nod. Apparently, she'd also noticed that Yukinoshita was behaving oddly.

"Fine, I'll call it a day." Perhaps even Yukinoshita noticed she was frazzled, as she miraculously took my suggestion. She tossed a few bills on the counter without looking at the receipt and stood. Yuigahama followed suit.

I called after Yuigahama as they walked away. "Yuigahama, I'll e-mail you later."

"Huh? U-uh. Oh, um, okay… I'll be waiting, then." Perhaps it was the indirect lighting, but Yuigahama's face looked particularly red as she fidgeted with her hands in front of her chest before waving to me. *That bearing is really incongruous with the classy vibe in here, so don't, okay?*

After watching the two of them go, I took a sip from my glass and turned back to Kawasaki, moistened my throat a little before I spoke. "Kawasaki. Meet me tomorrow morning. Five thirty at the McD's by the school. Okay?"

"Huh? Why?" Kawasaki's attitude was even frostier than it had been before, but I was confident that what I had to say next would change her tune.

"I want to talk to you about something. It's about Taishi."

"What?" The look Kawasaki gave me was now less suspicious than it was openly hostile.

I avoided meeting her eyes by downing the rest of my ginger ale and then standing. "We'll talk about that tomorrow. See ya."

"Hey!"

I ignored her as she called after me, attempting to make my exit from the bar with the sort of style and class a joint like this deserved.

"Hey! You didn't pay enough!"

Hey, Yukinoshita. You didn't pay for me?

I silently slunk back to the counter and handed her my meager thousand-yen bill. She gave me back sixty yen in change. U-uh… I couldn't exactly ask why now, could I? One ginger ale cost me almost a thousand yen… Was there some kind of rush on ginger ale?

× × ×

It was the next morning, but I hadn't slept. I was nodding off just past five AM at the McD's while sipping my second coffee. The sky was already bright, and sparrows were lighting on the ground, restlessly pecking at it and then flying up into the sky again.

After leaving the Hotel Royal Okura, we'd all gone home. When I got there, I asked Komachi to do a couple favors for me before heading out again to kill time here. I could have stayed at home and slept, but I wasn't sure I could actually wake up at five.

All this effort had been exerted to stay awake with a singular purpose in mind.

"So she came…"

I heard the sound of the automatic doors opening, and Saki Kawasaki appeared, sluggishly dragging her feet. "What did you want to talk about?" she asked. Maybe she was tired, as she seemed grumpier than usual. She was so intense that, for an instant, I felt the urge to get down on my hands and knees and grovel before her, but I suppressed the impulse and acted as calm and composed as possible.

"Hey, dalm cown. I mean calm down." I really fumbled with my words there. Pretending to be calm: gigantic fail. Kawasaki was just *too* scary; I couldn't even. But perhaps my slip-up had loosened me up a little because everything came out smoothly after that. "Everyone will be here in just a bit. Give them a little longer."

"Everyone?" Kawasaki's expression turned doubtful as I heard the automatic doors open again, and Yukinoshita and Yuigahama made their entrance.

Immediately after we'd parted ways the night before, I'd sent Yuigahama a single e-mail saying that she should stay over at Yukinoshita's place that night, tell her parents where she was, and then come to the McD's by the school with Yukinoshita in the morning at five. The message had contained just those three bullets; a simple, bare bones business e-mail.

"You guys again?" Her demeanor saying she was fed up, Kawasaki sighed deeply.

But there was another grump in our midst. Yuigahama was pouting and wouldn't look at me.

"What, has she not slept enough?" I tried asking Yukinoshita, but she seemed perplexed as well.

"Who knows? I think she did, but…actually, I feel like she's been in a plainly foul mood since receiving your e-mail. Did you write something obscene?"

"Come on, will you stop treating me like a sex offender? And all I wrote were basic instructions to come here, so there wasn't anything for her to get upset about."

Yukinoshita and I swapped glances, and then Komachi hopped in between us. "Man, that's my brother, all right! He's got no tact when it comes to important stuff."

"Hey, Komachi. Can you not pop up out of nowhere just to put me down?"

"Bro, people usually use errands as an excuse to talk to someone. If you're all businesslike about it, it sounds like you don't want to talk to them."

"You invited your sister, too?" Yukinoshita asked, slightly surprised.

"Yeah, there's something I wanted her to do for me. Komachi, did you bring him?"

"Yep," Komachi chirped, pointing just a little ways off toward Taishi Kawasaki.

"Taishi…what are you doing here at this hour?" Her expression in a gray zone between anger and shock, Kawasaki glared at her little brother.

But Taishi held his ground. "At this hour? That's what I'd like to ask you, Sis. What have you been doing all night?"

"That's none of your business." Kawasaki refused to engage him and tried to cut the conversation off. But while those techniques might have worked on others, they were wasted on Taishi—he was family. Up until now, Kawasaki and Taishi had always been talking one-on-one, so Kawasaki had had ample opportunities to evade him. She could do anything—end the conversation, or just walk away.

But now she couldn't do that. The rest of us encircled the two of them, and we definitely wouldn't let her get away. More than anything, she was restrained by the fact that it was morning and we were in public.

"It *is* my business. We're family."

"I'm saying you don't need to know," Kawasaki replied.

Taishi stood firm, and Kawasaki's voice grew weaker. But even so, it was clear that she wasn't going to talk to him. Considered from another angle, though, couldn't that mean that all of this was something that she specifically couldn't discuss with Taishi?

"Kawasaki, I can guess why you were working and needed money," I said, and she glared at me. Yukinoshita and Yuigahama considered me with deep interest.

Saki Kawasaki hadn't elaborated on why she'd gotten a job, but when you thought about it, the hints were there. She'd turned delinquent around the time she started her second year of high school, according to Taishi Kawasaki. And indeed, from his perspective, that was true. But that wasn't how it looked from Saki Kawasaki's vantage. From her point of view, she'd started working when her little brother entered his third year of middle school. That meant Taishi Kawasaki's circumstances were her impetus for getting a job.

"Taishi, has anything changed since you started your third year of middle school?"

"U-um... Just that I started going to cram school, I guess?" Taishi seemed quite perplexed as he racked his brains, but that was enough for me. Perhaps Kawasaki had already guessed what I was about to say because she was biting her lip and looked frustrated.

"I see. To pay for her brother's tuition—" Yuigahama seemed convinced, but I cut her off.

"No, Taishi was already going to his cram school in April, so that shouldn't have been an issue. His entrance fees and tuitions would already have been paid. Their family probably took that into account beforehand. So when you think about it, that means *only* Taishi's tuition got covered."

"Indeed. You're right; he isn't the only one who would need money."

Apparently, Yukinoshita understood everything, as she turned sympathetically to Kawasaki.

Yes, our school, Soubu High, is higher education oriented. The majority of attendees either want to or are actually going to university. That meant more than a few students were thinking about entrance exams around this time during their second year while others were seriously considering taking summer courses. Both in preparation for as well as to actually go to college, you need money.

"Didn't Taishi say his sister had always been the kind and serious type? Basically, that's what's going on," I concluded, and Kawasaki's shoulders slumped weakly.

"Sis… I-it's because I'm going to cram school…"

"This is why I said you didn't have to know." She patted Taishi's head as if to comfort him.

Oh-ho! Apparently, this had all wrapped up with a nice, touching conclusion. Yeah, how nice, how nice. And they all lived happily ever after. Or so I thought, but Kawasaki was biting her lip again.

"But I still can't quit my job. I intend to go to college. I don't want to burden Taishi or my parents with that." Kawasaki's tone was sharp with clear determination. Her firm resolve eradicated Taishi's earlier assertiveness.

"Um…can I say something?" Komachi's happy-go-lucky voice broke the silence.

Kawasaki turned her head toward my sister as if she found this tiresome. "What?" Her expression and curt tone together made her seem almost hostile.

But Komachi ignored that, smiling brightly. "Well, both of our parents have always worked, too. So when I was little, I always came home to an empty house. I'd call, 'I'm home!' but nobody would answer."

"Come on, it'd be freaky if somebody did. What's with this random story time?"

"Oh, uh-huh. You be quiet for a bit, okay, Bro?"

Totally shut down, I had no choice but to shut my mouth and listen.

"So I didn't like going back home, and I ran away for about five days. And then who came to find me? Not my parents, but my brother. And ever since then, he's come home earlier than me. So I'm grateful to him for that."

I'd been thinking, *Oh, this brother sounds like such a great guy,* before realizing it was me. This unexpected anecdote almost brought me to tears. My intention at the time hadn't been to keep her company. I'd just been going home early because I had no friends to hang out with and wanted to watch an anime that aired at six o'clock on TV Tokyo.

Kawasaki gave me a look reminiscent of something like empathy, and Yuigahama's eyes were a little damp.

Only Yukinoshita shook her head. "You only went home early because that's when you stopped having friends, isn't that right, Hikigaya?"

"Hey, how did you know that? Are you Yukipedia or what?"

"Oh, no, I'm totally aware of that," Komachi said with a bold non-chalance. "But I think putting it my way is worth more Komachi points."

Yuigahama opened her mouth, her expression weary. "You are Hikki's sister, after all."

"Hey, what's that supposed to mean?" *She must have meant that I'm cute, too. Definitely.*

"So what's your point?" Kawasaki demanded, irritated. Frankly, she was pretty terrifying, but Komachi faced her head on, her smile unbroken, as usual.

"He's a pretty crappy brother, but still, he'll never make me worry. And that's enough to make me feel grateful as his little sister. I'm happy about that. Oh, and that just now was worth a lot of Komachi points, too."

"Enough with this 'Komachi points' thing."

"Nooo. It's obviously just my way of hiding my shyness! Oh, that just there was also worth a lot of—"

"Enough, already, enough." *Good grief. This is why I can't trust girls. My own sister spouts this stuff so casually.*

When I indicated that I found her annoying, Komachi voiced her dissatisfaction with a *murg*. I decided not to engage with her, and she gave up and went back to talking to Kawasaki. "Well, in other words, just like you feel like you don't want to be a burden on your family, Taishi doesn't want to be a burden on you, you know? I think if you understood that, he'd be happy as a younger sibling."

Kawasaki was silent. And so was I. Oh man, just what was this feeling? I'd had no idea that Komachi felt that way. She was usually a constant burden, so I hadn't noticed at all.

"Yeah, I'm kind of like that, too," Taishi added softly. He looked away, his face red. Kawasaki stood and softly stroked Taishi's head. Her smiling face was very slightly softer than her usual languid expression.

But still, the issue hadn't been resolved. All that had happened was that Saki and Taishi Kawasaki's relationship had been mended and they were talking again. Just because you're emotionally fulfilled doesn't mean everything else is fine. Material wealth may be fleeting, but that doesn't mean it's worthless. Money and goods are necessary, after all.

Money problems are a harsh thing for high school students to deal with. You feel that all the more keenly if you even start trying to earn some pocket money with a part-time job. Then you can calculate how many hours you have to work to make the millions of yen it takes to pay tuition at a private university. It would've been cool if we could have handed over a million or two right there just like that, but we didn't have that kind of money. Most importantly, though, that would have been counter to the principles of the Service Club.

At some point, Yukinoshita had said it: You don't give someone a fish; you teach them how to fish.

So instead, I'd offer her my plan for making big money fast. "Kawasaki. Do you know about scholarships?"

X   X   X

The air at five thirty in the morning was still unpleasantly cold. I saw off the two retreating shapes as I yawned. They stayed a fixed distance from each other, and if one got ahead, the other slowed its pace until the first caught up. Occasionally, I could see their shoulders shaking as if they were laughing boisterously.

"Is that what siblings are like?" Yukinoshita asked with a sigh in the morning mist.

"I dunno. Doesn't it depend on the person? They do call them 'the closest stranger.'" There are actually times when Komachi makes me so legitimately angry that I want to punch her, and those times don't feel like me at all. But then at another random moment, she'll do exactly the same thing, and it fills me with feelings of love and affection. Honestly, I think maybe with siblings, they always feel distant in a way you can't quite grasp. That's why I think the phrase *the closest stranger* is oddly fitting. Even though they're the closest, they're a stranger, and though they're a stranger, they're still closest.

"The closest stranger…indeed. I understand that quite well." Yukinoshita nodded, but then she never raised her head.

"Yukinon?" Puzzled, Yuigahama quietly peered into Yukinoshita's face.

Yukinoshita immediately jerked her head up and gave Yuigahama a smile. "Come on, let's go back as well. Another three hours, and it will be time for school."

"Y-yeah…" Yuigahama's expression said she wasn't fully satisfied with that response, but she nodded and turned the bag over her shoulder toward her back.

I unlocked my bicycle, too. "Yeah. Komachi, wake up." I slapped her cheeks lightly where she was sitting, nodding off on the green rock in front of the McD's. She mumbled something mumbly and rubbed her eyes. She stood up and took swaying steps over to my bike like a ghost and then sat down on the back. She would usually still be sleeping at this time. Oh well, today I'd ride slowly along even pavement. I threw a leg over my bike and put my foot on the pedal. "I'm going home, then. See ya."

"Yeah, I guess it isn't *see you tomorrow*, huh? See you at school today." Yuigahama waved her hand a little in front of her chest.

Yukinoshita stayed silent, watching Komachi and me with a vacant expression, but as I was about to pedal off, she said quietly, "I rather disapprove of two riding a bicycle, but…be careful not to get into another accident."

"Yeah, see ya," I replied and started pedaling. I was so sleep-deprived, my head wasn't working right, and it was occupied pretty much to capacity just keeping an eye on oncoming traffic and the condition of the ground below us. My weariness meant that I'd only offered a vague, offhanded response to Yukinoshita. I guess I'd told her about that accident, then…?

I rode slowly along a route that crossed Highway 14. The oncoming wind that always got in my face on my way to school was now at my back. While waiting at the second light, a fragrant smell from a bakery at the intersection greeted me. My stomach rumbled. "Komachi, do you want me to get us some pastries?"

"What?! You dummy, Bro. What you're supposed to do is either pretend you didn't notice or just casually stop by the bakery without asking! I'm hungry, so I'll go, though!!"

As she pounded her fists on my back, I turned my bike toward the bakery and started pedaling.

"Agh… You really are a crappy brother. If I knew you were gonna do this, I wouldn't have said all that nice stuff about you."

"Hey, that wasn't nice stuff about me. At the end, it was just about you turning into a good girl. And plus, it was mostly made up."

"Yeah, that's true," Komachi admitted, and she stopped punching me. "But I really am thankful." With that, she wrapped her arms around my waist and squeezed me tight, burying her face in my back.

"Is that worth a lot of Komachi points, too?"

"Tsk. So you could tell," Komachi pouted, but her arms remained firmly around my waist. The cold morning wind slowly eroded our body heat. Feeling her pleasant warmth against me, sleepiness gradually took hold. I guessed I would be late again today, too. Feeling like this, I could probably have slept well once I got home. It wasn't so bad having a friendly brother-sister late day once in a while.

"But I'm glad you got to meet, though," Komachi said behind me.

"Huh? What're you talking about?" My expression was probably suspicious.

Komachi couldn't see my face, though, and she kept talking. "You know, the sweets person. You should've told me you already met her. Aw, isn't that nice, Bro! Thanks to that broken bone, you got to know a cute girl like Yui."

"Oh, yeah, I guess…" I thrust out my foot mechanically to step on the pedal. It was an almost entirely unconscious motion with no feeling in it at all. That was why the moment feelings got interjected, the action went awry. My body suddenly swayed with a jerk, and pain radiated through my shin. "Aghh!"

"Tsk, tsk, tsk, what's with that? I've never seen anyone miss a pedal before." Komachi whined and complained, but this wasn't the time.

What did she just say? Yuigahama was the sweets person?

The sweets person was neither a familiar face from *chuugen* using the holiday to repay a debt with candy nor the Purple Rose. It was some-one from my past. The day of my high school entrance ceremony, I got into a traffic accident. On my way to school, there'd been a girl walking her dog nearby, and her dog had gotten off its leash. Then at the worst possible moment, an expensive-looking limo rolled up. I saved that dog's life and broke a bone in the process. I was in the hospital for about three weeks starting from the first day of school, and that sealed my fate as a loner from day one of high school. The owner of the dog was this "sweets person" Komachi was talking about.

"What's wrong, Bro?" Komachi eyed me worriedly, but all I could do was give her a vague grin. I'd been thinking a little bit about a bunch of stuff.

I laughed at myself in mild self-deprecation. "It's nothing. Let's get some pastries and go home," I said, starting to pedal, but inexplicably, the pedals spun around and hit me in the shin again.

Hachiman's mobile

FROM Hachiman ▮▮ 21:12

TITLE Re

Sorry, but who is this?

FROM Hachiman ▮▮ 21:20

TITLE Re

(´ -`) 。o O (Her personality is totally different in texts.)

Hiratsuka's mobile

FROM Hiratsuka ▮▮ 21:09
TITLE Hikigaya, how is your studying for the exams going?

I think it would be a good idea for you to improve your reading comprehension for your entrance exams in the future as well, not just your upcoming Japanese midterm. Please study hard.

FROM Hiratsuka   ▮▮ 21:15
TITLE Sorry, this is Shizuka Hiratsuka.

Though it might be easier for you to understand if I said I was your teacher.

Hachiman Hikigaya goes back the
way he came again.

Exam week was over, the weekend had passed, and it was Monday
again. This was the day the exam results would be distributed. All we
did in class that day was get our exams back and listen to each teacher
go over the problems. At the end of each subject, Yuigahama would
make her way to my desk to report her results. "Hikki! My grades in
Japanese history went up! That study party really was awesome after
all," she declared, rather exhilarated.

I, however, was less enthusiastic. "That's great."

"Yeah! Man, this is all thanks to Yukinon! And you, too, Hikki,"
Yuigahama said, but frankly, I hadn't done anything. There was no way
that single study session could have given her instant results. Studying
together like that was fundamentally pointless. So if Yuigahama was
getting better grades, it was probably due to her own efforts.

As for my exam results, as usual, I had fiercely defended third place
in Japanese. Nine percent in math. *Hey, what's a recurrence formula? It
sounds like some technobabble Zaimokuza would come up with.*

Not only was that the day we were getting our exam results back, it
also happened to be the day of our long-looming workplace tour. When
lunch hour rolled around, all the students were sent off to visit the workplaces they'd selected.

Where we were headed was Kaihin-Makuhari Station. The area

had quite the office district and, surprisingly, even some head offices. It was also the same shopping district I'd gotten to know the other evening. They didn't call it Makuhari New City Center for nothing. You could actually call this place the capital of Chiba.

I was in a group with Totsuka and Hayama. Or rather, I was supposed to be. But when we actually got there, a bunch of people were crowding around Hayama. What was this guy, a feudal lord?

Well, I hadn't intended to go with Hayama in the first place, anyway, so I looked around for Totsuka, figuring I'd stroll around with him and pretend we were on a date. Totsuka, though, had his own small entourage of girls. This gaggle was so intense that anyone who didn't know what a timid guy Totsuka was would think he was being bullied.

With Hayama, there were three boys who were supposed to constitute a separate group as well as Miura's clique. I caught sight of Yuigahama with them, too. My attempt at a sporadic headcount told me about five groups had arrived at our site.

I wasn't really good with crowds. Sometimes when I went out on weekends, I ended up wanting to go home just because there were a lot of people around. So naturally, I ended up just trailing along at the heels of their group. Good old Hachiman, taking rear guard. If I were a general of the Warring States period, this would be deserving of a medal of honor.

We—or rather, Hayama—had picked some familiar-sounding electronics manufacturer. The location wasn't just the office building and research facility; there was also an adjacent museum. The company even had the perfect entertainment draw: The museum had a theater with a full 360-degree movie screen. If Hayama had picked this place randomly, he either was just lucky or had been born with some amazing intuition. If he'd chosen this place deliberately, though, anticipating the throngs of hangers-on, I was impressed by his consideration.

For me, though, the mecha-style exhibits were what held the most appeal, perfect for a loner. I was like a kid pining for a trumpet on the other side of the display window. Just pressing myself up against the glass and gazing at the machines whirring about excited for me.

The phrase *we are not machines* was likely originally coined by people resisting authoritarian control and sentences of hard labor, but it's still absolutely true. We are not machines. That's why sometimes cogs like me show up: they don't fit in with the other parts, and you're not quite sure what to use them for. If this were a model car, I'd call Tamiya about it.

But in reality, these kinds of extraneous parts do exist in machines. It's what's commonly referred to as *play*. This is what you call stuff like an extra length of chain or excess gear ratio. These things give the machine a bit of flexibility and apparently extend its service life. One of the researchers said that today. That both machines and humans need play.

Not that I ever got invited over to play, though…

Keeping a moderate distance from the group, I went to tour the machines. Boys and girls were having fun chattering and joking around with each other in front of me. Had I turned around, though, there'd have been no one behind me. The vacant space behind me was so utterly silent it hurt.

But the hard sound of heels clicking on the floor broke that silence. "Hikigaya. So you came." Miss Hiratsuka was, uncharacteristically, not wearing her white coat. It was probably because if she had worn it here, she'd have been indistinguishable from staff, making things confusing.

"Patrolling?"

"Yeah, something like that," the teacher replied, but her attention wasn't fixed on the students at all. That was wholly devoted to the mecha-esque machines. "Phew… Japanese technology is amazing, huh? I wonder if they'll make a Gundam in my lifetime."

She really did have the brain of a little boy. She had this enchanted look in her eyes gazing at the steel bodywork, as if she was falling in love. *Come on, please get yourself a real relationship, seriously.*

I started to stroll with the thought that perchance I'd just leave her in my wake, but apparently, Miss Hiratsuka had noticed the sound of my footsteps, as she strode up beside me, matching my stride. "Oh, that reminds me, Hikigaya. About that contest…"

The contest… She meant the Service Club competition Yukinoshita and I had going over who would help the greater number of people. The winner would get to order the loser to do whatever they pleased.

Even though she was the one who'd broached the subject, Miss Hiratsuka hesitated. I prompted her to continue with a glance. She steeled herself and pressed on. "There was too much interference from variable elements, and the current framework isn't manageable. So I think I'll change some of the specifications." The way she put it made it made it sound like the kind of excuse a video game maker would give, but basically, it sounded like the teacher was overwhelmed and running around with too much on her plate.

"I'm fine with that." Either way, Miss Hiratsuka was the rulebook for this contest. I could protest, but her rules would change when they changed. The standards of the competition would be arbitrary and biased, anyway. Resistance was futile. "Have you decided on anything specific?"

"No… There's just one kid I'm having trouble dealing with," she said, scratching her head.

Hearing *trouble dealing with* brought Yuigahama suddenly to mind. The Service Club had originally been just me and Yukinoshita. Yuigahama had joined after that. Her presence could be called irregular. She was unquestionably the "variable element" Miss Hiratsuka had referred to. She hadn't been part of the original plan, and yet now she was central to the Service Club. Then I supposed the competition would now be among the three of us: Yukinoshita, Yuigahama, and me.

"Huh… It looks like Mecha Mecha Road ends here," the teacher said.

What the heck was Mecha Mecha Road?

"Once I've come up with some new specifications, I'll update you. Come on, I won't sabotage your chances," Miss Hiratsuka teased, grin-

ning brightly. I've only ever heard that line from villains, though…
Miss Hiratsuka eased back down the Mecha Mecha Road from whence
she came. I watched her go and then headed toward the exit.

Miss Hiratsuka had chewed my ear a little too long. Hayama and
the others were already gone, and the empty bamboo thicket swayed in
the early-summer wind, rustling like a flood of whispers. As the western
sky began growing orange, I looked around the empty entrance area
and found a familiar bun there. Unfortunately.

She was sitting on a big green rock, her knees drawn up as she
occasionally fiddled with her cell phone. For an instant, I wondered if
I should really talk to her. While I vacillated, though, she noticed me.
"Oh, Hikki, you're slow! Everyone already left!"

"Oh, yeah. Sorry, my robot soul got excited in there. So where did
this 'everyone' go?"

"Saize." High schoolers in Chiba really do like Saize, huh? They're a
little too biased to it, in my opinion, even if the family restaurant chain
did originate in Chiba. It's amazingly cheap, and the food is good,
though.

"You're not going?"

"Huh?! Oh, well, like, I was sort of waiting for you, ish. Um…it's,
like, I'd just feel sorta bad if you got left behind…" Yuigahama glanced
at me, tapping her pointer fingers together in front of her chest.

Her fidgeting made me smile. "You're a nice person, Yuigahama."

"Huh?! Uh, what? N-no, not really." The sun was in the west, so
maybe that was why Yuigahama's face looked red as she violently flailed
her hands to signal no.

I don't know why she was denying it. I still thought she was nice.
I considered her a good person. That was why I felt like I should let her
know. "Listen, you don't have to worry about me. It was just a coinci-
dence that I saved your dog, and even if it hadn't been for that accident,
I'd probably still be a loner in high school, anyway. There's absolutely
no need for you to feel awkward about it. I guess I'm kind of burning
myself saying this, though." I really was burning myself, but given that

this was about me, I knew it better than anyone. I'd probably never have been surrounded by friends, even if I'd started my high school career normally. No, definitely never.

"H-Hikki... You...remembered?" Yuigahama opened her big eyes wide and stared at me, her face full of shock.

"No, I don't remember. But I heard you came to our house once to say thanks. Komachi told me."

"Oh...Komachi, huh...?" she tittered, that shallow smile on her face again as she quietly looked down.

"Sorry. I guess I've actually made you weirdly careful around me. Well, from now on, you don't have to worry about it. I'm the reason I'm a loner, anyway, and the accident had nothing to do with it. There's no need for you to feel indebted to me or feel sorry for me... If that's why you're being nice to me, then just stop." I was aware that my tone had gotten a little rough. *Oh, this isn't good. What am I getting so touchy for? This kind of thing isn't important at all.* I scratched my head to conceal my irritation. An oppressive silence flowed between us. This was the first time I'd ever found silence unpleasant. "So, uh, like..." Though I'd been inclined to open my mouth, I couldn't find the words, and nothing definite came out.

Both of us at a loss for words, Yuigahama smiled faintly. "W-well, I dunno, but...it's not really like that, though. It's more like...like... It's just not like that..." Still smiling, she looked down awkwardly. With her face turned away, I couldn't see her expression anymore. I could only hear her thin voice shaking a little. "That's...not it... It's not..." Yuigahama trailed off, her voice quiet.

Yui Yuigahama was always kind, and she'd probably be kind until the end.

If the truth is cruel, the surely lies are kind. That's why kindness is a lie.

"Oh, well, you know," I began, and Yuigahama glared at me. There were tears in her eyes, but her gaze was strong and unwavering. I was the one who looked away.

"You jerk." Leaving that remark behind, Yuigahama ran off, but once she was a few meters away, her steps became heavier, like she was trudging along.

I watched her go, then spun away from her again.

Maybe Yuigahama was going to Saize where all her friends were waiting. But that had nothing to do with me. I hate crowds, anyway. I also hate nice girls. They follow you around everywhere, like the moon above in the night sky, but they're always unreachable. But I can't keep them at a distance like I should. Just a simple exchange lingers in my mind. If we e-mail each other, I feel unsettled. If one calls me, I'll dwell on my call history and feel my face falling into a grin.

But I know…I know that they're just being nice. People who are nice to me are nice to others, too, and I feel as if I might forget that. I'm not dense. I'm actually pretty perceptive. Sensitive, even. And that causes an allergic reaction in me.

I've been through this sort of situation before. An experienced loner doesn't fall for the same trick twice. Confessions of love as part of a punishment for losing at rock-paper-scissors don't work on me, and neither do fake love letters from a girl written by boys. I'm a hardened veteran schooled in a hundred battles. I'm the best when it comes to losing.

Always having these expectations, always getting the wrong idea, constantly hoping… I've given up on all that.

That's why I'll always hate nice girls.

Afterword

Hello, this is Wataru Watari.

Recently, I've been thinking back on my youth, but my memories are so faint, I've been having trouble with it. That's probably because there were nothing but unpleasant memories, and I don't want to remember any of it, but also perhaps because those memories are still too close to be reflecting on just yet. It's been years since I graduated from high school, so it's not chronologically close, but rather, emotionally too close, I think.

Let me compare how I was back then and how I am now. It's like this:

In high school: Late 1,100 times in three years. Late so often that they called my parents to school to talk about it. Thinking in the future I'd like to marry a rich, beautiful woman and lead a life of indulgence and depravity. Had a high probability of skipping on rainy days.

Midtwenties: Late so often that they called me out at work to talk about it. Thinking in the future I'd like to marry a rich, beautiful woman and lead a life of indulgence and depravity. Forget rainy days; I don't get much writing done even if it's sunny.

I really haven't lost my boyish spirit, man. Wow.

When I think about it, I figure maybe being a boy is about always acting like you're in the middle of your youth. So I think I can keep dragging around the feelings of awkwardness, jealousy, and inferiority from my high school years, keep occasionally getting drunk on baseless confidence, keep maintaining the incomprehensible contradiction that is *I'm the best at feeling inferior. I've got, like, a superiority complex about it*, and keep writing the things I've dreamed of writing forever.

But there are still things that are most definitely lost to me forever... I wanted to go on a date with a high school girl in uniform...

Now then, for the acknowledgments.

Holy Ponkan®. Thank you so much for your wonderful illustrations in Vol. 2 as well. Yui is so cute on the cover that I started doing a Yui-nique dance in celebration. I will offer prayers to you a full five times a day.

My editor, Hoshino. I've been causing all sorts of trouble for you for Vol. 2, too, but somehow you managed everything for me. I plan to continue causing trouble for you, so please keep working hard. Thank you very much.

Manta Aisora. You wrote some comments on the obi of this book even though you didn't know me, and for that, I am grateful. Also, thank you for sending me chocolates. Those delicious morsels are what enabled me to write this.

My family, especially my father. Thank you for all your hard work over the years. You working yourself to the bone has enabled me to be a writer. Please take it easy, enjoy your life, and live a long one. Also, I don't think our cat likes me at all. Maybe it's just my imagination, though.

All my readers. Your support for *My Youth Romantic Comedy Is Wrong, As I Expected* (also known by the abbreviation *Oregairu*) is the reason I was able to publish Vol. 2. I'm really happy about this. Thank you very much. I will try my very best to write a third volume that you will all enjoy.

And now I shall say something conclusive and set down my pen here. Once you start running, you can't stop; it's because you've got momentum! And the same happens with teen rom-coms. I hope you will stay with me for the next volume, too.

A certain day in June,

A certain place in Chiba,

While eating a plain Italian gelato with relish,

Wataru Watari

Chapter 1 ... And that's how Yui Yuigahama decided to study.

P. 14 **"...like those on the Nio statues by Unkei and Kaikei."** The Nio are a pair of famous statues of guardian warriors of the gods at Todaiji in Nara. They were said to travel with Gautama Buddha to protect him and have very angry expressions to ward off threats.

P. 14 **"Shocking First Bullet!"** This is a skill that is a special attack of Kazuma Torisuna, the main character in the *shonen* anime *S-CRY-ed*.

P. 15 **"...Annihilating Second Bullet...Exterminating Last Bullet."** These are more special attacks of Kazuma Torisuna from *S-CRY-ed*. As you might assume, Shocking First Bullet is the weakest; Exterminating Last Bullet is the most powerful.

P. 17 **"It's a Yutori education–style program that just cuts into the curriculum..."** Yutori education or "relaxed education," is a general government policy to reduce classroom time while adding things like extracurriculars. This began in the 1970s. It's constantly under criticism in the vein of "students these days don't learn anything anymore, and school is too easy."

P. 20   **"...a disco monster truck?"** The original novel references a *dekotora* (an abbreviation of "decorated truck"), which is a part of a Japanese trucker subculture. Long-haul truckers (who own their own trucks) will deck out their rigs with LEDs and glittery custom artwork.

P. 21   **"...the Ayrton Senna of fingertips."** Ayrton Senna is a Brazilian race car driver and winner of three Formula One championships.

P. 24   **"...that hero who says that love and courage are his only friends..."** This is a line from the opening song of the children's anime *Anpanman*. It's about a hero made of *anpan*, a red bean jam bun.

P. 24   **"...soccer balls aren't friends, either."** Hachiman is referencing the soccer manga *Captain Tsubasa*. The protagonist's catchphrase is "The ball is my friend."

P. 26   **"...Devilman, whose devil ears could hear all the way to hell."** This is a rather loose translation of the opening song of *Devilman*, an old Go Nagai anime from the 1970s. There's a bit of wordplay here. In Japanese, *jigokumimi* ("hell ears") means sharp ears or the ability to remember everything one hears.

P. 28   **"Misuzu Kaneko would probably be angry..."** Misuzu Kaneko (1903–March 10, 1930) was a poet and songwriter. The poem Hachiman is quoting is called "Watashi to kotori to suzu to" ("Me, a Birdie and a Bell") and is one of her most well-known children's poems. It compares one's self, a bird, and a bell, noting how all three have different abilities and that while they are all different, they are all good.

P. 32   **"...if they were to pilot an Eva, they wouldn't even be able to activate an AT field."** In the original 1995 *Evangelion* anime, an AT (Active Terror) field is a shield barrier created by the giant "robots" known as Evas. These fields can only be activated when the pilot has a metaphorical barrier around their heart, that is to say a certain degree of psychological damage.

P. 37   **"...Saize in Purena?"** Saize is short for Saizeriya, a cheap and ubiquitous Japanized-Italian food chain (their menu includes dishes such as *mentaiko* pasta), with meals in the three hundred to six hundred yen range. Purena is the name of a mall in Chiba.

Chapter 2 ... **Komachi Hikigaya** is gonna marry her big brother when she grows up. (says me)

P. 41   **"...the great monk of old, Shinran."** Shinran (AD 1173–1263) was a Buddhist monk and the founder of the *Joudo Shinshuu* sect of Buddhism. This school preaches reliance on another power, that is to say relying on the Amitabha Buddha, rather than engaging in specific acts.

P. 42   **"...a snake, a frog, and a slug..."** This comes from an old folklore belief that these three animals have a rock-paper-scissors-like relationship, where snake swallows frog whole, frog traps slug with its tongue, and slug melts snake with its ooze. Of course, if all three meet at once, none of them can move, because going for the animal they can defeat would spell their own doom at the hands of the one they can't. Anime fans might be most familiar with this concept as referenced in the *Naruto* anime and manga: Orochimaru summons a giant snake, Jiraiya summons a giant frog, and Tsunade summons a giant slug.

P. 44   **"I can explain *Grappler Baki* instead..."** The series *Grappler Baki* sometimes called *Baki the Grappler*, is a very long-running martial arts manga that began in 1991, with a sequel manga ongoing as of 2014. There is also an anime adaptation, an OVA, and a video game.

P. 44   **"...a boy wearing a *gakuran*."** A *gakuran* is an old-fashioned style of boys' school uniform based on military uniforms. It has a raised collar, unlike a blazer, and is often associated with public middle schools (as opposed to private schools) in particular.

P. 44   **"No little sister can surpass her older brother!"** This is a reference to the 1980s post–apocalyptic manga *Fist of the North Star*. The protagonist Kenshiro's older brother Jagi is known for the line "No man can surpass his older brother!" The line has reached meme status on the Internet.

Chapter 3 ... **Hayato Hayama's** presence always shines.

P. 52   **"Make me my miso soup every morning."** This is actually an old-fashioned way to propose marriage. A man would not ask a woman to marry him directly by getting down on one knee, Western-style. Rather, he would just casually ask one day, "So when are you quitting your job?" or "I'd like to eat your cooking every day." The growth in popularity of Western-style proposals and weddings as well as greater participation of women in the workforce has turned this into a rather quaint and old-fashioned thing to say, and many young people (like Totsuka) might not even be sure what it means.

P. 53   **"...Fearow is surely a master loner."** Fearow is a bird-type Pokemon with a skill called "Mirror Move" that copies enemies' attacks back at them. In Japanese, the move is called *oumugaeshi*, which means to parrot someone's words back at them.

P. 58   **"...as bad as the Haunted Housekeeper in Uptaten Towers..."** The notorious Haunted Housekeeper is the first boss of *Dragon Quest V* and one of the most infamous "But Thou Must" moments in the series. It's completely obvious that the boss is leading the player into a trap, but if you try to pick the dialogue option to avoid the trap, the game just asks the same question again and again until the player goes into it.

P. 59   **"...the game I'm working on in RPG Maker..."** RPG Maker is a software series that allows users to create RPGs video games with little to no knowledge of programming. There is a stereotype that most games made with RPG Maker are uninspired garbage, but there are exceptions, and many have enjoyed varying amounts of success.

P. 59   **"...BL that is all the rage these days."** BL stands for "boy's love," and is also known as "yaoi" or as "slash" among Western fans. It refers to romantic stories about male/male couples written and enjoyed largely by women.

P. 61   **"...sleeve-pulling imp?"** A *sodehiki kozou* ("sleeve-pulling kid") is a *you-kai* (a sort of spirit) of Japanese myth. When you're walking along, it will pull your sleeve out of the blue, but when you turn around, nothing's there. When you go back to walking, it will pull your sleeve again. They are purely mischievous, not actively malicious.

P. 64   **"...and Hikitani..."** The kanji in Japanese names can be pronounced in many different unique ways, and it's often difficult to know how it's said just by seeing it written—you need to be told how it is pronounced. "Hikitani" is a misreading of the characters that spell Hikigaya. The character for "valley," which is the last character in Hikigaya's name, is often read as *tani*. *Gaya* is the less common reading.

P. 70   **"Finding the courage..."** Hachiman is parodying a tanka by the poet Machi Tawara. The original goes, roughly: So you said to me, / "I like this flavor a lot," / so, well, that means the / sixth of July is now the / Salad Anniversary.

P. 74   **"...I was basically Nobita."** Nobita is the main character of the children's anime *Doraemon*. He's good at cat's cradle...which is notable, since he's not good at much else.

P. 77   **"...totally an *uke*...the arrogant *seme*."** *Seme* and *uke* are terms generally used by *fujoshi* (women who like BL) to describe sexual roles of characters in BL manga: *Seme* is the top, and *uke* is the bottom. It's notable that gay men do not use these terms—that would be *tachi* and *neko*, respectively.

P. 79 **"…Ebina was a *fujoshi*…"** *Fujoshi* literally means "rotten woman" and refers to women who enjoy BL manga and fantasizing about sexual or romantic relationships between men. The Japanese counterpart of the slash fangirl.

P. 80 **"…a flash of insight like a tranquilizer bolt…"** This is a reference to *Detective Conan* (also known as *Case Closed*) by Gosho Aoyama. The protagonist, Conan, is an adult trapped in the body of a child. He uses a tranquilizer gun to knock out a certain detective and then impersonates him in order to be taken seriously by adults.

P. 80 **"This mystery is solved!"** This is the famous catchphrase of the hero from the mystery manga *The Kindaichi Case Files* by Youzaburou Kanari and Seimaru Amagi.

P. 81 **"It used about as much MP as Magic Burst…"** Magic Burst is a spell from the Dragon Quest series of video games. It uses up all of the user's remaining MP, and damage of the spell is based on amount of MP spent.

P. 83 **"Skipping out of class as swiftly as the wind, nodding off at your desk as quietly as the forest, jealousy raging hot as fire, steadfast as a mountain."** This is a horribly twisted interpretation of *fuurinkazan*, meaning "wind, forest, fire, mountains." It was the slogan written on the Sengoku-era feudal lord Takeda Shingen's battle flags. The real meaning of the slogan is "swift as the wind, silent as the forest, attack as fire, and steadfast as a mountain."

P. 85 **"Three for the Kill: the Next Generation!"** *Three for the Kill* is a historical drama that ran from 1987 to 1995. The story is about three swordsmen who work together to take down villains. Depending on the episode, they sometimes acted together and other times independently, occasionally even on opposing sides but would invariably come together in the end to enact justice and root out evil.

P. 87   **"...tour in Iga or Kouga or something."** Iga and Kouga are cities in southern Japan rumored to have been the home provinces for ninja during the Sengoku Period, a tumultuous era that was characterized by constant warfare and warlords competing with one another throughout Japan. In the present day, these provinces are only affiliated with ninja as a tourist thing.

P. 89   **"...the Minovsky particles around here are thick."** Minovsky particles are part of the lore of the Gundam franchise. They confound sensors and jam sensitive electronics like preternaturally effective chaff.

P. 89   **"Beast Hachiman, respond to my call!"** This is an incantation from the fantasy light novel, manga, and anime series *Sorcerous Stabber Orphen*. "Beast, respond to my call" is also the title of the first volume of the light novel.

P. 89   **"Darkness beyond twilight, crimson beyond blood that flows..."** This is the beginning of the incantation for the Dragon Slave spell in the *Slayers* series, another fantasy light novel series that was also adapted into an anime and manga. The spell essentially blows up everything.

Chapter 4 ... **Saki Kawasaki** has some stuff going on, so she's sulking.

P. 91   **"I wish someone on Pixiv would draw..."** Pixiv is a popular site for users to upload their art to share and display. It's like the Japanese equivalent of Deviantart.

P. 98   **"...Gooo Magnum! ...Don't lose now, Sonic!"** Magnum and Sonic are the names of cars in *Bakusou Kyoudai Let's & Go!!*, a manga by Tetsuhiro Koshita about racing toy cars that ran from 1994 to 1999.

P. 98   "...kind of like how *Iitomo* is over 50 percent funnier..." *Waratte Iitomo* (*Of Course You May Laugh!*) is a very long-running daytime talk and variety show that was notorious for being unfunny in its later years. It ran from 1982 to 2014.

P. 99   "...the planet Vegeta..." Vegeta is the home planet of Goku and the other Saiyans in the *Dragon Ball* series by Akira Toriyama.

P. 100   "Swift death to evil." This is Hajime Saitou's motto in the Meiji-era swordplay manga *Rurouni Kenshin* by Nobuhiro Watsuki.

P. 103   "...the water over here is sweet!" This is a reference to a children's song "Hotaru Koi" ("Come Firefly"). The song goes, "Come, come, firefly, come. The water over there is bitter, the water over here is sweet." It's basically about catching fireflies.

P. 103   "If the wind blows..." The correct idiom is "If the wind blows, the bucket maker makes good money." It means something similar to "A butterfly flapping its wings creates a hurricane in China." That is to say, that events have far-reaching and unforeseen consequences.

P. 105   "Chiba is famous for festivals and dancing." This is a line from the chorus of "Chiba Ondo," a traditional song and dance celebrating Chiba prefecture.

P. 105   "...the Bon Odori of Chiba." The Bon Odori is a dance performed at Bon, an annual festival to commemorate the dead. The festival is generally regarded by most Japanese people as one of the major holidays. The dance generally differs depending on the region.

P. 105   "...about as big a deal as 'Nanohana Taiso.'" Nanohana Taiso, meaning "rape blossom calisthenics," is a government-sponsored calisthenics video from the 1980s that is often played in gym class for local schools.

It's extremely cheesy music by modern standards, and the accompanying video features some extremely tacky calisthenics.

P. 106 **"...less *Ah! My Goddess* and more *Shin Megami Tensei*."** *Ah! My Goddess* is a long-running manga series originally published by Kodansha from 1988 to 2014, spanning forty eight volumes, and generally featured cheerful, pleasant interactions with characters who were goddesses. Shin Megami Tensei, meaning "Resurrection of the True Goddess," is a very long-running series of videogames (the first one released in 1992) published and developed by Atlus. These games revolve around the theme of summoning demons. In this series, "goddesses" are usually not the benevolent kind.

P. 108 **"Don't troll me, Bro."** In Japanese, Komachi is saying *matamata gojoudanwo*, a very polite way to say, "Oh, you and your jokes again." This is a quote from the ballet instructor Mr. Cat in the magical girl anime *Princess Tutu*. As an Internet meme, this line is usually accompanied by ASCII art of the character.

P. 114 **"...adding 'Kabuki-cho' to the word *angel*."** Kabuki-cho is major red-light district in Shinjuku, Tokyo, and is generally considered a seedy area.

P. 115 **"...ask Santa for *Love and Berry* cards?"** *Oshare Majo: Love and Berry* (*Stylish Witch, Love and Berry*) is a trading card arcade game. Trading card arcade games use physical, collectable cards that can then be inserted into arcade machines to play. *Love and Berry* has fashion as a theme, and the main target market consists of little girls.

P. 128 **"...why did middle schoolers like Yokado so much?"** Ito-Yokado is one of the larger general merchandise chains in Japan and is a part of Seven & I Group, which is the parent company of the much more familiar (for Americans) Japanese chain, Seven Eleven.

P. 128 **"Go to Mother Farm or something."** Mother Farm is a farm-themed amusement park in Chiba.

P. 128   **"…it's Chiba's thing to obsess over being Chiba-ish in weird ways…"**
The New Tokyo Airport, the Tokyo Game Show (an annual videogame
expo), and the Tokyo German Village (an amusement park) are all actually in Chiba. Chiba is right next to Tokyo and is often just treated like
an extension of Tokyo, thus the inferiority complex.

P. 128   **"…the high-class residential area Chibarly Hills…"** Chibarly Hills is
a nickname for a wealthy residential district that is actually called One
Hundred Hills.

P. 128   **"…the center of a certain type of Chiba subculture."** Animate and
Tora no Ana are retail chain stores for anime, manga, and *otaku* goods.
Animate leans more toward merchandise while Tora no Ana sells *doujin-
shi*, but there is a lot of overlap.

P. 130   **"…my ghost is whispering to me…"** These famous words are a quote
from the film and anime series *Ghost in the Shell*. Motoko Kusanagi, the
cyborg protagonist, tends to say it when she has a hunch about something. This quote alludes to "the ghost in the machine," a turn of phrase
discussed at length by the philosopher Arthur Koestler.

P. 130   **"…the holy kingdom where all men are loved."** This is a rough translation of the title of the gag manga *Shinsei Motemote Oukoku* by Ken Nagai.
It's about an alien father and son trying to get women to like them.

P. 132   **"Come back once you've read *Shirley*!"** *Shirley* is a manga by Kaoru
Mori (author of *Emma* and *A Bride's Story*) about a maid.

P. 132   **"…Miku cosplay at Comiket…"** Zaimokuza is referring to Hatsune
Miku, the vocaloid, and the massive biannual *doujinshi* (fan comic) market hosted at the Tokyo Big Sight in Tokyo.

P. 138   **"Are you Perfect Cell?"** Cell is one of the antagonists in the
long-running *shonen* manga series *Dragonball Z* by Akira Toriyama. Per-

fect Cell is his final form, and he's basically good at everything and has no weaknesses.

P. 139 **"The opposite of approval is approval."** Hachiman is playing with a quote from Bakabon's father in the gag manga *Tensai Bakabon* (*Genius Bakabon*) by Fujio Akatsuka. He's always saying things like "the opposite of approval is disapproval" or "The opposite of approval! An approval of opposition!" It's all slightly nonsensical and generally just means "Whatever, that's fine."

P. 140 **"Believe it."** Hachiman is adopting the catchphrase of the titular character of the *shonen* ninja manga *Naruto* by Masashi Kishimoto.

P. 141 **"...muster all his strength to HeartCatch Kawsaki..."** *HeartCatch Pretty Cure!* is the seventh installment of the Pretty Cure magical girl anime franchise.

P. 144 **"For some reason he was wearing *samue*..."** *Samue* are a monk's working clothes that look slightly like medical scrubs. It's not uncommon for a ramen or sushi chef to wear them as a work uniform.

P. 145 **"...a Piiko-esqe fashion evaluation...do the same like Don Konishi."** Piiko is fashion critic and celebrity, and Don Konishi, aka Yoshiyuki Konishi, is a fashion designer. Piiko has more reserved taste, while Don Konishi's dress is quite garish. Both are baby boomer-aged.

P. 146 **"Have you ever heard of the no-waste ghost?"** The no-waste ghost is the star of an old public service announcement from 1982. The ghost scares children into eating their vegetables, crying, "What a waaaaaste!"

P. 148 **"...restaurants we went to were Saize and Bamiyan. The fanciest it got was Roiyaho."** Saizeriya is a cheap Japanese-style Italian restaurant chain. The meals are in the three hundred to six hundred yen range. Bamiyan is also cheap and serves Chinese food. Royal Host is not as fancy as it sounds. They serve simple and inexpensive dishes like omelette rice.

P. 148 **"I fluttered my jacket like Hiromi Gou..."** Hiromi Gou is a singer who was popular during the 1970s and 1980s. He often wore a blazer over his shirtless torso and did these iconic dance moves that involved fluttering his jacket. It looks extremely corny from a modern perspective.

P. 152 **"She doesn't know Shimamura. I bet she doesn't know Uniqlo, either."** Uniqlo and Shimamura are both cheap clothing chains and are considered the most basic of options when dressing yourself.

P. 154 **"Should I say Dom Perignon or Don Penguin?"** Don Penguin is the mascot for Don Quijote, the "palace of low, low prices," a bargain retail chain. The stores are famous for their low prices, the mascot, and the theme song played in every location.

P. 154 **"So that Perry guy...was a drink..."** Commodore Matthew Perry (1784–1858) was a famous foreign diplomat from the United States who is known as being a major player in the opening of Japan.

P. 155 **"I don't have to say Harris or Earnest Satow here, right?"** Townsend Harris and Earnest Mason Satow were also foreign diplomats who negotiated trade with Japan during the Edo and Meiji periods.

P. 155 **"...like Yamanashi having mountains."** Though the name of Yamanashi prefecture actually means "mountain pear," it's also a pun with "no mountains." But Yamanashi actually has lots of the largest mountains in Japan, with Mount Fuji nearby, thus the irony.

P. 169 **"...a familiar face from *chuugen*..."** *Chuugen* is a period in July when workers bring in gifts (usually edible) to give their superiors as tokens of appreciation.

P. 169 "**...nor the Purple Rose**" This is a reference to the classic *shoujo* manga *Glass Mask* by Suzue Miuchi. "Purple Rose" is the main character's anonymous fan who sends her bouquets of purple roses.

Chapter 5 ... Hachiman Hikigaya goes back the way he came again.

P. 175 "**If this were a model car, I'd call Tamiya about it.**" Tamiya is, as one may expect, a toy company that makes plastic models, remote-controlled cars, and other similar toys.

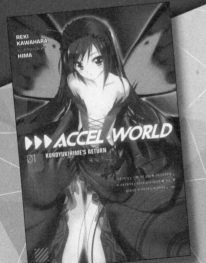